Susanne O'Leary

The
Lost Girls
of Ireland

bookouture

Published by Bookouture in 2021

An imprint of Storyfire Ltd.
Carmelite House
50 Victoria Embankment
London EC4Y 0DZ

www.bookouture.com

ISBN: 978-1-80019-406-9
eBook ISBN: 978-1-80019-405-2

For Gemma and Aisling (in no particular order)

Chapter One

Four months after her husband's death, Lydia found herself without a home. Listening to the careful, quiet voice of her solicitor as he broke the news to her, she felt as if she was waking from a dream. His words confirmed what she had secretly feared for some time, even if it sent a shock wave through her. When her husband had the heart attack, she had known somehow that it was just the beginning.

The past months had been harrowing, and she remembered that moment in late October like it was yesterday. She had got the phone call one Saturday afternoon after a shopping trip with her daughter in Dublin. It had been a fun afternoon with chats and giggles; they had been trying on clothes, and browsing in little boutiques in the narrow lanes behind Grafton Street. It was one of those mother and daughter moments that were so precious. Lydia had felt thankful, as she often did, to have Sunny in her life. *What a gift she is*, Lydia had thought, as she'd watched Sunny walking down the street, her long blonde hair gleaming in the sunlight.

Sunny had looked over her shoulder and smiled. 'Come on, Mum,' she'd said. 'I'm starving. Let's go for a yummy cream tea at The Shelbourne.'

Lydia had readily agreed and they headed up the street to St Stephen's Green and the old Victorian building, settling on a sofa in the plush lounge of the hotel, enjoying buns and scones with cream and jam in front of a blazing fire, laughing as rain began to fall outside, still on a high after the successful shopping spree. That was the moment when their happy, carefree life came to an end.

They had been discussing Sunny's part in the school play, joking about the silly costumes, when Lydia's phone had rung and she had heard a stranger's voice telling her Barry had collapsed and was in intensive care. Suddenly, her world had stopped and she had felt as if she was in a silent bubble, the only sound her own heartbeat. She'd tried to speak but no sound had come out, and she'd stared at Sunny, who'd stared back with fear in her eyes.

'What is it, Mum?' Sunny had asked.

'It's Dad,' Lydia had managed to say, her mouth dry. 'We have to go.'

They had rushed to Vincent's Hospital in a taxi, and Lydia had told Sunny what she had just heard while they had held onto each other. Lydia had tried to calm Sunny down – she'd been in floods of tears – by telling her that her father would be all right. But of course he hadn't been. He died only minutes before they arrived.

Feeling she was stuck in some kind of horrible nightmare, Lydia had done everything required of her, trying her best to help Sunny through the worst of the shock and grief. As if on autopilot, she'd arranged the funeral and everything else that had to be done, at the same time trying to console a grief-stricken fourteen-year-old girl who couldn't stop crying.

And that was not all she'd had to cope with. The doctor had told Lydia that Barry had been at the airport when the heart attack had happened. He'd said he was playing golf that day, but he'd clearly been lying to her. They had been planning to leave for a wedding anniversary weekend at a hotel in the country the day after, and now she had no idea if that would even have happened.

Then there were the whispers at the reception after the funeral, the veiled comments from his associates that told her all was not right with Barry's affairs. She'd tried to find out what they meant, but all she got was a little hint here and there about certain discrepancies in the finances and something about investments going wrong. She'd tried not to worry, but a few days after the funeral, she'd had a call to say the direct debits for her electricity bill and the house insurance had bounced and could she please check with her bank and get that corrected. The bank had told her there wasn't enough money in the household account as her husband had emptied it a few days before his death.

Puzzled, she'd transferred the money from her personal account and rang Barry's office, where she had been told his associate was away and his personal assistant had quit. And that had only been the beginning. There were the bills that had not been paid, Margarita, their housekeeper, asking for her salary, which hadn't been paid for months, and the gardener demanding his money up front, or he wouldn't come back. And as Lydia had checked her different accounts, trying to find the money to pay them all, it had slowly dawned on her that there was very little left.

She couldn't understand how that was possible, but now, sitting on a hard chair in the solicitor's office, she was finding out. She listened to him telling her that everything she owned, even the house she was living in, had to be sold.

'So there's nothing left?' she asked, just to make sure she had heard correctly. 'Not even the money from my inheritance that I gave to Barry to invest for me?'

'I'm afraid not,' Jonathan Martin said, a sad look in his eyes. An older man in his seventies and the senior partner in the firm, he had handled her family's affairs ever since Lydia was a small child. 'Your money went into some bad investment funds that sank.'

'Wonderful,' Lydia said, her mouth twisting in a bitter smile. 'Not a cent to my name, is that it?'

'Yes. And I'm afraid there's a little more bad news,' Jonathan continued.

Lydia stared at him. 'More? What could be worse than losing everything?' She frowned, bracing herself for yet more misery. 'Go on,' she urged.

'It's about some, ahem, irregularities with his business dealings. And an off-shore account that's now being looked into by the tax people. It appears Barry was moving money around in a way that's not quite… legal.'

'Not quite legal?' Lydia gripped the arms of the chair, feeling the blood drain from her face. 'You mean… Some kind of fraud?' she whispered.

The solicitor looked uncomfortable. 'Something like that, yes.'

'Oh God.' Lydia was lost for words. She couldn't believe it. Barry, her husband of nearly twenty years, had been involved in something like this? 'Are you sure?' she asked.

'Yes. It all came to light during the probate research into his accounts. It appears Barry gambled heavily on the stock market and never declared the income from that. And then there were other things...' He stopped for a moment. 'The debts have been piling up. And that's why the bank is repossessing your house and the contents in it.'

Lydia's stomach flipped. Not their home, the beautiful Victorian villa in Killiney with the wonderful garden and views of the sea. It couldn't be true. 'How is that possible?' she asked. 'Have you spoken to his associates about this? And Mike, his business manager?'

'We tried to get in touch with them, but it's impossible to contact anyone. We believe that everyone else who was involved with Barry's business has left the country. Gone abroad,' he added as if she wouldn't understand what it meant.

Lydia's hand flew to her mouth as she tried to take it all in. 'Just like Barry,' she whispered. Her thoughts went to her husband and those last days before he fled to the airport. What must he have been going through to act like this? The stress and worry had to be incredible, so bad he had to leave his family in the lurch. And that in turn had probably caused the heart attack. Lydia felt a dart of pity as she imagined his plight. Why hadn't he told her? Maybe they could have worked it out together... She had still loved him then and had hoped their weekend away would give them a chance to get close again. She would have been prepared to do anything to help him. Tears welled up in her eyes as she went through it all in her mind. 'He was on his way to London when it happened. Running away from this and abandoning us as well.'

'That's the way it looks, yes,' Jonathan said, pushing a box of tissues towards her. 'I have a feeling he was worried he might be prosecuted.'

'Does everyone know?' Lydia asked hoarsely, dabbing her eyes with a tissue, anger replacing her sorrow. 'I mean, is it out there in the media?'

'I don't think you need to worry about that,' Jonathan soothed. 'You had nothing to do with it and your family name will not be affected. You have a solid reputation and your charity work is well known. If this leaks to the press, you might have to answer awkward questions, I suppose. But I can help you to write up a statement and then you could just keep a low profile until it all blows over.'

'A low profile?' Lydia asked. 'How?'

'Maybe you should go away for a bit?' he suggested. 'Go out of town, perhaps?'

'Where?' she said. 'And how? You've just told me I have nothing, where could I go?' she asked, her voice suddenly much quieter. 'And what on earth am I going to do?' she said, finally, almost to herself.

'This brings me to something you might have forgotten about…' Jonathan said, shuffling the papers on his desk. 'I got this in the post this morning.' He handed her a stack of documents. '*You* might have forgotten all about it, but *we've* been looking after it for over ten years now. It might help you get back on your feet.'

Lydia took the documents and glanced at the first page. 'Oh,' she exclaimed, her heart beating faster. 'I haven't thought about this since I don't know when. My great-aunt's cottage in Kerry. Are you saying I still own it?'

Jonathan nodded. 'Yes. The rental agency sent me all the brochures and asked if we want them to let it again this year. But of course we don't if you're going to move there. It could be your salvation, Lydia. You inherited the property when your great-aunt died ten years ago, and it's been let ever since. I believe she left it to you because you were the only girl in the family. The rental agency in Kerry has been looking after everything, and they pay rent into an account in your maiden name – the one your father set up for you – and there's a nice sum in there. Selling your home and your belongings will cover Barry's debts. This is still yours.'

Lydia looked at the deeds. 'Starlight Cottages,' she said. 'Nice name.'

'It's a coastguard station on the outskirts of a village called Sandy Cove, I believe. It's near Ballinskelligs on the Iveragh Peninsula. A row of four houses on top of a headland. Have you never been there?'

'No,' Lydia confessed. 'I'm afraid I've never been to Kerry. I didn't even know this aunt at all. She was my grandfather's sister and they weren't close. We used to go to Courtown in Wexford on our holidays when I was a child, and to Norway now and then to visit my mother's relations. And when I married…'

'You spent most summers in St Tropez,' the lawyer interjected. 'Barry liked the house you had there very much, I believe.'

'He loved it,' Lydia said wistfully, thinking of the beautiful villa overlooking the Mediterranean and all the fun they had had there. Glitzy poolside parties, trips on yachts, swims in the turquoise sea, champagne, gorgeous food… She pushed the memories away and returned to the harsh reality. 'But that house is gone now, I suppose.'

He nodded. 'I'm afraid so. Repossessed by the bank. In any case it belonged to the firm, just like the chalet in St Moritz.'

'I thought so.' Lydia looked at the document in her hand. 'Starlight Cottages.' It had meant little to her at the time and she had forgotten about it as she had been busy with looking after Sunny and organising charity events. But now here it was, like a security net that would save them. She felt suddenly grateful to her aunt, who had left it to her in her will, and to Jonathan, who had looked after it all these years. 'So you're thinking we might go there?'

'It would be the wisest thing to do, I think.'

'Coastguard station,' Lydia said as if to herself. 'On a headland by the Atlantic…'

'That's right. There are four cottages and the one you own is at the end of the row. I believe the other cottages are occupied by artists. Nice little community, I've been told by the letting agent.'

'You spoke to them?'

'Yes, earlier today,' Jonathan replied. 'I took it upon myself to tell them to take it off the website.' He handed her a brochure. 'Here's the advertisement. And…' Another piece of paper crossed the desk. 'A statement with the amount of rent that's in the account. This could tide you over until you get back on your feet, so to speak.'

'Back on my feet,' Lydia said with a bitter little laugh. 'I'll never get back to what we were. I just have to survive, I suppose.' She flicked through the brochure and glanced at the photo of the white house at the end of the terrace. It had a slate roof and a small sunroom facing the ocean. Not much of a garden except for a patch of grass on the edge of the cliff with some kind of flowering shrub. The views seemed nice and the interior clean and tidy but sparse, with a living room and a kitchen downstairs and two bedrooms and a shower room upstairs. Oh God. Sunny would have a fit if she had to share a bathroom with her mother. But that was a minor matter. How would she react to the idea of moving there? Away from everything – her school, her friends and big city life – to a tiny village in the west of Ireland? 'It'll be such a huge shock to Sunny,' she said, looking at Jonathan as if he could help her. 'It's like falling into a ravine,' she added. 'What a disaster.'

'I know,' he said. He paused for a while looking at Lydia thoughtfully. 'But I know you will cope,' he added.

'Cope? How do you mean?' Lydia stared at him. 'Sunny will be devastated.'

'Maybe at first,' the solicitor said. 'But kids are very adaptable. And you're made of strong stuff, Lydia, I've seen that all through the years that we've known each other.' He leaned forward and looked at her sternly. 'It might even be what you need right now to turn your mind away from your grief. A new challenge, a move to a wild, beautiful part of Ireland, where you're not judged for what you have but who you are and how you treat others.' He sat back and drew breath. 'You have a roof over your head at least and a little bit of money to tide you over for a while. You'll have to get a job, of course, but right now you can take a little time to get used to your new life.'

'I suppose.' Lydia nodded and gathered up the papers, stuffing them into her handbag. 'Thank you,' she said, meeting Jonathan's kind eyes with a dart of guilt. It wasn't his fault this had happened and he had done his best to help her. 'You've been wonderful, as always.'

He stood, walked around the desk and took both her hands in his. 'I wish you the very best of luck with everything. Let me know how you get on.'

Lydia smiled and got up. 'I'll send you a postcard. From the edge,' she said in an attempted joke. 'The edge of the west coast.' And as she said it, she had that flash of something strange. A feeling of freedom. How strange to feel free when she was facing such a huge change. That feeling gave her a tiny glimmer of hope in the midst of all the misery. A moment that allowed her to face the idea of breaking the news to Sunny.

Chapter Two

Later that afternoon, Lydia was going through the contents of the kitchen trying to decide what to bring to Kerry, when she heard the front door slam. Sunny was home from school. Lydia waited for the usual forage for snacks in the walk-in pantry but Sunny's footsteps could be heard going upstairs instead. Lydia's stomach churned as she put down the saucepan she was holding and walked out of the kitchen, down the long corridor, into the large hall and up the staircase that curved gracefully to the upper floor. She paused on the landing for a moment, looking down at the gleaming parquet floor below, the big antique hall table and the paintings that adorned the walls. It was a beautiful house that she had been so proud of and she knew she would miss it terribly. The house that had once been the venue for so many parties and gatherings – where friends had loved to come and where she and Barry had been so happy – would now be someone else's home.

She had spent the morning wandering through the rooms, running her hand over the smooth mahogany of the beautiful antique dining table, gazing at the paintings in the living room and looking at the many silver-framed photos from holidays and family events, feeling like someone drowning, as if her whole life was flashing before her eyes. One of the photos in particular gave her a jolt of pain. It had been taken during a skiing holiday in February last year. Sunny, Barry and her standing against the backdrop of the snow-covered Alps, about to take off down the slopes. She and Sunny looked so alike: tall and slim with light blonde hair in contrast to Barry's darkling good looks. It was exactly a year ago. The memory of that carefree day had felt so sharply painful – it had made Lydia gasp. And now, looking down at the beautiful rooms below, she felt the same dart of pain at the thought of having to leave all this behind. But what was the use of grieving for a life that was over?

Lydia turned her back to the view and padded down the thickly carpeted corridor to Sunny's room and gently knocked on the door. 'Sunny?' she said. 'May I come in?'

'Okay,' Sunny replied from inside.

Lydia walked in to the bright, airy bedroom that had stunning views of the sea from the bay window. The room was furnished with a four-poster bed with a handmade quilt and piles of cushions in bright colours. Sunny's favourite cuddly toys lay strewn across the bed where she loved to lie and read a book on her Kindle or talk to her friends on her phone or iPad. A pair of ballet shoes hung by their pink ribbons beside the bookcase, the shelves of which were crammed with books, framed photos and a collection of china animals.

Sunny wasn't on the bed, as usual, however; she was sitting on the window seat staring out to sea, her schoolbag thrown on the floor. Her blonde hair was messy, strands escaping from the scrunchie that held up her ponytail and her thin shoulders slumped in the blue school uniform sweater, the shirt collar sticking up.

'Sunny?' Lydia said softly as she entered.

Sunny turned and looked at her mother with eyes red from crying. 'Yeah?' she said and wiped her nose with the back of her hand.

Lydia ran to her side and sat down, putting her arm around Sunny's shoulder. 'Sweetheart, what's wrong?' Lydia immediately wondered if Sunny was still grieving for her father, but she hadn't seen her cry in weeks. 'Just a bit sad?' she asked her.

'No,' Sunny mumbled, leaning her head against Lydia's chest. 'It's… Someone at school said something about Dad. Something awful.'

'What?' Lydia asked.

'Just lies,' Sunny mumbled. 'Something about Dad having cheated and stolen money.'

'Who said this?' Lydia asked, appalled that the story was now out there in public.

'Maria Lonergan. You know, the most popular girl in my class. She said her mother had read it in the evening paper. Oh, Mum, I wish I could leave that stupid school. Everyone is so mean.'

Lydia stroked Sunny's hair. 'Not everyone, darling. Lizzie is your best friend and she's lovely.' If Sunny felt she wanted to leave her school, it might help her cope with moving to Kerry. She mightn't take the news of the move so badly after all.

'Yes, she is,' Sunny agreed. 'But she has left. They've moved to Cork. So I'll be all alone now. Oh, Mum,' Sunny wailed while Lydia continued to stroke her hair. It dawned on her that what Sunny had heard in school meant that the press had got hold of the story about Barry's fraud. He was a well-known businessman in Dublin; it suddenly didn't seem impossible that soon reporters might try to contact her, or worse, turn up on their doorstep.

And though Lydia didn't want to encourage Sunny to run away from her problems – from the girls at school or to let Lizzie's own move affect her – in some ways, it did present an opportunity for Lydia. A little village in the west might seem enticing to Sunny right now. And it was sounding better to Lydia by the minute. It would be remote, windswept, possibly very boring – but safe. And the house was hers and would provide a cheap place to live. A good place to start their new life until the storm passed.

'Mum?' Sunny's voice interrupted Lydia's thoughts.

'Sit up, darling,' Lydia said. 'I have something to tell you. Something important.'

There must have been a tone in Lydia's voice that made Sunny shoot up out of her crumpled state and stare at her mother. 'What, Mum? Is it about Dad? About what Maria Lonergan's mother read in the paper?'

Lydia nodded, asking herself if it would be fair to tell Sunny the truth about Barry. 'Not quite,' she said, struggling with the dilemma of just how much to reveal. 'Just listen to me for a moment.'

Sunny pushed the strands of hair from her face and looked expectantly at Lydia.

'We…' Lydia started, then stopped and swallowed, her throat suddenly dry. *Is it fair to tell a fourteen-year-old that her father committed a crime?* she asked herself, even though she knew the answer. She cleared her throat and continued. 'What Maria said is just a nasty rumour. Your father was on his way to London to… sort things out with his company, you see,' Lydia said. 'That's why he was at the airport. The things he's being blamed for are the company's problems. He was going to sort it all out.'

Sunny started to say something but Lydia held up her hand. 'Listen before you say anything. I was at old Jonathan's office this morning and that's what he told me. But what we have to deal with now, is that your father didn't get a chance to sort things out, and so we need to give up the house to help pay some of the company's huge debts.'

'Oh,' Sunny said. 'That's awful. But that wasn't his fault, was it?'

'No,' Lydia said, hoping Sunny wouldn't ask too many questions. She didn't want to lie to her – but then, she didn't know for certain what Barry had been planning to do that day. 'Not really,' she replied. 'He was just a little unlucky. We loved Dad, didn't we?'

Sunny nodded, her eyes again glistening with tears.

'So then we know that he couldn't do anything wrong. We have to go on living and remember him the way he was,' Lydia said more to herself than to Sunny. She knew that keeping the truth from Sunny might not be the right thing to do, but she couldn't bear to tell her daughter that the father she loved had committed a crime. She knew deep down that she would never understand or forgive Barry for leaving his family in the lurch. But it would be unfair to burden Sunny with all this right now. She had enough to cope with. As she went on talking, the enormity of what she had heard that morning hit her like a sledgehammer. 'As I told you, we have to sell the house,' she said, her voice shaking. 'Everything inside is being sold to help the company too. It sounds to me like the media have found out now, and they'll want a statement and more from me, plus all the juicy little details those tabloids love. I can tell them it's not true, but they won't believe me. Do you know what I mean?'

'Yes,' Sunny replied. 'And they'll try to take photos of us with telephoto lenses and chase us down the streets like they did to the Kardashians. It was all over the news on TV last year, remember?'

Lydia laughed. 'Not quite. We're hardly celebrities.'

'I know. But you and Dad were famous in Dublin, going to all those charity parties and film premieres and stuff because of all the money you helped raise.'

'Not exactly a low profile, I suppose. But anyway,' Lydia said. 'I'll tell you what we're going to do.'

'Yes?' Sunny's eyes lit up.

'We have a house, you see, a house that belongs only to me and nobody else. A little house in a village far away. By the ocean.'

Sunny stared at her mother. 'A house by the ocean? Where?'

'In Kerry. On the Iveragh Peninsula.' Lydia took the brochure that she had brought with her and gave it to Sunny. 'Here. Take a look. It's an old coastguard station. My great-aunt Nellie used to live there and then she left it to me in her will. It's been let as a holiday home for years.'

Sunny looked through the brochure in silence, turning the pages, carefully studying every picture. 'It looks like a beautiful place,' she said, her voice full of wonder. 'The house is small but okay and I'm sure we can make it better.' She looked thoughtfully at her mother. 'We have no choice, do we, Mum?' Sunny continued bravely, clenching her fists. 'And we will manage. We *will*.'

'Of course we will,' Lydia said, moved close to tears by both the sadness and determination in Sunny's voice.

'At least we have a house,' Sunny said, looking at the picture of the coastguard station on the front of the brochure and the sweeping views of the ocean. 'If it's half as beautiful as this photo, it will be the best place to start a new life.' Her voice wobbled slightly but she looked at Lydia with a mixture of hope and fear.

'Of course it will,' Lydia tried to reassure her. 'The very best place.' *Or the worst*, she thought with trepidation. It looked like a wonderful place, but one couldn't eat the view. How on earth would they survive in the long run in such a remote little village?

She took the brochure from Sunny and looked at the photo. The terrace of houses perched on this rocky headland above the blue ocean, the ragged tops of the mountains, the green slopes and the road winding around the coast… She suddenly felt something pulling at her emotions as she kept looking at the scene, as if it was meant to be and they would somehow find what they had lost over there, on the wild west coast of Kerry. Even through her grief and sorrow, this felt like the biggest challenge in her whole life and it excited her. She had never had to try hard or cope with anything remotely difficult. Life had been easy and pleasant – and maybe a tad boring. *This is it*, she suddenly knew. A test of her strength and resilience. She felt a dart of excitement, which surprised her.

'It's going to be fun,' Sunny chirped beside her, echoing her thoughts. 'And isn't Kerry close to Cork, so I'll be able to visit Lizzie all the time? Don't worry, Mum, everything will be fine. It'll make men out of us, like Norwegian Granny used to say.'

Lydia smiled at the excitement in Sunny's voice. Being so young, she seemed to take their changed circumstances very well. The fact that she would now be close to her best friend probably had a lot to do with it. Sunny had had a hard time fitting in to the exclusive school, where most of the girls already sported designer handbags and shoes at the tender age of fourteen. Sunny had been labelled as a 'nerd' by the clique of popular girls in her class because of her top marks in maths and her love of reading and ballet, and wasn't even on any of the social media platforms. Lydia had wondered if this was quite normal, but as Sunny seemed content not to follow the stream, she stopped worrying and instead felt grateful that her daughter was strong enough to be different. Her best friend Lizzie was much the same and the two of them had built a bond between them that would never break.

Lizzie's move to Cork would have been devastating for Sunny in the middle of her grief for her father, but now that problem would be solved by their move to Kerry. And Sunny was right, it would probably 'make men' of them. But first they had to sort out their belongings, leave their home, and try to dodge the press. The latter was the more serious problem. Journalists loved a sensation, especially if it involved the bad luck of someone wealthy. They simply had to disappear from the radar altogether, which seemed like an impossible task. But as Lydia sat on the window seat with Sunny, she suddenly knew how they might manage it.

Chapter Three

'Brilliant idea, Mum,' Sunny said as they left Dublin in their hired van at daybreak a week later. 'It's a bit like that movie we watched about the people who had to adopt new identities as part of a witness protection programme.'

Lydia had to laugh as she drove down the M50 heading south toward the motorway to Limerick. 'Not quite that bad, sweetheart. We'll just change our last name. We're still the same people, only now we're using my maiden name instead of Harrington.'

'Sunniva Butler,' Sunny said as if tasting the sound. 'I like it. And Lydia Butler is very nice too.'

'I'm glad you like it.' Lydia glanced at Sunny sitting there in the front seat, looking excitedly out the window, her phone in her hand. It was amazing how Sunny had accepted everything and been such a huge help with this big move. She hadn't even worried about going to a new school. She said she thought it would be fun to try the new one in Cahersiveen, who had accepted her application at once when they learned Sunny had been a top student at her school in Dublin. But Sunny, in her youthful innocence, had no idea of the huge upheaval this move was. To her, it was a kind of adventure, but Lydia knew that what lay ahead would be hard. They would have to adjust to being unable to afford what they used to take for granted. No more shopping trips, meals in nice restaurants or trips abroad. Lydia thought of the carefree life she had enjoyed, now gone forever. And here they were, running away from the press and the wagging tongues of the gossipmongers. Lydia only hoped the reality would not hit Sunny too hard once the excitement of the trip and the new place had worn off.

They had spent a few days closeted in the house, sorting out what they should bring and what had to be sold, finally deciding on just their clothes, some books, their laptops, the little TV set from the study and the items of kitchen equipment that they would need in a small cottage in Kerry. They left everything else behind, which was a huge wrench for Lydia but didn't seem to faze Sunny in the slightest. She kept saying she couldn't wait to go to that beautiful place by the ocean.

Lydia had made a last-ditch attempt to stay in Dublin by calling the advertising firm where she had worked as a copywriter before she married, but they had said they weren't hiring right now. They would, however, keep her in mind if things changed. So that was that.

Lydia and Sunny both had many tearful moments during that last week, but the big life change they were facing helped turn their minds away from the grief and sorrow of Barry's sudden death. Lydia sold all her jewellery, including her wedding and engagement rings, which gave her only a brief pang of guilt. But she was beginning to realise that the marriage had been over for a long time. When she thought about the last few years she was aware of just how much Barry had been drifting away from her, hiding what was happening while pretending everything was going well. She barely recognised the man she had last seen, the man who had being boarding that plane to London. The man she was sure had been running away from his problems.

Lydia cast her mind back to when she and Barry had first met twenty years ago, when she was working at the high-profile advertising firm. Barry was then executive director of one of Ireland's largest supermarket chains and had hired the firm where Lydia worked for their Christmas advertising campaign. The budget was large and they wanted a series of advertisements for TV and radio that would grab people of all walks of life. 'Think the Coca-Cola ads,' Barry had said at the first meeting, during which he had fixed Lydia with his dark velvet eyes, never letting his gaze wander. Charmed by his handsome, boyish face, brilliant smile and tall, lean frame, she had been instantly smitten. She'd put everything she could think of into the campaign, as she always did, and it had been a huge success. Barry had asked Lydia out to dinner when the campaign was over and he was no longer a client. Good food and plenty of champagne had made them both a little giddy and when Barry kissed Lydia goodnight outside her parents' house in Ballsbridge, she had kissed him back with fervour, leaving him in no doubt as to how she felt about him.

And straight after their first night out, he had proposed. Lydia had never heard anything crazier in her life. But crazy or not, she knew at that moment he was the right man for her. And though her parents had thought it was a little too quick, six months later they were married in the nearby church.

The wedding reception at the K Club in Kildare – the most exclusive country club in Ireland – was spectacular. Barry was soon made a partner in the firm and also started his own investment company. She remembered how happy she felt when they bought their large Victorian villa in Killiney – even if she was overwhelmed with its sumptuous gardens and terrace overlooking the sea. She remembered how relaxed she'd felt – when Barry had arranged for them to go to the Bahamas for their honeymoon, she'd wondered if it wasn't all a bit too extravagant, but she'd let him decide, like she had with many things all those years ago…

'Left here,' Sunny said, jolting Lydia out of her thoughts. 'It says Adare; isn't that on the way to Killarney?'

'You're right,' Lydia agreed and steered the van up the slip road to the exit. 'Do you want to stop in Adare for a coffee? We've been on the road for two hours. Two more to go. Maybe you're hungry?'

'No,' Sunny replied. 'I want to keep going.' She consulted the map on her phone. 'We have to stop off in Killarney to look at that second-hand car you're buying after you've given the van back to the rental people.'

'That was supposed to be tomorrow,' Lydia said. 'We were to drive to the house and unload all the stuff and then sort out everything the day after.'

'Yes, but I think you should look at that car now,' Sunny argued. 'Then you'll be able to organise the registration and the tax and insurance so you can get the car quicker.'

'Good idea,' Lydia said, yet again taken aback by her daughter's practical thinking. 'In any case by the time we get to Killarney, we'll want to eat something. We had breakfast so early.'

'Okay,' Sunny agreed. 'That's a great plan, Mum.' She sighed deeply and put down her phone. 'I was sad leaving the house, you know.'

'Yes, me too,' Lydia said softly, touching Sunny's cheek. 'Very sad.'

'It felt like leaving a little bit of me behind.'

Lydia blinked away tears as she thought of how she had felt leaving the house this morning. She knew that her solicitor's assistant would take care of the sale of the furniture and art, and then pay the bank who would be selling the house eventually. All they had taken was the kitchen equipment and their clothes and personal belongings which had been packed into the van the night before. There had been a few journalists outside the gates during the afternoon, cameras ready to take shots should they venture outside. But they had closed the curtains and busied themselves with packing and then took off through the back gate just before sunrise. Lydia had been relieved to see nobody around but as they drove down the street lined with sumptuous villas, she felt a wave of despair and sorrow. It was as if she had been stripped of everything that mattered in her life, suddenly thrown off a cliff into an abyss, deep and dark and impossible to survive. She glanced at Sunny and their eyes met for a moment.

'It's not fair that this is happening to you,' Lydia said. 'I'm so sorry, Sunny.'

'It's not your fault,' Sunny replied. 'It's not fair to you either. But at least we know Dad didn't do what those people said.'

'Yes, that's true,' Lydia said, wondering how long she would have to keep lying. But she couldn't bear to see Sunny any sadder about her dad. She had already lost him once. How would she feel if she found out that he had lied to them? 'But it's so hard to come to terms with all we have lost. I'll never get used to that.'

'You should never say never,' Sunny said.

'I suppose,' Lydia replied without much conviction. 'But right now all we can do is try to survive, and look forward.'

'And we have to count our blessings,' Sunny stated after a moment's silence. 'We have somewhere to live... And a lot of designer clothes,' she added with a giggle. 'Just imagine what an impression you'll make in that little country village.'

Lydia had to smile, feeling proud. What a brave little trouper Sunny was, and such a comfort to her mother. If Lydia was in a mood to count her blessings, Sunny would be at the top of her list. And in a way, she was right. And they had each other.

They drove through the pretty little village of Adare, only glancing at the cute cottages and the quaint pubs and shops, pressing on down the road through other villages, only stopping an hour later as Killarney came into view.

Sunny gasped with delight when she saw the beautiful town and its church spires outlined against the mountains, the lakes, woods and green fields dotted with sheep. 'We're in Kerry,' she said, her voice full of wonder. 'I never knew it was this beautiful. I think we're going to be happy here, Mum.'

Lydia rolled down the window and breathed in the soft air, her tense shoulders finally relaxing. 'We might, you know,' she said with a dart of hope. 'Eventually.'

Chapter Four

After lunch in a café that served freshly made sandwiches, and stocking up in the nearby supermarket, Lydia and Sunny continued to the garage that sold second-hand cars. Lydia had already looked at what was available for her budget online and decided on a Toyota Yaris that seemed in good nick and didn't have a huge mileage even though it was ten years old.

'She's a beauty,' the salesman said, slapping the little red car on the roof. He was a dapper red-haired man who had introduced himself as Sean Keating. 'Just one lady owner – a teacher who only used it for shopping locally. Perfect for you, my dear.'

'Manual transmission?' Lydia said, glancing into the car. 'I'm not used to that. I only ever drove an automatic.'

'But you must have learned to drive on a manual,' Sean replied.

'I did, but that was a long time ago.'

'Sure it'll come back to you in no time,' he assured her. 'Just like riding a bike.'

'I suppose,' Lydia said hesitantly.

'You could go for a spin in it right now, if you want,' he said. 'Just to get a feel for her.'

'Yeah,' Sunny said behind Lydia. 'Go for it, Mum. I love it already. It's so cute.'

Lydia hesitated. 'I don't know… I'm very busy today.'

'But Mum,' Sunny groaned, 'you have to make up your mind. Remember what we agreed about saving time by doing it all today?'

'Your daughter is right,' the salesman said. 'It'd take a lot of pain out of it. Are you bringing back the van to the Hertz people?'

'That's right,' Lydia replied.

'They're just around the corner from here. I think you should hang on to the van until we have all the paperwork ready, then you can take it back and pick up your new wheels. Easy-peasy.'

'Perfect,' Sunny said. 'We'll take it. We'll go for a little drive around town and then we'll sort everything out. Would that be okay?'

'That'd be grand, ma'am,' Sean said and bowed theatrically. 'With an attitude like that, your daughter will go far,' he remarked, turning to Lydia.

'We're just going to Sandy Cove,' Sunny said. 'For now anyway.'

Sean smiled, obviously realising that Sunny had understood what he meant. 'A good springboard for greater things,' he replied. 'Sandy Cove is the best little village in Ireland.' He looked at Lydia. 'So it's a deal, then?'

Lydia laughed. 'Okay. But only after I've had that test drive.'

It didn't take Lydia long to get the hang of the manual transmission and after a short drive around Killarney, they sealed the deal with a down payment and a handshake and Sean promised to have everything sorted in a couple of days. 'Hang on to the van until then,' he suggested. 'Once we get the money into our account, the car is yours and you're away in a hack.'

'Brilliant,' Lydia said, smiling at his turn of phrase. 'We'd better get going. Thank you so much for all your help.'

'Pleasure, ma'am,' Sean said with a grin and a little salute. 'It's not every day we get such fine customers. Say hello to my cousin Sorcha. She runs the grocery shop in Sandy Cove.'

'We will,' Sunny promised.

They set off down the road past Killarney National Park with its views of mountains and lakes smiling at each other, both cheered by having settled the problem of a car so easily and reasonably. 'What a nice man,' Lydia said, her mood lifting. Buying the car had given her a sense of freedom and control after all that had happened. She was finally in charge of her life again.

'Lovely,' Sunny agreed. 'People in Kerry seem so friendly. He was, anyway. And he has a cousin in Sandy Cove, so we can go into the shop and say hello to her. I feel I know her already.'

'I'm sure it won't be long until we meet her,' Lydia said, turning her thoughts to the challenges ahead as they drove down the road lined with green fields. They would soon be near the coast and they could already glimpse the ocean in the distance. There was so much to get used to, so many problems to sort out. She had the keys to the house in her bag and she wondered in what state she would find it. It had been empty since last August so it was bound to be cold and damp. But she had brought their electric blankets with them, alongside two warm duvets and all their ski clothes, which had made Sunny laugh. But Lydia had no illusions and her stomach churned with dread as she thought of the old house on the edge of a rugged, windswept headland with the Atlantic Ocean roaring below. It must be lovely in the summer, but in February? She shivered as she turned off the main road onto a narrow country lane with the signpost that said 'Sandy Cove'. They were nearly at their destination and she felt something ominous as the first little house came into view. She barely heard Sunny's comments about the village as they drove down the main street with the quaint little houses, the cute shop fronts and a donkey in a field.

Following the directions Lydia had memorised, she continued through the village, taking the Ballinskelligs road that hugged the cliffs with stunning views of the ocean below and the majestic mountains on the other side. Then, as a violent shower accompanied by gusts of winds shook the van, the row of houses on the edge of the cliff came into view. Lydia drove carefully down the rough path, trying to avoid the worst of the potholes and finally pulled up outside the house at the end of the row. They had arrived. This was it. The beginning of their new life.

Chapter Five

As they sat in the van, waiting for the rain to ease, Lydia looked
at the house. Like the others in the row, it was white with a green
door. The original sash windows with two panels – one of which slid
upwards – were still in place, which was charming but possibly not
very practical. The slate roof looked solid and she could see smoke
coming from one of the houses further down the row, which meant
that there must be a fireplace and they could light a fire to keep warm.

'It's lovely,' Sunny said from beside her. 'So cute. It looks like
it's waiting for us.'

Lydia smiled, trying her best to feel positive. 'It's a nice house,'
she said and opened the door of the van. 'Let's get inside now that
it has stopped raining.' She rummaged in her bag for the keys that
the rental agency had sent her and found them at the bottom of the
bag. Then she stepped out of the van, closed the door and walked up
the short gravel path. She inserted the key in the lock of the green
panelled door, trying to open it. But it refused to budge. Lydia had
to give it a shove with her shoulder before it gave in. 'The wood
must have warped during the winter,' she said to Sunny, who was
standing behind her, hugging her rucksack and peering inside, her
eyes wide with excitement.

The door opened with a loud squeak and they found themselves looking into a small porch with a hallstand and a pot with a dead plant. 'Geranium,' Lydia said, after a quick glance. 'It'll probably bloom again in the spring.'

'Just like us,' Sunny said with a smile. 'We'll bloom again in the spring, won't we, Mum?'

'I hope we will,' Lydia said, smiling at Sunny's positivity. She opened the inside door and could see that it led to a narrow hall with a steep staircase rising to the upper floor. They walked through the hall and into the living room that was surprisingly large and bright. It was sparsely furnished with a dark grey sofa facing a large wood-burning stove with logs in a basket, two matching armchairs, a rug in various shades of blue and a bookcase with tourist brochures and books about nature trails and local wildlife. The room was freezing cold and smelled of damp and salty sea air – but at least Lydia couldn't smell the slightest hint of mould as she stood on the dusty wooden floor. She could see a sunroom through the French windows, with wicker furniture, a shelf full of seashells, binoculars and pieces of driftwood. Despite the cold, the whole place had a charming, beachcomber atmosphere that appealed to Lydia. It was much larger than she'd thought.

'Can we light the stove?' Sunny asked, rubbing her arms. 'It's freezing in here.'

'We'll see to that in a minute,' Lydia promised. 'Nice room, don't you think?'

'It's great,' Sunny replied, opening the French doors to the sunroom. 'And this is such a cool room. I can see the Skelligs from here.' She pointed to the horizon where two jagged shapes rose out of the sea.

Lydia walked across the creaking floorboards and joined her daughter in the sunroom. It overlooked a small back garden, which was separated from its neighbour by a tall hedge. The views took Lydia's breath away as she stared at the ocean and the waves sending sprays high in the air as they crashed against the rocks below.

'Look, there's a little beach down there,' Sunny said, pointing at it. 'And a path down the cliffs. Must be fantastic in the summer.'

'Yes, but that's a long way off,' Lydia remarked, suddenly noticing the cold draught from the cracks in the window frames. 'Let's see if we can light that stove.'

'Do you know how?' Sunny asked.

'I've seen it on TV. Shouldn't be too hard,' Lydia said, trying to remember if she had ever lit a fire in her life. Before marrying Barry she'd lived with her parents. Things like this had nearly always been done for her, she realised. She walked back into the living room to the stove and opened the door, peering inside. 'I suppose we just put the logs in there and light them?'

'With what?' Sunny asked. 'Did you think of buying matches?'

'No,' Lydia had to admit.

'It didn't occur to me either,' Sunny said. 'I was too busy deciding which bags of crisps to get.'

'That's important, too,' Lydia replied. 'But it's my fault for thinking we were on some kind of holiday. I should have thought about the practical things instead of worrying about snacks and treats and getting here quickly.'

'We're not very good at surviving,' Sunny remarked in a sad voice. 'Let's go and look in the kitchen. There might be matches there.'

Together they walked into the adjoining kitchen, the windows of which overlooked the front garden with a view of the mountains towering above. The room was a little darker than the living room and had a big ceramic sink, old-fashioned cupboards, an electric cooker and a fridge-freezer. A pine table with four chairs stood in the middle of the flagstone floor and a half-open door revealed a utility room with a larder and a washing machine.

'Not bad,' Lydia said and closed the fridge door. She flicked a switch and the fridge started to hum. When she had spoken to the lady from the lettings agency, she'd ensured that they left it switched on for them. The last thing she wanted was to deprive Sunny of WiFi, and she would sort out that problem as soon as she could, but she was kicking herself for assuming the heat would be electric too.

'There's plenty of crockery and some saucepans,' Sunny announced after a quick rummage in the cupboards. 'No matches, but maybe we can light a bit of paper off one of the rings on the cooker. I learned how to light a fire at girl guide camp last year,' Sunny said. 'So I think I can light that one, if I can find some paper and kindling.'

'Kindling?' Lydia asked. 'You mean like little sticks?'

'And bits of bark and stuff like that.' Sunny patted her mother's arm. 'Don't worry. I'll get it going. We could look around for matches in the living room. But can we take a look at the bedrooms first?'

They climbed the stairs to the bedrooms under the eaves of the house, the slanting ceilings and wallpaper with tiny rosebuds giving the rooms a romantic old-fashioned air. The larger bedroom with a double bed overlooked the ocean while the smaller one with two singles was over the front garden with views of the mountains. The shower room had a tiny round window to the back of the house, and was adequate but certainly not luxurious, Lydia thought, as her en-suite bathroom in Dublin briefly popped into her mind.

'I can pretend I'm on a ship,' Sunny said bravely as she stood in the small space. 'And I can see the ocean through that little window that's like a porthole. Isn't that cool?'

Lydia agreed that the bathroom was cute but very old-fashioned, wondering how they were going to share it. Sunny had started spending long sessions preening herself, like most teenagers. 'I think you should take the big bedroom,' she told Sunny as she watched her exploring the room, but unable to find any matches. 'I'll be fine in the small one.'

'Are you sure?' Sunny asked, looking a little happier.

'No, but grab it before I change my mind,' Lydia replied, knowing she would have loved going to sleep to the sound of the waves.

'How are you going to get all your clothes into that tiny wardrobe?' Sunny teased. 'You brought everything you owned, even all your handbags and shoes. I don't think you'll need them here.'

'Can't you see me walking down the village street in my high heels?' Lydia asked Sunny and the two of them looked at each other and giggled. 'I'll just unpack the jeans and sweaters and store the fancy stuff somewhere else in the house,' she said.

'Good plan,' Sunny said, nodding wisely. 'You never know. You might get to use it all again one day.'

Lydia nodded. 'But right now, we have to settle in.'

'I know.' Sunny pointed at a door beside the bathroom. 'What's in there?'

'No idea. I think it's a boxroom.' Lydia turned the doorhandle. 'It's locked. It'd be a great place to put our suitcases and things,' she said, and Sunny nodded her agreement, squeezing past Lydia to peer into the keyhole. 'I'll see if I can find a key,' Lydia said. 'But first, let's get that fire going and make something to eat. I'll put one of those frozen pizzas in the oven and then we can have the apple pie and ice cream for dessert.'

'Sounds great,' Sunny replied. 'Thank you for giving me the best bedroom, Mum,' she said and gave Lydia a brief hug. Over Sunny's head Lydia could see the little window seat in the big bedroom. There was a beautiful view of the ocean, where the sun, partly obscured by dark clouds, slowly sank behind the horizon, casting a golden glow across the dark churning waves. Seagulls glided over the water, their plaintive cries echoing around the bay. Lydia suddenly sighed, not from sadness but from something deep inside that told her they had landed in a good place.

Chapter Six

Two hours later – as the stars appeared in the black winter sky and the wind dropped, heralding a cold night ahead – Lydia and Sunny had moved everything from the van, lit the stove, lugged their suitcases upstairs and turned on the electric radiators in the bedrooms. They'd even made the beds with the sheets and duvets they had brought. Then they ate pizza followed by apple pie in front of the stove in the living room that Sunny had managed to light, dressed in their warmest sweaters and ski socks. The sofa sagged in the middle, they found, as the springs had gone, but Lydia promised to see if they could buy a better one when she found a second-hand furniture shop. Then Sunny started to yawn and announced she wanted to go to bed.

While Sunny was in the bathroom, Lydia tidied up the kitchen and went back into the living room to check the stove. It was still warm, the logs inside smouldering. The nearly full moon cast an eerie light through the windows of the sunroom, and Lydia suddenly felt an urge to go outside to look at the stars. She put on her jacket, walked out through the sunroom and opened the door, shivering in the cold air, feeling she should go back inside. But the immense black sky dotted with glimmering stars beckoned her and she walked out and closed the door, leaning against it, staring out across the diamond-studded blackness, the waves crashing against the rocks below the only sound.

'Ooh,' she whispered, overwhelmed, her hand to her heart.

'Wonderful, isn't it?' said a man's voice on the other side of the hedge.

Lydia gave a start and looked in the direction the voice had come from. But the hedge that separated her garden from next door was too high to see anyone on the other side. 'Yes,' she said. 'Incredible.'

'You just moved in, I saw.' His voice was deep with a strange twangy accent. Not Irish, she thought.

'Yes,' she said, feeling it was a little weird to talk to someone she couldn't see. But maybe that was just as well, as him not seeing her was a good thing. She must look a mess in her strange mish-mash of clothes with no make-up and her hair flat. 'We just arrived from Dublin.'

'You're here for a vacation?'

'Vaca—?' She let out a hollow laugh. 'No. This is certainly no holiday.'

'I see,' he said as if her tone of voice had revealed everything. 'Welcome to Starlight Cottages, in any case.'

'Thank you.' Lydia hesitated, not sure she should be speaking to a strange man like this. But he was their neighbour, so it seemed churlish not to reply. 'I'm Lydia, by the way,' she said.

'Hello, Lydia. I'm Jason O'Callaghan. A Bostonian with Irish roots.'

'Ooh, that explains it,' Lydia said, trying to peek through the gaps in the hedge so she could have a look at him. But the hedge was dense and it was too dark to see anything at all.

'Explains what?'

'Your accent.'

'The Boston twang?' He laughed. 'Yeah, that's hard to lose. Lydia – what?'

'Butler,' she said, still unused to her maiden name after so long.

'Lydia Butler,' he said. 'Nice name.'

'Thank you.'

'You must have had a long day.'

'That's putting it mildly,' Lydia said with a laugh. 'Long and very strange.'

'In what way?' he enquired, his voice soft in the still night. 'Moving house and so on?'

'Yes, well… A bit more than that.' His sympathetic voice and the feeling of anonymity made Lydia lose her reticence. It was nice to talk to an adult for a change – and someone who had nothing to do with her life. 'I bought a car today that cost less than my handbag,' she blurted out. 'And I realised that I can't do the simplest things like lighting a fire. God knows how my daughter and I are going to survive if we have to rely on my skills.'

He laughed. 'But you bought a car for less than a handbag. Isn't that a great achievement?'

'Not really. A designer handbag is very expensive. Buying a car for less isn't that much of an achievement.'

'I have to confess that's an area of expertise I don't have a clue about.'

'Not worth knowing, really.' Lydia shivered in the cold air, realising she had to go inside and get warm or she'd catch her death out here. But his voice was so comforting, she didn't want to stop talking to him. 'My life is…' She paused, not knowing how to go on.

'Your life has changed suddenly?' he asked softly. 'And now you're trying to pick up the pieces?'

'Yes,' she whispered into the darkness. 'Something like that.'

'So coming here is the first step of a very hard journey?' He laughed apologetically. 'I'm sorry. I'm presuming too much. I take it you own the house, though? If your name's Butler, you must be related to Nellie – the lady who lived there before.'

'My great-aunt,' Lydia replied. 'She left the house to me and it's been let as a holiday home since she died ten years ago.'

'I see. I didn't know her as I only came here two years ago. But I believe she had a very exciting life.'

'Exciting? Old Aunt Nellie?' Lydia asked, her interest piqued. 'I never heard that.'

'She wasn't always old.'

'Of course not,' Lydia protested. 'But exciting? Here in the—'

'Sticks?' he filled in. 'Oh you don't have to live in a city to have excitement, you know.'

'Of course,' Lydia mumbled, feeling stupid. 'I'm sure there's excitement everywhere if you look for it.'

'I have a feeling she did, judging by the way people talk about her. I would have loved to have met her.'

'I did. Once. But then I was very young and not interested in older people,' Lydia said, feeling a pang of regret. Her father's aunt had seemed boring and old to a teenage girl, but now she wished she had made the effort to get to know this woman and ask her what her life had been like here in this beautiful but remote part of Ireland. It could have been fascinating to talk to someone of that generation.

'I know what you mean,' Jason said. 'I was the same. Never bothered to talk properly with the older generation. If I had, maybe my life would be different.' Lydia was intrigued by the touch of sadness in his deep voice. She wanted to ask what he meant, but before she could get her words out he carried on. 'I have to turn in. It's a chilly night and I have much to do in the morning. Goodnight, Lydia Butler. Enjoy the stars,' he said.

'But…' Lydia protested. She wanted to get him to meet her at the front of the house so she could see him. But she heard him go inside and close the door and she was alone again.

She looked up at the bright stars and the swathe of the Milky Way that spanned the heavens like a diamond-studded belt, the feeling of infinity making her dizzy. The conversation with her neighbour had made her feel a little less lonely and more hopeful. He seemed so nice and so empathic, somehow. And what he had said about Aunt Nellie intrigued her. She hadn't known much about her father's old aunt. She remembered that he had spoken about her being an artist who did illustrations for postcards or something. But that didn't seem like the exciting life her new neighbour had mentioned.

Lydia slowly turned to get back inside, her thoughts on Nellie Butler and what her life had been like here in this remote part of the country. It would be interesting to find out more about this woman who had left her house to Lydia and in this way saved her. But right now, she needed to settle in, make the house as comfortable as she could manage and figure out a way to earn some money, the latter a seemingly impossible task.

Most important of all, Sunny was taking the school bus to her new school in Cahersiveen tomorrow and would have to try to cope with being the new girl and fit into a rural lifestyle. It wasn't going to be easy, and Lydia knew that it was something Sunny would have to manage on her own, which made her sick with worry. Would the other students accept Sunny? And if they didn't, how would a fourteen-year-old deal with that on top of all her other sorrows? Lydia only hoped the Viking spirit from her Norwegian grandmother would help Sunny through it.

Chapter Seven

The next morning, Lydia got up after a restless night, finding Sunny in the kitchen, dressed in her school uniform that they had bought before leaving Dublin. She was already busy making tea and toast. 'Hi, Mum,' she said brightly. 'I lit the stove and turned on the radiators, as it was so cold this morning. Hope that was okay.'

Lydia hugged her cashmere robe tightly around her. 'Perfect.'

Sunny did a twirl. 'How do I look?' she asked and squinted down at the white shirt and grey pullover with a blue stripe around the neck.

'Nice,' Lydia replied. 'Not the most stylish of uniforms, but you'd look good in anything.'

'You would say that. You're my mother,' Sunny said with a sigh. 'But to me it's like prison clothes.' She flicked at the pleated skirt. 'Why is everything grey?'

'I know what you mean.' Lydia remarked. 'It is a little bit dreary. But grey is a practical colour, and everyone will look the same. At least the blazer is blue.'

'I suppose. Sit down,' Sunny ordered and put a teapot on the table that she had laid with mugs and plates. 'I have made a pile of toast and loads of tea.'

'You're a treasure.' Lydia poured tea into a mug and added a dash of milk. Then she spread butter on a slice of toast from the little breadbasket. 'Come on, sit down and have your breakfast.'

Sunny added a few slices to the basket and sat down. 'Did you sleep well?'

'So-so,' Lydia replied through a bite of toast. 'I think I'm not quite settled yet. How about you?'

'The sound of the waves helped me get to sleep,' Sunny said. 'I thought I heard you talking to someone, but I might have dreamed it.'

'No, it did happen. I was looking at the stars and then our neighbour said hello over the hedge.'

'Really? Who's our neighbour, then?'

'A man called Jason O'Callaghan from Boston. That's all I know for now. But I'm sure we'll meet him soon. He seemed nice enough, though.'

Sunny nodded and spread butter on a slice of toast. 'Okay.'

Lydia started to get up. 'I should make you lunch for school.'

'I already did. Banana and peanut butter on brown bread, an apple and a piece of cheese. Nice and healthy, but I'm sure I can get crisps and stuff in town during lunch break.'

'Probably.'

'But maybe they don't let you out for lunch?' Sunny said. 'There might be rules about things like that. I've heard country schools are very old-fashioned.'

'I wish I could come with you.' Lydia met Sunny's eyes that were full of fear, despite her cheery tones. 'But I'm sure you'll be fine.' She put her hand out to touch her, but Sunny pulled away.

'Don't try to make me feel better, Mum. You can't help me with this. I just have to get through the first day,' Sunny said, looking miserable. 'Then it might be easier. Or harder. I'm sure country kids don't like girls from Dublin.'

'Don't expect the worst,' Lydia soothed. 'I've heard nice things about people from Kerry.'

'Teenagers are different,' Sunny argued. 'If you don't fit in, they'll either ignore you or make you feel inferior. Either way it sucks.'

Lydia felt a dart of pity. Sunny looked so vulnerable and scared. But she had no choice and Lydia secretly hoped this school full of country kids might be better than the school in Dublin where Sunny had never fitted in either. 'Try not to worry. You don't know what it's like until you've started. Give them a chance before you make a judgement.'

Sunny sighed. 'That's easy for you to say. I just know it's going to be awful.'

'You'll be fine and they'll love you,' Lydia promised, trying to look cheerful while she glanced at the old clock on the wall. 'The bus leaves from the main street in half an hour. I'll go to the bus stop with you.'

'Thanks, Mum,' Sunny said. 'I'll get my lunch and my schoolbag. They said they'd have all the books for me at school, didn't they?'

'That's right.' Lydia finished her tea and got up. 'I'll just get dressed while you get ready.'

Lydia ran upstairs and after a quick shower in the cold bathroom, fished out a pair of Armani jeans and a cashmere polo neck from the suitcase she hadn't yet unpacked. She pulled on her suede boots and brushed her hair. After applying foundation and a coat of mascara, she ran downstairs again, finding Sunny at the door, her schoolbag on her back.

'Let's go, then,' Sunny said and opened the door. 'It's only a few minutes' walk to the bus stop.'

'I know.' Lydia grabbed her Canada Goose jacket and locked up, glancing at the silver Audi outside the house next door, wondering if it was Jason's car.

'Is that his?' Sunny asked as they walked away. 'That neighbour you were talking to last night, I mean.'

'Must be.'

'Not short of money, then.'

'Who knows?' Lydia said. 'You can't judge a person's income by just looking at their car.'

'Or their clothes,' Sunny said, smirking at her mother. 'Looking at you, anyone would suppose you're well off. Armani jeans, Ralph Lauren cashmere, Canada Goose jacket and the Birkin handbag… Not quite a poor woman's wardrobe.'

'What was I supposed to do?' Lydia asked. 'Throw it all away? I prefer to wear it and make it last so I don't have to buy anything new for a long time.'

'You look lovely, Mum,' Sunny assured her. 'I was only teasing you.'

Lydia took Sunny's hand and they walked up the main street. 'By the way,' she continued, 'our neighbour said something about old Aunt Nellie that was very interesting.'

'What did he say?'

'That he'd heard she had an exciting life. He didn't know any details, but it made me feel we should try to find out more about her.'

'How could we do that?' Sunny asked. 'Is there anything of hers left in the house?'

'I don't think so,' Lydia replied. 'But I'll have a look around.'

'I'd love to do some research on her,' Sunny said. 'That'd take my mind off… stuff.'

Lydia squeezed her hand. 'I know what you mean. We could certainly try to find out more later on, when we've settled in.' She stopped as a big white bus lumbered up the street ahead of them and stopped outside the post office. A number of children in the same school uniform as Sunny's gathered around the front of the bus and climbed aboard once the doors opened.

'Okay,' Sunny muttered, her face pale. 'Here I go. Wish me luck.'

'Good luck, darling,' Lydia whispered.

'Thanks. See you later.' Sunny pulled her hand from Lydia's grip and walked swiftly to the bus and got on. Lydia saw her talk to the bus driver and then move down the aisle, probably looking for a seat. Then the bus drove off and Lydia stood there, staring at it until it turned a corner and disappeared.

A group of mothers at the bus stop studied her curiously and then nodded and smiled before they walked away. Hardly noticing the glances in her direction, Lydia stifled a sob, silently praying that all would be well and that Sunny would be treated with kindness instead of the scorn she expected. But it was her battle and she had to fight it alone.

'First day in a new school?' a voice said behind her.

Lydia turned and found a small, wiry woman with red curly hair standing behind her. 'Yes,' she replied. 'My daughter was a little nervous. We've just arrived, you see, so everything is a little strange to her.'

'I know,' the woman said. 'You moved into Nellie's house yesterday, didn't you?' She held out her hand. 'I'm Sorcha Keating. I run the grocery shop down there.' She pointed at a shop with a bright sign. 'My son goes to the same school. Fourth year. Also known as Transition Year.'

'Same year as Sunny, my daughter,' Lydia said, feeling a little brighter. The woman seemed so nice which had to mean her son was too. 'Lucky it's a year when there are no important exams,' she continued. 'She'll have plenty of time to settle in and get used to things.'

Sorcha nodded. 'I know. I never thought much of a whole year doing next to nothing but now I have a son in that year, I realise it's good for them to have a chance to mature before they have to prepare for their final two years. And the work experience thing is a good idea too.' She looked Lydia up and down with interest. 'So you've come here for a sabbatical? A break from the rat race in the big city? Forgive me if I appear nosy, but we don't often get such glamour in these parts.'

'Oh,' Lydia said with a laugh, realising she was dressed as if going to lunch with her girlfriends in Dublin. 'You have the wrong idea, I'm afraid. I'm not here to take a break from anything. I've moved here for good. Or until I can get back on my feet, so to speak. I've just lost…' She stopped. 'We've had to reduce our costs,' she continued, trying to explain without revealing too much. She didn't want anyone to connect her to her earlier life. What if someone found out and then told Sunny? 'And we needed a change of scene,' she added, trying to look cheerful. 'Country air is so healthy.'

'It is,' Sorcha agreed. She looked at Lydia quizzically, and Lydia wondered if perhaps Sorcha could tell that she wanted to keep her business to herself. 'But would you like a cup of coffee in my shop? I have a little café corner where customers can have coffee, and we can chat while I stack shelves and so on.'

Lydia brightened, cheered by the kind invitation. 'I'd love some coffee and a chat.'

'Grand,' Sorcha said. 'Let's get going, then. I have a lot to do with deliveries coming in, so I'll talk while I work.' She started to walk swiftly down the street, Lydia half-running behind her and came to a stop outside the shop where she unlocked the door and pushed it open, making bells jingle. 'Here we are. Coffee machine over there in the corner. Help yourself. And grab a bun from the basket if you feel like something to munch on.'

'Thanks,' Lydia said, following Sorcha inside, feeling as if she had stepped back in time. The interior of the shop, with its light green wainscoting, the little lamps hanging from the ceiling, the wooden kegs with apples and bananas, the shelves lined with jars and bottles of all kinds was charming and cosy. The coffee corner even had a little wood-burning stove, the warm glow of which was welcome after the chill of the winter's day outside. The whole shop smelled of newly baked bread and apples.

'Not exactly The Shelbourne,' Sorcha said with a laugh.

'Are you kidding?' Lydia said. 'It's much better than The Shelbourne or any place I've ever been in.'

'Thank you,' Sorcha said happily. She grabbed an apron hanging from a peg and put it on and then proceeded to unpack cans from a stack of boxes near the checkout. 'So,' she said as she started to put the cans on a shelf. 'How are you settling into Starlight Cottages?'

Lydia helped herself to coffee at the machine and sat down on one of the chairs beside the stove. 'So far, so good. We arrived late yesterday afternoon, so we haven't even unpacked yet. And the living room is still full of boxes. But I'll be able to get stuck in while Sunny's at school.' She looked at Sorcha, suddenly remembering something. 'I've bought a car from your cousin Sean in Killarney.'

'Really?' Sorcha dragged a stool to the shelves and stepped up. 'Would you mind handing me up those cans? I'm too short for these high shelves.'

'Of course.' Lydia put her mug on the little table beside her and got up. 'Do you run this shop all by yourself?' she asked as she handed the cans to Sorcha. 'Seems like a lot of work.'

'Yes, it is, I have to admit. Especially being a single mother. But it's easier now that Fintan is older. When he was a toddler, it was a nightmare. But it's hard to find anyone who'd want to work here, what with the long days and the carting stuff around and then doing the accounts.'

'Oh,' Lydia said. 'I suppose that takes a degree of dedication.'

Sorcha jumped down from the stool. 'Definitely. And young people are so demanding, don't you think? Always looking to be entertained. Everything has to be *fun* or they're not interested.' She took a paper mug and helped herself to coffee from the machine.

'I know what you mean,' Lydia said. 'My daughter used to be like that. But now…' She stopped, not wanting to share the story of her life with someone she had just met. But the comment about teenagers had made her realise how much Sunny had changed from the typical teenager to a young woman with amazing strength and maturity, shouldering the burdens of this huge shift in their lives with enormous courage and acceptance, without which Lydia was sure she wouldn't have been able to manage.

'Now life has slapped you both in the face?' Sorcha said, looking at Lydia with empathy.

Lydia let out a little laugh. 'Yeah, you could say that. Or that I'm suddenly finding myself on the edge of a precipice, so to speak.' *The precipice of having to lie to my daughter*, she thought. It really felt like that, as if telling Sunny the truth about her father would push them both into some kind of abyss, with Sunny's grief that was just beginning to heal ripped open again by the ugly facts of the fraud Barry had committed.

'That bad?'

Lydia nodded. 'Nearly.' She sat up, straightening her back. 'But I won't fall down. I'll get back up again,' she said as if talking to herself.

'Of course you will,' Sorcha said with feeling. 'Look at you. You're young and pretty and I have a feeling you're strong and sassy.'

Lydia laughed. 'Not so young at forty-five. But thanks for the compliments.'

'Forty-five is not exactly ancient, you know. I'm nearly that age myself. We still have a few years to go before we hit old age.'

'I suppose. But oh God, I'm learning the hard way that I've been living in some kind of fantasy world. I feel as if Sunny has done more of the practical stuff than me. She's coping amazingly well with this change in our lives. She's more adult than me sometimes. How hopeless is that?'

'Not your fault,' Sorcha soothed. 'And maybe kids don't actually understand how serious some situations really are. But she seems to be a very practical girl.'

'She certainly is. That reminds me,' Lydia said. 'I need matches. We had to light a piece of paper on the cooker last night. Sunny's idea.'

'Very clever.'

'She certainly is. Helpful, thoughtful and smart. She used to be a bit spoiled but she seems to be growing up. I sometimes worry that she isn't quite normal. She doesn't behave like other teenagers these days. Never sulks or rebels. And she is a top student, which didn't make her very popular in her last school.'

'Why worry?' Sorcha said. 'Just thank your lucky stars you got yourself such a gem of a daughter. She's probably just one of those old souls who are born sensible. And maybe she rebels against her own age group rather than her parents.'

'I never thought of it that way,' Lydia said, relieved to talk to another adult about her daughter. She suddenly realised this was what it was like to be a single parent – not being able to discuss her child with a partner. 'Maybe you're right.'

'Of course I am.' Sorcha went to a shelf and took a box of matches from a pile. 'Here,' she said and tossed the box in Lydia's lap. 'On the house. I'll throw in a packet of firelighters as a house-warming gift,' she continued, giving Lydia a box. 'Put that in first, then the kindling and logs and it'll light quickly.'

'Thank you,' Lydia said, so grateful to this woman for making her feel so at home. 'Where can I get firewood?'

'You could go to Moroney's yard up the mountain road. He sells logs. I think it's twenty euros for a big load. Should last you a while. He delivers as well. I'll give them a call, if you like.'

'That would be so kind,' Lydia said, overwhelmed. Was everyone around here this helpful, or was it only Sorcha? Suddenly Dublin felt like a cold place to Lydia. Nobody there had ever gone out of their way to help her like this.

Sorcha took her phone from the pocket of her jeans. 'Actually, let me have your number so I can give it to Moroney's. I'll ask them to send some down to you. They'll call you as soon as they've loaded the logs and are ready to bring them. Then they'll unload and stack them for you if you give them another fiver. All cash, of course.'

'Perfect,' Lydia said and read out her phone number. 'Send me a text with yours so I have it.' She was amazed at how comfortable she felt with this woman after only a few minutes of conversation. Maybe it was simply Sorcha's empathy, or more than that – the support of another single mother who had the experience of raising a child on her own.

Sorcha texted Lydia with her number, and while she added it to her contact list, Sorcha called the yard. 'Hiya, Matt,' she said. 'Would you be free to deliver a load of logs to Starlight Cottages? I have Lydia here, who's just moved into old Nellie's place. You know the house, don't you?' She listened to the reply, nodding, and then gave Matt Lydia's number. 'Yeah, that's right. She's moved in to live here for a while. Okay, if you could do that in a few hours, she'd be very grateful. Thanks a million, Matt.' She hung up and beamed at Lydia. 'All done. You'll soon have enough wood to last you a while. And when you run out, you can call Matt yourself and he'll deliver another load.'

'Wonderful,' Lydia said with a sigh of relief. 'It would have taken me a long time to figure out where to get logs. And he seemed not to mind doing it at such short notice.'

'Of course he doesn't. You've landed in a good place, you know,' Sorcha continued as if reading Lydia's thoughts. 'People around here are very supportive.'

'Even to a blow-in like me?' Lydia asked, touched by the kindness and understanding in Sorcha's voice. Sympathy but not pity, she thought.

'This village is full of blow-ins,' Sorcha said with a laugh, leaning against the coffee machine. 'Take Starlight Cottages for a start. That whole row is inhabited by artists from all over. American, French, Dutch and now a Dubliner. They're a great bunch. Especially Jason next door to you.'

'What does he do?' Lydia asked, sipping the rest of her coffee.

'He designs furniture. Works in a place in Waterville where they make very expensive bespoke pieces. They've sold furniture all over the world. Very exclusive. Jason's a nice man, but likes to keep himself to himself, too, if you see what I mean. I think he's been through some rough times, but hey, who hasn't?'

'That's for sure.' Lydia looked at Sorcha, wondering what rough times she had been through. Single mother, that might mean a lot of things…

'Nellie Butler,' Sorcha continued. 'Your great-aunt, was she?'

'That's right. On my father's side. I only met her once.'

'Interesting woman,' Sorcha said. 'Talk about rough times. She had them in spades. During the war, I mean. But she was a bit of a heroine, too, I believe.'

'Really?' Lydia looked at Sorcha, wanting to know more. 'In what way?'

'I don't really know. I can just tell you what I've heard. There was an old man in the village who knew everything about everybody, but he passed away last winter. Mad Brendan he was called. Not mad at all. Very sharp, actually. He told me once that your aunt Nellie was a spy, but I think he was joking.'

Lydia laughed. 'A spy?'

'I know,' Sorcha said. 'That's impossible. What kind of spying could she have done around here? He was pulling my leg as usual. He loved having people on.' She finished her coffee and threw the paper mug into the recycling bin as the chime on the door tinkled and the door opened to let in the first customers. 'I'd better get back to work. I'll see you later, Lydia. Let me know if you need a hand with anything.'

'Thank you,' Lydia said getting up. 'And thanks for the chat.'

'Pleasure,' Sorcha said and went to sit at the checkout. Lydia heard her say, 'Howerya, Maureen, grand day,' to a customer browsing among the shelves.

With a warm feeling of having made a friend, Lydia walked back to the cottage. At least her first day in Sandy Cove had got off to a good start.

Chapter Eight

The pleasant feeling disappeared as Lydia faced a cold house, the mess of unpacked boxes and suitcases and the remains of their hasty breakfast. She had never been completely alone before, and now the time until late afternoon when Sunny would come home stretched before her like a month of Sundays. In her old life, her calendar would have been full of appointments for lunches, meetings and dinner parties. She would often go from a lunch to afternoon tea and then a short break at home with Sunny before she sailed out again with Barry to a dinner party, all dressed up in evening clothes. It had often been quite stressful to try to fit everything in and she had sometimes wished to have more time for herself. And now she did, but it felt empty and lonely rather than relaxed.

She shivered as she took off her down jacket, thinking with a pang of longing of their warm, comfortable house in Dublin: the things she had taken for granted, now lost for ever. Hopefully that man would arrive soon with the logs. She sighed and sat down on the sofa, staring at the stove knowing she had to learn how to work it and keep it lit all day in this cold weather.

There were two small logs left in the basket with a few sticks and some scrunched-up newspaper. Maybe she could light a fire and keep it going until the new load of logs arrived. Lydia got up and got a firelighter, put it on the cold embers and arranged the sticks and the last logs on top. Then she struck a match and held it to the firelighter, not expecting it to light. But as the first flame started to flicker, she jumped back – staring at the sticks starting to glow, followed by the beginning of a fire – with a feeling of having achieved something amazing. *Silly*, she thought, *this is what most people do every day and here I am like a five-year-old, thinking I've done something amazing.* She laughed as she realised she wanted to tell someone, to say, 'Look, Mummy, I did it,' and get a pat on the back. But as there was nobody around, she took a photo with her phone to show Sunny later, just to make her laugh.

As the fire slowly warmed the room and a pale winter sun shone in through the windows, Lydia went to the kitchen to wash the breakfast dishes. That done, the little kitchen tidy, she went upstairs to unpack and sort her clothes. She would have to put away all the fancy designer stuff – the skirts, silk tops, dresses, high heels and accessories, even her expensive handbags that she had brought just because she couldn't bear to part with them. All she needed were jeans, shirts, warm sweaters and good rainwear, which would mean some of their ski clothes she had worn in St Moritz. Later in the spring and summer, she could wear some of the resort clothes she had bought last year for their month on the Riviera. Too dressy for the wilds of Kerry, but it was cheaper to use what she had, rather than buy anything new.

She had already raised a few eyebrows with what she had put on today, but the looks she got hadn't seemed unfriendly, just slightly bemused. Well, so what? In any case, once she had recovered and found herself a job, they might move back to Dublin and pick up some sort of life again with the help of the few friends who hadn't backed away when Barry had died and the money was gone. With their help, she had managed to get through the first horrible period of grief and reached a kind of acceptance. When everything had crashed and she had been packing up the house, she had said she'd be away for a while and they had understood that she needed space to start a new life. 'Call us if you're desperate,' they said. 'We'll miss you and think of you always.' It had felt like a farewell, but she hoped it was more of an 'au revoir'. Knowing those women were there was a comfort in her despair.

Lydia sank down on her unmade bed, thinking of those good friends, all from different walks of life, that had been her soul sisters since her teenage years. She missed them but had decided not to call any of them until she was settled. She wanted to put some distance between her new life and the revelations about Barry and what he had done before she could face anyone from her old life, even true friends.

She looked at the two big suitcases on the floor, bulging with clothes, and got up from the bed, smoothing the duvet. Then she opened the first suitcase and picked up a black skirt with a matching jacket that looked like a tuxedo with a feminine touch. She had worn it two years ago, when she and Barry were on a trip to Vienna, staying in the Sacher Hotel just across the square from the opera house.

They had tickets to *The Marriage of Figaro* and decided to walk the short distance to the opera. In her short skirt and stilettos, Lydia had wobbled across the street, and just as the traffic lights changed, they had been hit by a squall of wind and rain. Lydia quickly put up her umbrella, but the wind turned it inside out, and there she stood, struggling with an umbrella in her short, tight skirt and high heels, nearly toppling into a puddle. Barry had laughed and helped her, saying she looked like something from an ad for perfume. 'With those legs and the black stockings, and your hair... Wow,' he said, kissing her. Then they had enjoyed the opera and made love afterwards in the big bed in the gorgeous hotel suite. For some time Lydia had been worrying that they'd lost their spark, and that night she began to hope that it was still there. But it hadn't lasted for long.

She didn't know for certain when their differences had become so apparent, or when they'd started to drift away from one another. She remembered their desperate attempts to conceive early in their marriage. The painful disappointment, the desperation, the hospital appointments. Barry had been so happy when eventually their baby girl was born. They named her Sunniva after Lydia's Norwegian grandmother. The name meant 'gift of the sun' which was the name of the first Norwegian saint, who was also an Irish princess. But the happiness didn't last for long. Barry wanted a large family, but Sunny was all that Lydia could give him. And once they gave up trying, they seemed to give up on one another too...

Lydia threw the outfit on the other single bed, deciding it would have to be taken to a charity shop. Why keep happy memories gone sour? More clothes were added to the pile as she kept sorting, the useful pile not nearly as big. Some outfits were worth keeping and would be put away for later, better days. Memories of parties, travels to exotic places and weekends in five-star hotels kept popping into Lydia's mind as she sorted through her vast wardrobe, but she pushed them away, trying to stop lingering in the past. This was now and the harsh reality had to be faced and coped with. *No use moping and crying over what could have been*, Lydia told herself sternly, fighting with her thoughts.

Lydia gave a start as there was a loud knock on the front door. Glancing out the window she saw that an SUV with a trailer full of logs had pulled up behind her hired van. Good. The logs had arrived. She ran down the stairs and threw the door open, smiling at a tall man with dark, greying hair dressed in blue baggy trousers and an Aran sweater that had seen better days. 'Hello,' he said. 'Matt Moroney with the logs you ordered. Sorry, should have called to say I was on my way. Do you want me to stack them in the usual place?'

'Eh, okay,' Lydia said wondering where 'the usual place' was. 'Go ahead.'

'Could you open the back gate so I can get to the shed, then,' Matt suggested. 'I have a small wheelbarrow here so it won't take long.'

'Great,' Lydia said and ran through the house and out the back door to open the gate at the side of the house. She spotted a small lean-to shed in the back garden that she hadn't noticed when they arrived the day before. Matt was soon beside her with a wheelbarrow loaded with logs and it didn't take him long to fill the small shed to the roof with firewood. 'There,' he said when he had finished. 'All done.'

'Thank you so much,' Lydia said. 'Come inside while I get the money to pay you.'

'Thanks,' Matt said, rubbing his hands together. 'Just what I need on such a cold day. Old Nellie used to give me a cup of tea when

I had finished stacking logs for her. Long time ago, of course, but seeing you brought back memories.'

'Oh? How did you know she was my aunt?' Lydia asked.

'Sorcha told me. I popped in to pick up a few things for my wife on the way. Nellie was a lovely lady, you know. A bit reclusive but really nice. We had some good old chats through the years.'

'You must have been very young then.'

Matt laughed. 'That's for sure. I started working at the yard when I was only a lad. Then I took it over when my dad died. Been in the family for over a hundred years. We do all kinds of timbers, and we even supply the furniture place over in Waterville and other places too.'

'You sound busy,' Lydia remarked. 'But come in and I'll put the kettle on. I wouldn't mind a cup of tea myself.'

Matt followed Lydia inside and sat down at the kitchen table while she switched on the kettle, took two mugs from the cupboard, putting teabags into them, then adding boiling water. 'I'm not a great teamaker,' she said apologetically as she pushed a mug across the table at Matt. 'I'm sure you're used to a proper cup from a teapot and all that.'

'Not really,' Matt said. 'The missus isn't into that kind of thing. She makes tea likes this, too and that's fine by me.' He helped himself to milk from the carton that was still on the table since breakfast, looking around the kitchen. 'Haven't been here since your aunt died. This place was let to summer visitors after that, so there wasn't much need for firewood. Nice to have the place lived in again properly. And this kitchen hasn't changed much since Nellie's time.'

'Tell me about her,' Lydia said, taking a sip of tea. 'I didn't know her at all. I never came to visit her and I think she only came to see us once when I was young.'

'What a pity. She was an interesting woman,' Matt said. 'Nice and kind but there was a fire in her that never went out. You could see it in her eyes when she talked about things that she cared about. Like women's independence. And nature. She never married but the story goes that she was in love with someone who left her way back in her youth. Must have happened during the war. Things were tough here then, like everywhere else, I guess.'

'What else can you tell me?' Lydia said, fascinated. As Matt talked, old Aunt Nellie suddenly became a real person, a woman with passions who had lived in this house all her life.

'Oh,' Matt said, pushing his empty mug away. 'I don't know much more. I believe she was educated and spoke at least two foreign languages, French and German, which she learned when she travelled in Europe with her mother. Then she went to the university in Cork to study and got some kind of degree there. That was all before the war broke out. Then she had to stay put here, which must have been a little boring for someone with so much knowledge in her head. But she worked as a translator, so that would have helped keep her interests up.'

'What did she look like?' Lydia asked, yearning to know more.

'I only knew her as an old lady, but I've heard she was very pretty with dark hair and lovely brown eyes.' Matt checked his watch and rose from his chair. 'But I must get going. The yard is very busy these days. Thanks for the tea, Lydia. And welcome to Sandy Cove. I hope you'll be happy here.'

'I'm sure I will,' Lydia said, getting up. She saw Matt to the door and said goodbye before he expertly backed the SUV and trailer down the little lane, turning as he reached the main road, hooting his horn.

Lydia was about to close the door when she saw someone approaching from one of the other cottages: a tall woman with long dark hair blowing in the wind, dressed in an ankle-length flowery skirt, thick green wool sweater and dangly earrings. Her arms were covered in bracelets that jingled as she walked. She increased her pace and waved as she spotted Lydia. 'Hello, there!' she shouted.

'Hello,' Lydia replied, staring at the woman as she came up to the door. 'You must be one of my neighbours.'

'I am,' the woman agreed, holding out her hand and grabbing Lydia's. 'I'm Saskia De Vries and I live next door but one. I'm from the Netherlands,' she continued. 'Just in case you were wondering about my accent.'

'It's hardly noticeable,' Lydia replied, studying the woman surreptitiously. She looked to be in her early sixties and was about six feet tall. Despite her height she was very attractive, with expressive dark eyes, a full mouth and a heart-shaped face. She was beautiful, Lydia thought.

'Well, I suppose the Irish accent has rubbed off on me,' Saskia said. 'I only have a Dutch accent when I'm angry. Which happens mostly when I have to deal with my neighbour on the other side. She can be a huge pain at times, when she does the sergeant major bit. Beware of her, by the way.'

'Who is she?' Lydia asked, intrigued.

Saskia darted a look over her shoulder. 'Ella Caron,' she said under her breath. 'A painter. Does these dramatic seascapes. Abstract art too. You know, those daubs of colour that are supposed to represent something nobody can see. She illustrates children's books as well.'

'Strange combination.'

Saskia shrugged. 'Yes, but she's *French*. And a great intellectual, she thinks. Not the cosy person she pretends to be at all.'

'Now I'm dying to meet this woman,' Lydia said.

'She's quite a character, I'll give her that. Right now she's in Paris for a *vernissage* of her new collection of abstracts. On the Left Bank, of course. The *vernissage*, I mean.' Saskia took a step back. 'But enough about her. I came here to invite you to my house for lunch. Are you free?'

Lydia let out a laugh. 'In my old life, I would have had to check my diary and say that I might be free in three weeks. But this is the new me, so yes, I'm definitively free.'

'Oh, good. One o'clock, would that be all right?'

'Lovely,' Lydia said, cheered by the invitation.

'See you then,' Saskia said and turned to run back to her house, her bracelets jingling.

Lydia shook her head and laughed, feeling as if she had been hit by a whirlwind. She looked forward to lunch with a spark of excitement. Then she went back inside to finish sorting out her belongings and put away not only her clothes, but also the memories of a life that she had once held so dear.

Chapter Nine

Saskia's house was warm and cosy, with a fire blazing in the open fireplace and colourful rugs on the floor. The wall between the kitchen and living room had been knocked down to make one large space which was flooded with light from the French windows that led to a deck. The period feel of Lydia's cottage was absent here and she secretly thought the soul of the house had been lost. The white-washed walls were covered in a multitude of prints and posters and the furniture consisted of a huge corner sofa and beanbags strewn across the floor. A table at the far side of the room was littered with stones and seashells; Lydia was immediately curious.

'My sea glass collection,' Saskia said. 'I make jewellery from whatever I find on the beaches around here. Go and take a look while I make lunch.' She walked over to the kitchen area and the round table set for two. 'I've made carrot soup. Then I thought I'd grill us some mackerel that I caught this morning. I hope you'll like it.'

'Sounds great,' Lydia said, walking over to the work table. The stones and pieces of glass of all colours polished smooth by the sea gleamed in the sunlight. Lydia picked up a piece that looked like a large aquamarine, turning it in her hand, astonished at its silky feel. An array of gold and silver strands lay in rows at the side with some small pliers and hammers. Finished pieces had been put on a shelf above the table; Lydia marvelled at the beauty of the stones and sea glass, polished by the ocean and set in gold or silver. There were bracelets, pendants and earrings, all exquisite and unusual. 'Gorgeous stuff,' Lydia said, admiring the handmade jewellery. 'This beats Cartier and all the others by a mile.'

'The most expensive pieces are not always the most beautiful,' Saskia said as she carefully placed two bowls of soup on the table. 'And the ocean delivers some of the most beautiful gifts.'

'I can see that,' Lydia said, running her finger over a smooth piece of glass the colour of the sky. 'This is all so fabulous.'

'I'm glad you like it,' Saskia said. 'Lunch is ready. I'll turn on the grill while we eat the soup and then I'll throw on the fish.'

Lydia sat down and tucked into the soup and newly baked bread, followed by the grilled mackerel and a salad of chopped kale and tomatoes. She quickly realised that Saskia's cooking was a little hit-and-miss, with the lumpy soup and underdone fish. The salad was the best part of the meal, as this didn't require any cooking skills. 'You're a good cook,' Lydia lied, feeling she had to say something positive.

'Not really. But this was easy. I can cook simple things,' Saskia said. 'But don't ask me to make a sauce or any kind of casserole.'

'I can't even boil an egg,' Lydia confessed. 'But I'm willing to learn. In fact I'll have to. Takeaways are not very healthy and my daughter needs to eat good food.'

'How old is she?' Saskia asked.

'Fourteen.' Lydia smiled. 'But she's more mature and sensible than me sometimes.'

Saskia nodded. 'Some girls are like that. Just like my daughter. She's in her thirties now, but when she was in her teens she was like a wise old woman. Must have been because of all the things she had to deal with then. My husband and I broke up at that time. Quite amicably, but it was traumatic for the children.'

'How many do you have?'

'Two. A son and a daughter. They live in Amsterdam. Both married with children. So I'm an old grandma,' Saskia added with a laugh.

'You don't look old to me.'

Saskia sighed. 'Depends on your attitude. I'm sixty-four but I don't feel a day over thirty. Some days I feel even younger, like twelve or so if I'm having a good day. Then I put on some music and dance all by myself. In my underwear.' She laughed and swung her dark hair out of her eyes, making her earrings dance, the blue stones catching the light. 'You must think I'm quite mad.'

'Not at all,' Lydia said, looking at Saskia, fascinated by her lively brown eyes and dancing eyebrows. She was so joyous and full of life, which made Lydia feel envious. 'I think it's wonderful that you feel like that. And you're such a talented artist. How did you start? And what made you move here?'

'I studied art and crafts in Amsterdam,' Saskia replied. 'I came to Kerry for a break after my divorce fifteen years ago. I cycled all over the area and just happened to come to this village. I fell in love with it instantly and just knew I had to live here. This house was for sale and I decided to buy it over a weekend.'

'How come there are so many artists in these cottages?' Lydia asked. 'Is there some kind of condition from the county council concerning who can buy them or something?'

'Not as far as I know,' Saskia replied. 'I think this terrace just appeals to artists. It did to me, anyway. It seemed so perfect, perched on the cliffs and so close to that private little beach where I could find material for my line of jewellery. I make all kinds of things with seashells too.'

'I can see that the location would be perfect for an artist like you,' Lydia remarked as she finished the mackerel on her plate. 'So inspirational.'

'Absolutely,' Saskia agreed. 'But it wasn't only that, it was the village too and the people in it. They're so warm and friendly and don't mind strangers like me arriving on their doorstep. You'll see. You'll feel at home very quickly. You just have to make a few adjustments and you'll fit right in.' Saskia drew breath and reached out for Lydia's empty plate. 'Can I get you some more salad?'

'No, thank you. It was all delicious,' Lydia said politely, although she had found the mackerel hard to finish. But as she wouldn't have a clue how to cook any kind of fish, who was she to complain?

'We can have coffee by the fire,' Saskia announced when she had piled the dishes into the sink. 'I got apple muffins from the bakery this morning too.'

'Lovely.' Lydia got up from the table and walked across to the sofa where she settled, enjoying the warmth from the still blazing fire.

Saskia joined her, putting a tray with two steaming cups of coffee and a plate with apple muffins on the table in front of the sofa. 'Dig in,' she ordered. 'They're delicious.'

'Oh, but…' Lydia protested, staring at the huge muffin she was supposed to eat. 'That's a bit much for me. I put on weight easily, so I have to be careful.'

'Why?' Saskia asked, taking a huge bite of her muffin. 'So you'll be a little fatter? Won't do you any harm. And in any case, who cares? I mean, it's not as if you're going to be modelling for *Vogue* or something, is it?' She munched on the muffin while she looked at Lydia with amusement.

'I suppose you're right,' Lydia said with a laugh and bit into her muffin, feeling she was doing something sinful. She closed her eyes for a moment while the sweet taste of apple and cinnamon filled her mouth. Then she looked at Saskia and realised she was right. There was no need to stick to any kind of diet or workout routine any more. No need to look fashionably thin to impress anyone. When she attended charity functions and business dinners with Barry, she had to look her best. And when she was running fundraisers herself, she needed to look both glamorous and professional, fitting into fashionable tight dresses. Those days were gone forever, even if it felt strange to let go of a discipline that had become second nature. She looked at Saskia and saw how natural she was, her face free of make-up and her hair long and a little unkempt. There was a wild charm about her that was very alluring and Lydia felt very relaxed in her company. 'It's a bit strange to sit here like this, in the middle of the afternoon, eating muffins and not doing anything remotely useful.'

'But you are,' Saskia countered. 'We're getting to know each other. Isn't that useful?'

'Well, yes,' Lydia said. 'But in my old life, I had a diary packed with appointments and a schedule for lunches and dinners weeks in advance.'

'Sounds like hard work,' Saskia said. 'What did you do in that old life of yours?'

'Fundraising.' Lydia hesitated, not wanting to reveal everything about herself to a stranger. 'I was in marketing before I got married. And then I organised events to raise money for charities. But then I lost my husband.'

'He left you?' Saskia put her hand on Lydia's arm.

'He died,' Lydia murmured. 'Leaving his affairs in a mess.'

'Oh,' Saskia exclaimed, putting her hands to her cheeks, staring at Lydia. 'What a horrible tragedy. I am so sorry.'

'Thank you.' Lydia was suddenly lost for words and hoped Saskia wouldn't start asking questions. Saying it out loud suddenly made all the sad memories rush back in a wave of sorrow.

'It's okay,' Saskia said, patting Lydia's shoulder. 'No need to talk if you don't want to.'

Lydia nodded, blinking back her tears. 'Thank you. I had begun to accept it and the grief is beginning to ease. But then, when I talk about it, the memories rush back for a moment.'

'Maybe it's best not to talk at all?' Saskia suggested. 'Look forward not back is my motto.'

'That's what I'm trying to do,' Lydia said, grateful for Saskia's discretion. 'I need to focus on tackling my new life and looking after my daughter. I have a lot to learn here in Sandy Cove: about myself, about how to stand on my own two feet.'

'Learning new things is good,' Saskia stated. 'And making new friends. And here, at Starlight Cottages, we're all friends, even if we argue sometimes. You have a lot of nice neighbours.'

Lydia couldn't help but think of Jason. 'I had a little chat with Jason over the hedge last night,' she said. 'He seemed nice. Has he been here long?'

'No. He moved in two years ago. But I don't know him that well; he doesn't spend much time in his house. I think he prefers his work over in Waterville. We say hello and good morning and so on, but that's all.' Saskia shrugged. 'No big deal, though. Some people are just like that. Better to leave them alone, eh?'

'I think you're right,' Lydia agreed. But as she sat there, she remembered that warm voice in the still night and wondered what kind of man it belonged to. Part of her wanted to know more about him, and his reticence felt reassuring – if he wasn't comfortable sharing his story maybe she wouldn't have to explain her own situation to him. She hoped she would hear his lovely voice again while she looked up at the stars.

'I knew your old aunt,' Saskia said, breaking into Lydia's thoughts.

Lydia sat up and blinked. 'Aunt Nellie? You knew her?'

Saskia nodded and wiped her fingers on a paper napkin. 'Yes. We became quite good friends during the year before she went to the nursing home where she died. She was a lovely lady. Very sharp even in her old age. Knew a lot about politics and history. She was a librarian in Waterville before she retired and then she used to write little articles for the local newspaper.'

'Really? I had no idea,' Lydia said, astonished. 'I didn't know her at all. I don't even know why she left me this house in her will, but I was told it was because I was the only girl in my family.'

'That would fit,' Saskia said. 'She wanted to support girls and give them independence.'

'She saved my life in a way,' Lydia said as she was suddenly filled with gratitude towards old Nellie. 'If I didn't have the house, I would have had no place to go.'

'But what about your family?' Saskia asked.

'My parents died a few years ago,' Lydia explained as the usual sadness settled on her when she told people about them. 'My mother died of cancer and then my father had a heart problem and just kind of faded away. I have two much older brothers but they live abroad. Australia and Canada. No other relations except some distant cousins in Norway.' Lydia drew breath and sighed, regretting having burdened Saskia with her sorrows when they had only just met. 'Sorry. That came out as a bit sad. Which it is of course. But I've got used to having no family through the years.'

'And then your husband died,' Saskia said, her eyes full of sympathy. 'And here you are in a new place, trying to make ends meet.'

'Oh, it's not that bad,' Lydia protested. 'I have some money to live on for a while. So I have a bit of a margin. And life isn't that expensive around here, I've noticed already.'

'No, here you can live very cheaply,' Saskia agreed. 'At least I do, but I don't have a teenage daughter. They can be very expensive to run,' she joked.

'Don't I know it,' Lydia said with a laugh, glad that the atmosphere had lightened a little. She finished the last of her muffin and drained her cup and then got up. 'I'd better get back and get a fire going before Sunny comes home. She'll want a warm house and some food, I'm sure. And I'm dying to know how she coped with the first day in the new school.'

'Of course,' Saskia said and jumped to her feet, brushing crumbs off her skirt. 'She'll want you there when she comes home.'

'Thanks for lunch,' Lydia said, walking to the front door. 'And for inviting me to your house.'

'It was lovely to get to know you,' Saskia said and gave Lydia a kiss on the cheek. 'Come and see me whenever you want.'

'Thank you.' Lydia smiled back at Saskia, charmed by her warmth. 'And you must come to dinner with me and Sunny as soon as we're more settled. And I've learned to cook something,' she added with a chuckle.

'We can get a takeaway pizza from the Harbour Pub,' Saskia suggested. 'Or better still, go there on Saturday night and eat in. It's very cheap and then you'll meet the locals. There's always a good crowd at the weekend. How about that?'

'Oh, well, maybe not quite yet,' Lydia said with a regretful smile. 'I'm not sure I'm ready to socialise.'

'Oh, no, of course not,' Saskia said, looking contrite. 'I shouldn't have suggested it.'

'I'm glad you did.' Lydia hesitated, her hand on the door. 'It'd be fun to do that sometime in the future.'

'We'll go when the time is right,' Saskia promised.

Lydia said goodbye and walked slowly back to her own house, cheered by the afternoon and marvelling at how much she had enjoyed spending time with someone so completely different from anyone she had ever met before. *I've lived in some kind of bubble all my life*, she thought. She realised that this had meant missing out on meeting unconventional and interesting people like Saskia and Sorcha. If her time here was as eventful as today had been, she was excited. Even if the next few months would be the hardest, before she found her feet and some way to earn money. She had already made a big dent in her bank account, what with buying the car, and other expenses necessary to set them up in the new place. Their survival depended on her alone and she had to find a way.

She looked up at the darkening sky and the stars that were beginning to appear and made a wish that she couldn't quite spell out, but was there, in her heart like a tiny seed waiting to be nurtured and allowed to grow. Then she suddenly realised that it was late afternoon and Sunny would be home soon, expecting dinner. Lydia ran the last bit of the lane and arrived breathless at the door just as Sunny came walking up the road from the bus stop.

Chapter Ten

Lydia could tell by her daughter's slumped shoulders that things hadn't gone well. She opened the door to let them in, putting her arm around Sunny, giving her a little squeeze. 'How did it go, sweetheart?'

Sunny didn't reply, just grunted something and threw her schoolbag on the hall floor. 'I'm going to call Lizzie,' she said before she stomped upstairs and slammed shut the door to her room.

Lydia stood in the hall, looking up after Sunny with a sinking heart. It didn't surprise her that the first day had been difficult, but she had hoped that the students would have been welcoming and understanding to someone who was new to both the school and the area. But children could be cruel, and Kerry kids were probably no exception. Lydia felt a dart of guilt as she thought of all the things Sunny had had to go through lately. It didn't seem fair that she would have to suffer for her father's sins like this. But how could she help Sunny?

Lydia knew there was no answer to that question, so she went into the kitchen to see what she could make for dinner. She found the frozen lasagne they had bought when they stocked up the day before in the freezer and she put that in the oven. Then she made a salad and went into the living room to light the stove with the new logs she had carried in from the shed. That done, she sat back on her heels and looked at the flickering flames, happy she had finally mastered this task at least. She could hear Sunny talking upstairs and thought she sounded a little brighter. It was hard to judge from far away, but Lizzie was the kind of girl who could cheer up a whole army. She was only a little over an hour away in County Cork, and Lydia intended to invite Lizzie over as soon as they were more settled.

As Lydia took plates and glasses out of the cupboard, she heard the door of the neighbouring house slam. It must be Jason walking to his car, she thought, realising it was a chance to find out what he looked like. She peeked carefully out the kitchen window to catch a glimpse. She could only see him from behind, while he got something out of the car, but when he walked back into the house, she could see him clearly for a second. He was a short man with a bulging midriff and a bald head. He had dark eyes and a solid black moustache. He was dressed in a leather jacket under which he wore a black shirt open at the neck that showed a glint of a gold chain against a very hairy chest. Fat fingers with a multitude of rings held the doorknob. Then the door closed and Lydia stood there, weak with disappointment, before she laughed out loud at herself. What had she expected? A tall dark and handsome man with soulful eyes to whom she could bare her soul? Some gorgeous hunk with the tortured soul of an artist? *Get a grip*, she told herself. *You've watched too many Hollywood movies*. But he was still a nice man, she thought. And his voice was lovely. She could have had a worse neighbour.

'What are you laughing at?' Sunny asked coming into the kitchen.

'Myself,' Lydia said. 'I just had a silly thought. Nothing important.'

'Oh. What's for dinner?' Sunny asked.

'Lasagne. Nearly ready. We can eat in front of the fire that I lit all by myself.'

'Good for you, Mum.' Sunny took the plates and cutlery. 'Do you want me to bring this in?'

'Yes please. Then I'll put the rest on a tray and take it inside as soon as the lasagne is ready. And I won't ask you about your day.'

Sunny shot Lydia a wan smile. 'It's okay. It wasn't that bad. Nobody was mean or anything, except when a boy put a spider in my locker and I screamed. Everyone laughed and a girl called Elaine told them all to shut up. But they sniggered at my Dublin accent. Nobody spoke to me much. That's the bad bits.'

'Any good bits?' Lydia asked.

'Yeah. The maths teacher. I liked her a lot. And the classroom looks out over the ocean. See you inside, Mum,' Sunny said before she walked out of the kitchen.

Lydia frowned. Sunny looked decidedly glum, but at least she was talking about her day. She checked the lasagne, and deciding it was ready, took it carefully out of the oven. Then she spooned a large helping onto a plate for Sunny, a smaller amount for herself, put that and the bowl of salad, two glasses and water in a jug on a tray and carried the lot into the living room, where Sunny had put more logs into the stove, making the fire blaze.

While they ate, Lydia told Sunny about her day, keeping it light-hearted and fun.

'Saskia seems like an interesting person,' Sunny remarked, scraping her plate. 'Yummy lasagne, Mum.'

'I'm glad you liked it.' Lydia pushed the bowl of salad to Sunny. 'Eat your greens, too, though.'

'Okay.' Sunny heaped salad on her plate.

'I also met Sorcha at the grocery shop,' Lydia started. 'She's lovely. And guess what? She has a son in your class. His name is Fintan. Did you meet him?'

Sunny made a face. 'Ugh, yes. He was the one who put a spider in my locker.' She rolled her eyes. 'Oh God, Mum, the boys are so immature.'

'I know. But they'll grow up, too, one day. I'm sure he didn't mean anything by it.' Lydia smoothed Sunny's hair. She could speak to Sorcha about her son, but she knew it was better not to get involved. 'Just ignore them, won't you?'

'I'll do my best.' Sunny put her plate on the table and took a swig of water. 'I'll be grand, Mum. It wasn't that bad today. I was just feeling a bit sad and lonely and I missed Lizzie so much. But she said her mother will call you and arrange for us to get together. Maybe meet up in Killarney or something in a week or two.'

'Good idea,' Lydia agreed. She sat back, enjoying the warmth of the fire. 'Not a bad first day, for either of us, I think.'

'Not really,' Sunny agreed. 'I suppose we'll survive.'

'Yes.' They sat quietly for a moment, watching the flames, then Lydia sat up and started to gather the plates. 'I want to do these and tidy up before we get too sleepy.'

'And I want to sort out my stuff,' Sunny said. 'I'll help you with the dishes, first, though.'

'No, it's all right. You go on.'

'Okay.' Sunny got up. 'Have you managed to open that door upstairs?' she asked, stopping in the middle of the room. 'Could be a great place to store what we don't need.'

'Oh, no, I forgot,' Lydia said. 'Let me just carry this inside and then I'll take a look at the bundle of keys the rental agency gave me. There was a lot of stuff in that big envelope, and I haven't looked at it all properly yet. I only discovered the woodshed this morning,' she added with a laugh. 'I'll get those keys and meet you upstairs.'

*

Moments later, they were outside the mysterious door with the keys Lydia had been sent by the rental agency. 'They're all bundled up,' Lydia said, trying to figure out which key would fit into the old lock. 'They said the boxroom had remained locked since Aunt Nellie died, as there were some of her things there that I needed to sort out. Of course I never came here to do that, as I was so busy with… well, you know.'

'Too busy,' Sunny said sternly. 'Dad and his business took up so much of your time. You didn't have any time left over for…'

'You,' Lydia filled in, giving Sunny a guilty look.

'No, for *you*,' Sunny countered. 'It was always all about other people. There was very little time for what you wanted to do.'

'Maybe.' Lydia sighed as she absentmindedly sifted through the keys. 'No need to go over that again.' She was relieved to find Sunny handling her grief so well. Not telling her about Barry's crimes had been the right decision after all, she realised. She picked out a brass key that looked worn. 'Maybe this is the one?'

'Let's try it.' Sunny grabbed the key, pushed it into the lock and turned after a little effort. 'It's stiff. I don't think…'

'Maybe if I give the door a shove at the same time?' Lydia suggested. 'Turn it now.' As Sunny turned the key in the lock, Lydia pressed her hand against the door and suddenly felt it give, the door scraping against the frame. 'It's warped, but…' The door slowly opened with a loud squeak and Lydia peered into the dark void. 'I can't see a thing,' she said.

'Is there a light?' Sunny groped on the wall and there was a click, but no light came on. 'If there was a bulb, it must have gone out.'

'It seems that nobody has been inside this room for over ten years,' Lydia said, her nose itchy from the musty smell that emanated from within.

'I'll turn on my phone,' Sunny said and hurried to get it from her room. Then she shone the beam into the dark space, revealing a tiny room that was empty except for cobwebs, dust and a small leather suitcase lying on the floor.

'Nothing much in here,' Lydia said. 'Except that thing over there.'

They stared in silence at the case until Sunny went inside and grabbed it, running back onto the landing, covered in cobwebs and dust. 'It's plastered with hotel labels,' she said and sneezed twice before dusting off the cracked leather. 'Look. Paris, Venice, Berlin, Hamburg, London. Your old aunt sure got around.'

'She travelled around Europe with her mother, the man who brought the wood told me,' Lydia said, taking the case. 'I'm sure this is full of souvenirs or something.'

'Amazing,' Sunny said. 'A relic from like a hundred years ago.'

'Not quite,' Lydia corrected. 'Around eighty years or so. Their travels stopped when the war broke out. And then Nellie lived here the rest of her life.'

'Poor thing. Stuck here forever,' Sunny said, her voice full of pity. She looked at the case that she had placed on the floor. 'I'm dying to look inside.'

'The room needs a good clean before we can use it,' Lydia said.

'Never mind the room, I want to open the case.'

Lydia laughed. 'Me too. Take it down to the living room and I'll give it a wipe with a damp cloth and then we'll open it. But change out of your school uniform first and give it a shake. It's covered in dust and cobwebs. Then we'll open the case.'

'It'll be full of jewellery,' Sunny said dreamily as Lydia carried the case downstairs. 'And we'll be rich again.'

'Yes, of course,' Lydia said ironically. 'Just like in the movies.'

The suitcase was placed on the living-room floor and quickly cleaned with a damp cloth from the kitchen, and then when Sunny, dressed in jeans and a hoodie, joined her, Lydia snapped the rusty locks and opened the suitcase. They stared at the contents which seemed to be mostly pieces of fabrics, ribbons, odd gloves and colourful postcards. At the bottom, they found an empty leather case that had some kind of insignia on it.

'Strange,' Sunny said, looking disappointed. 'Bits of fabric and all kinds of junk. Why would anyone save that?' She picked up a faded postcard of the Eiffel Tower and looked at the back. 'It's blank. She must have bought it as a memento.'

'Probably,' Lydia said. 'And they might have saved all these bits of fabric in case they needed to patch their clothes. People did that in the old days.'

Sunny looked at a grubby once-white kid glove. 'And this was probably saved because they hoped they'd find the other one sometime.'

Lydia got up off the floor. 'Well, that was a bit of an anti-climax after all that excitement. We'll sort through this and see what we can recycle and then just throw away the rest. But I'm glad we could open the door, so we can use the room. I'll hoover it tomorrow and then it'll be a great space for our suitcases and boxes.'

'Okay,' Sunny said and got up off the floor. 'I have to go and sort through the new books and stuff.'

When Sunny had gone upstairs, Lydia started to put back everything into the suitcase, sad that there had been no letters or photographs to throw any kind of light on old Aunt Nellie and who she had been. She was about to close the suitcase when she noticed something left on the floor. It looked like the bit that sits on the shoulder of a uniform. She picked up and looked at the stripes. A lieutenant, she deduced. But it didn't look British or Irish, but German.

Later that night, when Sunny had gone to bed, Lydia was again drawn to the immense starry sky outside. She put on her warm down jacket and ski gloves and went out to sit on the step outside the sunroom. The stars glimmered and glittered and the full moon slowly rose over the bay, casting a beam of light across the dark water.

Lydia hugged herself, shivering more from the eerie beauty of the night than the cold. A wisp of smoke rose from the other side of the wall and she could smell faint cigar smoke that reminded her of her father and the occasional cigar he would smoke on festive occasions.

'Lydia?' the voice said. 'Are you there?'

'Yes,' Lydia said softly. 'I am. Good evening, Jason.'

'Good evening. I hope the smoke doesn't bother you.'

'Not at all,' she replied, smiling even though he couldn't see her. 'I like it. My father used to smoke a cigar on special occasions.'

'Just like me,' Jason said. 'I'm celebrating the completion of a project. Something that took a long time and required some special material that was hard to find. But I did and now I can send it off to my client. I design furniture,' he explained.

'I know. Saskia told me.'

'Ah,' he said, blowing out a plume of smoke. 'You have met my other neighbour. Very nice, I believe.'

'Yes, she's lovely. I never met anyone like her.'

'Really? She's a bit eccentric, I've heard, but not that unusual.'

'Possibly,' Lydia replied. 'I didn't mix with artists much in my old life. At least not that kind of artist.'

'Only well-behaved ones?'

'I suppose.'

'But I thought you used be – wealthy? Judging by your collection of handbags, I mean.'

'Oh, that. Well…' Lydia suddenly felt a little uncomfortable. 'Yes, we were well off,' she continued. 'But our social circle was quite narrow.'

'I can imagine. Wealthy people are often very clannish.'

'That's true,' Lydia said, thinking of the people they had mixed with. Businessmen and bankers and the odd politician would have been the usual mix of guests at parties she went to. 'I suppose we were quite limited, really. But that's in the past. I'm looking forward now,' she said, remembering Saskia's philosophy.

'That's the best policy,' Jason said. 'I'm doing the same. Not always succeeding, but trying my best.'

'I know what you mean,' Lydia said. 'But sometimes you fall down into that dark hole and have to claw yourself up. It's very tiring.'

'Exhausting,' he agreed.

As she listened to the waves, Lydia could feel herself relaxing. 'In any case I have my daughter to think of. I need to stay positive for her. I need to do more than survive. We have to have some kind of life for her to thrive.'

'You love her very much, I take it.'

'More than I have loved anyone in my entire life.'

'I know. I'm a father,' Jason said, his voice suddenly sad. His voice trailed away as Lydia heard him pull on his cigar. 'Well, it's difficult.'

'It is.' Lydia stood up and tried again to see through the hedge. 'It's weird to share so much with someone I can't see.'

'I find it quite interesting. But we could meet out front if you prefer.'

'No,' Lydia said after a moment's hesitation. She didn't want to break the spell of the stars and the sound of the waves. This way, it was like being in a dream with a mystery man who listened to her without the distraction of facial expressions or polite smiles. 'Maybe another time.'

'Yes. Right now it's nice to be somehow anonymous. Like in a confessional,' he suggested, his voice light.

Lydia laughed. 'Well, not quite. I'm not looking for atonement for my sins.'

'I wouldn't say there were that many.'

'Depends on your definition of sins,' Lydia said, smiling into the darkness.

'I suppose,' he replied. 'But let's not get into that. Tell me more about you.'

'Like what?' Lydia asked, suddenly on her guard.

'Like your likes and dislikes. Your hopes and dreams. You look strong and determined, so I have a feeling you'll be all right in the end.'

'How do you know what I look like?' she asked, taken aback.

'I saw you taking your daughter to school. Only from the back, but that was enough. I think you have what it takes to make your life a success.'

'Success?' Lydia let out a bitter little laugh. 'That's not possible at the moment.'

'I suppose it depends on what one means by success,' he said as if to himself. 'Wealth? The means to buy expensive things? Or just having survived by doing it all yourself, using your own talents? Success is probably simply being happy in your own skin.'

Lydia thought for a moment. 'Yes. That last bit sounds quite amazing. But right now, I'm just trying to survive.'

'I know. It's too soon to do anything else.' His chair scraped. 'But now I have to get to bed. Early start tomorrow, as always. Goodnight and sweet dreams, Lydia Butler.'

'Goodnight, Jason.'

His footsteps echoed in the still night and a door closed, leaving only a wisp of smoke and a faint smell of cigar. *How strange*, Lydia thought, *to sit here and be comforted by talking to a complete stranger about life and despair and survival. Someone who suffers himself, someone so different.*

She stood up and turned her eyes to the sky, looking at the stars and breathing in the cold fresh air, feeling oddly at peace. Her conversation with Jason had given her a ray of hope, and she began to realise that it wasn't looks but what was in a person's heart that defined them. Her thoughts drifted to the past few months and she realised that coming here and meeting new people was helping her to overcome her grief and to look forward with both hope and trepidation. It seemed ironic that she had had to lose everything and come to a cold little cottage in a small village on the edge of the west coast to find out what mattered most in life.

Chapter Eleven

The following day, Lydia got a message from Sorcha's cousin in Killarney saying that her car was ready to be picked up and she only had to register and pay the insurance and tax and everything would be in order. Lydia left in the van for Killarney as soon as Sunny had gone to school, and when she had returned it to the rental firm, she treated herself to lunch at a nearby café. When she had picked up the car, she drove through Killarney where the traffic had slowed to a near stop as a lot of visitors were arriving for a short break to play golf. Lydia glanced at the expensive cars and the people in them, watching them drive up to five-star hotels, where valets rushed out to park their vehicles. She spotted a few people she knew slightly from Dublin and couldn't help feeling a pang of nostalgia for those bygone days when everything had been so easy. But those people hadn't been true friends, she had discovered after the funeral; none of them had called or sent a note of sympathy. And again none of them had reached out when the story of what Barry had done came out. If those people saw her now, they'd judge her not only for Barry's actions but also for losing all she had. Being poor was the worst crime in their eyes.

A hooting of horns woke Lydia from her trance and she drove away, telling herself sternly to look forward instead of living in the past. But it was impossible to stop thinking about what had happened to her. The change was hard to cope with, but what hurt the most through everything was Barry's betrayal and his dishonesty. If she'd known, then they could have handled this together, and it would have been easier. They could have weathered the storm and worked hard to get back on their feet again. The problems with the business losing money were something Lydia couldn't even begin to understand. Why hadn't she noticed? Why hadn't Barry told her? Had they drifted so far apart that he couldn't share anything with her? She would never know. He had died, and she had been abandoned to deal with this mess all on her own…

Lydia arrived back in Sandy Cove still wrestling with what had happened. She was so lost in thought that she didn't even notice the small black dog as she drove up onto the pavement outside the grocery shop. She saw him just in time, and he ran faster to avoid her, as she came to a stop suddenly. Sitting in the car, she breathed hard, her foot still on the brake, trying to pull herself together.

The door to the shop opened and Sorcha stuck her head out. Lydia wound down the window. 'Sorry. I nearly flattened your dog,' she said apologetically.

'It's not my dog,' Sorcha replied. 'It's a stray that has been wandering around the village all day. We're trying to find out who owns it.'

'Oh.' Lydia looked at the little dog, who was now sitting on the pavement. It was a Jack Russell terrier with the saddest eyes Lydia had ever seen. She got out of the car and crouched beside it, putting out a tentative hand to touch it, ready to pull back should it bite. But the dog just whimpered softly as Lydia stroked its soft head. 'Hello,' she said. 'Are you lost? Where did you come from?'

'Could have been dumped,' Sorcha suggested. 'Happens sometimes. Isn't it sweet, though?'

'Adorable,' Lydia said. She gathered the dog in her arms and stood up. 'Look how he's cuddling into me.'

'Maybe it's a she,' Sorcha said and took a look. 'No, you're right. It's a boy.' She stroked his head. 'He's lovely. Quite young, I think. Maybe you should take him to the vet's across from the pharmacy? The vet's my cousin and he'll be able to tell if he's got a microchip. I'd go with you but I left a shop full of customers.'

'That's okay,' Lydia said. She agreed that she should take responsibility for it, and started to walk in the direction of the pharmacy further up the street. She soon spotted the veterinary clinic with its sign over the door and went inside, arriving into an empty waiting room.

A door opened and a tall man in dark green scrubs looked out. 'Hello,' he said. 'Your dog not well?'

'It's not my dog,' Lydia said. 'I found him in the street. I thought I'd try to find out if he has a microchip. I'm Lydia Butler, by the way.'

He nodded. 'I know. You just moved into Nellie's house.'

Lydia stared at him. 'How did you know?'

'I was in the pub last night and someone said a fierce stylish woman from Dublin had moved into Starlight Cottages. So then, as you fit that description perfectly, I deduced that you must be her.' He held out his hand. 'I'm Brian O'Connor.'

Lydia tried to hold on to the little dog while she shook Brian's hand. 'Hi, Brian,' she said, instantly charmed by his twinkly brown eyes and wide smile. His brown hair flopped over his forehead in a boyish manner even though he must be well over forty.

'Let's have a look at this little fella.' Brian took the dog from Lydia and walked back into the surgery, where he placed him on a clean white table. Brian examined the dog, taking out a machine to scan for the chip, running it over the dog's back. He patted the whimpering animal and looked at Lydia. 'No microchip. He's perfectly fine, although he's a little shaky. Perhaps he's traumatised, which is normal if he's been abandoned. He needs food and a lot of love. Are you planning to keep him?'

Lydia looked at the dog and hesitated for only a second. Then she took him in her arms. 'Yes,' she said, almost instinctively. The little dog reminded her of a puppy she had played with in the neighbour's garden as a child. She thought for a moment. 'It's probably not the most practical decision I've ever made,' she mused. 'But I'm not sure I care. I think he might have stolen my heart already.'

'I'm not surprised,' Brian said, laughing, looking at the two of them. 'He's probably the cutest dog I've seen in a long time.'

'But I don't know anything about dogs,' Lydia confessed.

'Not much to know,' Brian said. 'The most important thing is to love him. And it looks like you already do. He'll need to be fed – you'll find dog food in the grocery shop with instructions on the back. You'll also find doggy things like leads and collars and toys and treats. Sorcha could give you hand with all of that. She's used to dogs even though she doesn't have one right now. If you come back tomorrow, I can give him the shots he needs for his age which I think is around eight months.' Brian watched Lydia as she stroked the dog's head. 'If I were you, I'd still try to see if you can find his owner. Take a photo of him and send it to the Guards in Killarney and then perhaps you could post it on any social media platform you're on? Just in case he's lost?'

'I'm not on any social media platforms,' Lydia said. 'I closed all that down recently. Personal reasons.'

Brian nodded, looking sympathetic. 'I can imagine. You've been through a lot.'

'I…' Lydia stopped. 'Thank you. But… How do you know what I've been through?'

'Oh, well… Sorcha said you'd lost your job or something.' He looked suddenly uncomfortable. 'I didn't mean to intrude. Sorcha doesn't gossip, but she happened to mention that she'd met you. She's my first cousin, you see.'

'I know. She told me,' Lydia said, suddenly worried about people gossiping. What if they found out who she was and what Barry had done? And if someone told Sunny… Oh, God, that would be awful. Lydia decided there and then to tell Sunny as soon as she could. But she needn't worry about that now. 'So you're related to Sean in Killarney too?' she asked, trying to work out the family connections.

'No, I'm on her mother's side. Look, I'm sorry if I was tactless just now. It's really none of my business.'

'That's all right,' Lydia said with a little smile. 'No need to apologise.'

'Well, maybe you don't want to be reminded of your past all the time. Can't be easy.'

'No.' Lydia buried her face in the dog's fur for a moment and then looked up at Brian. 'You're very kind. It's difficult to know what to say to people like me who've suddenly become unemployed. But I know people generally mean well.'

'Of course they do,' he said, looking relieved. 'And they know you're Nellie Butler's grand-niece, so in a way that makes you one of us.'

'That's a lovely thought,' Lydia said. 'Did you know her at all? Or anything about her history? What happened to her during the war and that kind of thing?'

'Not much,' Brian replied. 'Only that she helped out with some war work, or something. But I have no idea what that was. But back to our little friend here. I could post his picture on our Facebook page and ask people to share it, if you'd like? I mean, if he's someone's pet, they might be desperate to find him. In any case, you might not have any contacts in this area as you've just arrived. But maybe your husband does?'

'I'm a widow,' Lydia said quietly.

'Oh God, I'm really sorry,' Brian said, looking embarrassed. 'I put my foot in it again, didn't I?'

'Not at all,' Lydia assured him, worried she might have made him feel bad. 'You couldn't have known.' She put the dog on the table. 'But back to the dog. How about taking his photo and then I'll go and see what kind of dog food Sorcha recommends?'

'I'll do the photo,' Brian offered. 'Leave him with me and pick him up when you've been to Sorcha's.'

'Great idea. Thank you, Brian,' Lydia said, touched by his kindness.

Once back in the shop, Lydia quickly explained what Brian had said to Sorcha and a line of customers who were all ears. An old lady with a walking frame, a man with a small child, two women who were filling their trolleys with treats for their bridge club evening and the parish priest all stopped in their tracks to listen to the story of the dog. They all agreed that Lydia had to find out if he was owned by anyone before she adopted him.

'Don't get too attached,' the old lady said. 'Pretend you're just minding him.'

The bridge ladies argued that the dog had probably been abandoned, the man with the child told her to take the dog to the pound, and the parish priest said it was in God's hands. Lydia thanked them all and bought a bag of food suitable for a puppy, a red leather collar and matching lead, amazed that Sorcha kept such things as this in stock.

'Most people have dogs here,' she said as she gave Lydia her change. 'I can't because I just don't have enough space in my flat above the shop, and Fintan is allergic. I love dogs, though. I hope you get to keep him.'

'I hadn't planned to get a dog,' Lydia said. 'But Sunny will love him. She begged me to get a dog when she was younger, but I was always so busy, so distracted…'

'It'll be very good for your daughter to care for an animal,' the old lady said behind them.

Lydia had to laugh at the way everyone took such interest in the matter. In Dublin, she would feel it was intrusive if someone volunteered their opinion, or stuck their nose into her business without being invited, but here it seemed caring and sweet, as if the whole village was looking after her, even though she was a complete stranger who had just blown in.

She only hoped the news of her whereabouts wouldn't reach the gossipmongers in Dublin. She wanted to disappear from their radar forever and felt that she was stepping into a new identity, that of a single mother who had lost her job in Dublin and was now trying to cope. There was a long hard road to walk before she could cast off from the past. But what worried Lydia the most was Sunny. She had decided to tell her about what had really happened. But how was she going to do it? On the one hand, she didn't want Sunny even more upset, but on the other, the fear of someone telling her became increasingly real. What on earth was she going to do?

When Lydia came home, she fed the dog in the kitchen and made up a bed in front of the stove with an old blanket she found in the sunroom, thinking he'd love the warmth. But he didn't settle and trotted after her wherever she went. He didn't like the hoover much, though, and ran down the stairs in a panic when she turned it on to clean out the boxroom. Lydia shook her head and carried on, determined to clear the room of dust and cobwebs so she could use it to store their suitcases and some of the boxes she hadn't unpacked. They were full of things she didn't really need but hadn't wanted to part with – her own things from her childhood home that had nothing to do with Barry. She'd unpack them later when she had more time and energy.

Once cleared and cleaned, all the little room needed was a lightbulb, but as Lydia had forgotten to buy one, she had to work in near darkness, the only light coming from the landing through the open door. She could see enough to put the empty suitcases into the room and push the two remaining boxes inside, but as she pushed in the last box, her foot caught on a loose floorboard. Pushing down on it with her foot, she noticed that something underneath was blocking it. A thick wad of papers. Lydia lifted the floorboard and removed the wad, putting it on the floor outside the door. Then she pushed the box inside and closed the door with a satisfied grunt. There. All tidied away.

She looked at the bundle on the floor and saw that it was a packet of old letters and cards tied together with a green ribbon. Intrigued, she picked them up, sneezing as the dust hit her nose, flicking through the pile. The letter on the top was yellow with age and the writing faded, but she could make out the date at the top of the page, which said, *29/1, 1941* and then the words *Liebe Nellie…* Lydia forgot all about the dog and tidying up the house as she looked at the letter, written in German. It was signed, *Liebe Grüße von deinem Hansi*, which, with the limited German she had learned in school, she took to mean 'with all my love from your Hansi' or something like that. There was nothing else in German, the rest of the bundle containing letters and postcards from friends and relatives, even a card from Lydia's father at a very young age, wishing Auntie Nellie a 'Happy Christmas' sometime in the early nineteen fifties.

There were also some photos of Nellie and her mother on their trips in Europe, the two women posing in front of the Eiffel Tower, the Brandenburg Gate and other famous monuments. Both Nellie and her mother were good-looking women with dark hair, strong features and charming smiles. Then there was a photo of Nellie in front of the cottage with the caption '*in our new home, 1940*'. That must have been just after her father died and she had inherited the cottage through his family, some of whom had been working with the coastguard ever since the houses were built. She must have lived here in the cottage with her mother, Lydia assumed.

Lydia brought the bundle downstairs and put it on the coffee table to show Sunny when she came home from school. They would go through them all together. But that letter in German kept popping into Lydia's mind. It looked like Nellie had received a love letter from a German man in the middle of World War Two. But that couldn't be true. Could it?

Chapter Twelve

Sunny was over the moon to find the little dog sitting in the middle of the sofa when she came home. 'A dog!' she exclaimed and threw her schoolbag on the floor. 'A gorgeous little doggie.' She knelt in front of the sofa and took the dog in her arms while he furiously wagged his tail and licked her face. 'Where did he come from?'

'I found him in the street outside the grocery shop,' Lydia explained, sitting down on the sofa, delighted to see Sunny's reaction to this nice surprise. This would cheer her up after that bad first day. 'I nearly ran over him, so he was lucky to escape.'

'Are we keeping him?' Sunny asked.

'I don't know. We have to try to find out if he's missing from someone first.'

'I hope he isn't. What's his name?'

'I don't know if he even has one,' Lydia replied. 'I don't think we should get too attached, you know.'

'Yes, but I want him to have a name,' Sunny argued, cuddling the dog.

'You're right,' Lydia said. 'I couldn't think of the right name, but I'm sure you will.'

'I want to call him Lucky,' Sunny said, staring into the dog's eyes. 'It seems he was lucky not to be run over by you. Do you like that?' she asked the dog, who barked twice and kept licking her face. 'He likes it,' she declared. 'So now he has a name. Welcome to our house, Lucky.'

'But he's not really ours,' Lydia protested. 'He might belong to someone else, a family who might be very sad to have lost him. So we have to find out if anyone has lost a dog. The vet is putting his photo out on Facebook and I've reported it to the Guards in Waterville.'

'Oh.' Sunny looked at Lydia, her eyes full of hope. 'But if no one claims him, can we keep him? He's so cute. I'll look after him and take him for walks and feed him and teach him to sit and all that.'

Lydia laughed. 'No need to make those sad eyes at me. Yes, we'll keep him if nobody comes forward. I'm in love with him already.'

Sunny set Lucky down on the floor and sat on the sofa beside Lydia. 'I hope he doesn't belong to anyone. I'd be so sad to have to let him go.'

'I'd say he doesn't,' Lydia soothed. 'He had no collar and wasn't microchipped. But we'll have to wait and see.'

'And love him and feed him and walk him and cuddle him and play with him,' Sunny filled in.

'All that,' Lydia said, laughing at Sunny's blissful expression. 'I bought him a collar and a lead and made up that bed over there by the fire. And some toys as well that Sorcha threw in for free. It's all in the kitchen with the dog food I bought. You can feed him while I make us some dinner. Fish fingers and chips with broccoli and carrots. Will that do?'

'Great.' Sunny's gaze drifted to the bundle of cards and letters on the coffee table and picked it up. 'What's this?'

'Oh,' Lydia said. She'd forgotten all about her discovery in the excitement about their new dog. 'I found these letters under the floorboards in the boxroom when I cleaned it out. Some of old Nellie's things.'

Sunny flicked through the bundle. She studied the neat writing for a while.

'One of the letters is in German,' Lydia remarked. 'So I assume she met someone German in Sandy Cove during the war. It's a shame you aren't studying the language.'

'Just type the whole thing into Google Translate,' Sunny suggested.

'Oh my God, that's brilliant!' Lydia exclaimed. She laughed and kissed Sunny's cheek, wondering why she didn't think of that herself. 'I'll do it after dinner.' She got up. 'You can feed Lucky while I cook.'

'Okeydokey,' Sunny chanted and followed Lydia into the kitchen with Lucky trotting behind them as if he knew he belonged to them from now on.

After dinner, they settled in front of the stove, Lucky asleep on Sunny's lap. Lydia turned on her iPad and clicked on Google Translate, telling Sunny to read out the German letter so she could type it in, Sunny doing her best to pronounce the words.

'It won't be perfect,' Lydia said as she typed.

'I know,' Sunny said, taking a break from her dictation. 'Let's not read it out until I've finished.'

Lydia nodded and kept typing until the end of the letter. Then she sat back and looked at Sunny. 'Okay. Here is the letter in English.'

My dear Nellie,

Just to let you know I'm fine and quite comfortable here at the internment camp at the army base in Cork. There are other German pilots here who have also crash landed in other parts of the south and west coasts of Ireland, some due to engine failure and then me and my crew who got caught in fog and managed to land on the slopes of the mountain just above your village. The few days I spent at the farm near your home were truly wonderful. I will never forget the kindness of the people of Kerry, or your gentle hands when you dressed my wounds, which have now healed – and your lovely brown eyes are forever in my mind. Our walks on the beautiful beach below your house where we shared our life stories will be the loveliest memories of this awful war.

I truly understand that your people had to contact the army and that they then had to take us to this camp. I have heard that they are building a special camp for us and other German soldiers who have arrived in Ireland by accident. We will have to stay there until the war is over. It's hard, but in a way, I think we have been lucky. I've been able to write to my family in Dresden to let them know I am fine and being treated very well. I thank God we didn't end up in England, where we might have been shot, as we are, after all, the enemy.

When we are transferred to the new camp at some place called The Curragh, we will be put to work at nearby farms, which might be hard but not too unpleasant. Write to me, dear Nellie, and I will write back, and then, after the war, I will return to your lovely village and we will once more walk together on that beautiful beach you told me was called Wild Rose Bay. The image of the wild roses all over the slopes, the white sand, the glittering ocean and your lovely face will keep me going through these dark times until we meet again, my very own Irish rose.

Love from your Hansi

'Oh my God,' Sunny exclaimed when Lydia had finished reading. 'How amazing! A German plane crash landed on the mountain up there and then the crew were captured by the people in this village.'

'Incredible,' Lydia said, looking at the text. 'He called her his Irish rose. Isn't that sweet? I must find out more. There must be some history of the village somewhere. Maybe at the tourist office?'

'Or on the internet?' Sunny said, grabbing the iPad. She started clicking but then let out a sigh. 'Died again. The hotspot phone signal is no use. We have to get broadband, Mum. Everyone in the village has it, so it must be able to reach the cottage.'

'I'll look into that,' Lydia promised, thinking with dismay of yet another bill to pay.

'One way or another, we have to find out more,' Sunny stated.

'Of course,' Lydia said. 'I'll ask Sorcha tomorrow where there might be a record of what happened here.'

'Brilliant, Mum.' Sunny got up and carefully placed Lucky onto the floor. 'I have a bit of homework, but I'll get into my pyjamas and do it in bed.'

'Good idea,' Lydia said. 'I'll come up to say goodnight later.' She watched as Sunny bounced across the floor with Lucky following behind her like a shadow, amazed at how Sunny's mood had changed for the better so quickly. She said a quick prayer that nobody would claim Lucky.

'It's amazing,' Lydia said to Jason over the hedge later that evening during their starlit chat that had become such comfort to her. 'I had no idea how much a dog could do for a teenager. She is so happy and now she has put his bed in her room and they're both asleep. That little dog has become a lifeline for her.'

'And you,' Jason filled in, his deep voice full of laughter. 'I have a feeling you're as much in love with him as she is.'

Lydia had to laugh. 'Yes. I have to admit I'm totally besotted. It's as if a happy spirit has come into our lives.'

'Dogs are wonderful company,' Jason said. 'I'm sure looking after him will help to comfort you in your sorrow.'

'I think he will,' Lydia agreed, trying to get comfortable in the folding deck chair she had found in the sunroom and had brought out so she could look up at the stars without having the crane her neck. Tonight was the third night of their acquaintance and though she was used to this unusual way of meeting, not seeing each other felt increasingly frustrating and she was dying to see Jason face to face. But maybe it suited him to stay like this? Having caught a glimpse of him the day before had surprised her, but now his appearance was only a faint memory, his voice and his wise words the most important aspect of his persona. It was like talking to a benevolent spirit who didn't judge her but simply let her talk.

But what about him? What had he been through and why was he so reclusive? He didn't volunteer much about himself and she didn't want to press him. He might be more ready to confide in her when he knew her better. But whatever it was that he had tried to escape must be serious as he had left his country and his family behind.

'Another exciting thing happened today.' Lydia proceeded to tell Jason about the letter they had found and what it had said. 'Did you ever hear a story about a German plane crash landing here in 1940?'

'Hmm… Maybe.'

'I'm going to try to find out more tomorrow,' Lydia said. 'I'll let you know if I learn something.'

'I'm afraid we won't be able to meet tomorrow,' Jason replied.

'Why not?' Lydia asked, alarmed. Was he getting tired of listening to her?

'Because the weather is breaking in the morning,' he stated. 'Wind and rain. It'll last a few days, unfortunately.'

'I see. But…'

'In any case I'll be away for a while,' he continued. 'I'm going to a furniture fair in Dublin with my firm. We're exhibiting some of our pieces there.'

'I must look up your firm,' Lydia said. 'Do you have a website?'

'No, we don't. We don't need one. We're known through word of mouth, and fairs and exhibitions. As everything is handmade for specific clients, we don't need a website or social media. But speaking of websites and such,' he added, 'I thought I'd tell you that I'd be happy for you to use my internet service. I'm sure you'll get a strong signal through the wall.'

'Yes. Sunny said someone's broadband comes up when she uses her phone.'

'That's mine. The password is simple. Just type in JASOC22 and you'll be connected.'

'That's very generous of you,' Lydia said politely. 'But we can organise our own, you know. I just haven't got around to it.'

'But then you'll have to pay,' he argued. 'This way it'll be free. No need to add to your expenses at this time, I think.'

'Yes but…' Lydia started, feeling uncomfortable. She didn't want to accept this kind of handout from someone she hardly knew, even though she had revealed a lot about herself to him because of the nature of their conversations. She wanted to be independent.

'Lydia,' he said softly, 'I know you feel that this is some kind of charity and you're too proud to accept it. But you should realise that accepting help from others, although hard, is just as helpful as giving it.' He paused. 'No, that was a clumsy way of explaining it. I think maybe I should say that taking is just as good as giving, and much harder in the end because it makes the person on the receiving end feel indebted. But it would make me happy if you accepted this offer from me, and you'll owe me nothing in return, that's all.'

'Then I will accept,' Lydia replied. 'Thank you, Jason.'

'You're very welcome,' he replied in the same gentle voice as before. 'Thank you for letting me help you. It makes me feel better about myself, too, you know.'

'Oh. I didn't think of that,' she said, feeling a dart of guilt. 'I've been going on about my problems and not asked you about yours at all. But I had a feeling you didn't want to talk about them,' she added.

'You were right. I didn't. Still don't. I don't want to burden you either when you're struggling with all that has happened to you and you're trying to settle into a whole new life.'

'I wouldn't mind listening if you want to talk about it,' Lydia said. She suddenly stood up. 'You know what? I'd like to see you. It's getting a little weird talking to you like this, as if you're some kind of disembodied voice in the dark.' She laughed.

She could hear him moving on his terrace. 'Yes,' he said. 'You're right. We need to say hello properly. I'll put on the light over my back door. Stand where you are. I think I'll be able to flatten the hedge a bit just there.'

Lydia waited while Jason went to turn on the light over his back door, and suddenly she could see the shape of him coming closer. She was astonished to discover that not only was he tall but he also had wide shoulders and a shock of dark hair. When he came closer and started to make a hole in the hedge she could see him a little better. This was obviously not the man she had seen at his door. 'I can see you,' she said, her voice tight with nerves. 'But... You're not what I imagined,' she ended lamely, deciding not to mention the man she had seen, whoever that was. It clearly hadn't been him.

'I'm sorry to disappoint you,' Jason said, his voice full of laughter.

'Oh, you're not a bit disappointing,' Lydia said. 'Quite the opposite,' she added, glimpsing a handsome face despite the dim light.

A hand was suddenly thrust through the branches. 'Glad to hear that. So let's shake hands, then, before we turn in. How do you do, Lydia? Nice to meet you at last.'

'Very nice to meet you, Jason,' Lydia said, laughing as they shook hands through the hedge.

'So,' he said, having pulled back his hand. 'After these few days, do you feel more settled?'

'A little bit,' Lydia replied after a moment's reflection, still staring through the shadows at his face, trying to see it more clearly. 'I like the house. And I love the views of the ocean. I feel that my father's aunt was happy here.'

'I think she was as far as I know,' Jason agreed. 'But I've only talked about her to Sorcha, that nice woman in the grocery store. I think they knew each other.'

'That's right,' Lydia replied. 'Sorcha knew her during her last years here. I must ask her if Nellie said anything about the German pilot. But if she doesn't know, where can I find out more?'

'I don't know,' Jason said. 'You'll have to ask around, maybe go to the library and look into the history of the village? Could be an interesting project for you.'

'That's a great idea,' Lydia said, her mood picking up. 'I should find out more about this area anyway.'

'It has an interesting history,' Jason said. 'Both ancient and modern. And who knows what you might find out about the time around the war,' he continued in a lighter tone.

'You know something,' Lydia exclaimed. 'And you're not telling me. You hinted at something just now. What do you know?'

Jason laughed. 'Much more fun for you to find out on your own.' The branches rustled as he moved away. 'And now it's goodbye for a while. See you next time the stars are out. Or perhaps better still, in daylight next time.'

'That would be nice.' Lydia said goodnight, looking at the tall figure at the door before he turned off the light. She was even more intrigued by him now that she knew he wasn't the man she had seen in front of his house. She went inside to prepare for bed, switching off lights as she went, thinking about what he had said. His offer of use of his broadband couldn't have come at a better time. Sunny would be happy to have her iPad working again, and she would need it for school projects. It was an expense she wouldn't have to meet, which was a relief.

But what about her own project? Finding out about what happened in the village during World War Two… She decided to go to the little library she had seen in the village square, housed in what in the old days had been the town hall, Sorcha had told her. And she had to call in to the vet for Lucky's shot and to find out if anyone had been in touch about the puppy. Trivial things compared to what she was used to, but it was something to look forward to all the same.

Life in a small village wasn't as busy as Dublin, Lydia thought, but the warmth and friendship she had found here already was heartening. And the quest to find out more about Nellie and her romance gave her a little thrill.

She thought again of Jason and how considerate he was. He seemed so full of compassion for other people, and that was still what impressed her the most about him. But who was he really? What had made him leave his home and his family to come here and live like a hermit in this remote place?

Chapter Thirteen

Jason's prediction about the weather proved to be right. Lydia woke up to the rain smattering on her window accompanied by the wind howling in the chimney. The house was chilly so Lydia quickly lit the fire and turned on the radiators, praying that it wouldn't result in a stiff electricity bill at the end of the month. But they had to keep warm, especially in the morning, before Sunny went to school. She'd turn them all off when she was alone.

Sunny appeared in the kitchen with Lucky, announcing that she had let him out in the back garden for a bit to 'do his business' and now they both wanted breakfast. Lydia quickly made some hot chocolate and a bowl of cereal for Sunny and tea and toasted soda bread with a slice of cheese for herself. Then they shared an orange and Lucky noisily wolfed down his bowl of dog food while Lydia made Sunny's lunch for school. Lydia felt at peace, despite Sunny's long loving farewell to Lucky, and as she poured herself another cup of tea and scooped Lucky onto her lap, she was truly relaxed.

It all felt so happy and normal that Lydia momentarily forgot about the miseries of the past months, even her intention to speak to Sunny about her father. She realised that today was the first day she had simply done her chores without thinking much about anything except the day ahead and planning what they'd have for dinner. She felt she had come through the worst of her grief and was now looking forward instead of back. There would always be a piece of her heart where sadness lingered, but now the pain was softer and a lot easier to accept. She was into a new phase of her life, where she was in charge of her own happiness.

'It's all your doing,' she said to Lucky, who wagged his tail and licked his mouth, looking for more food. But Lydia put him on the floor, quickly tidied the kitchen, and went upstairs to get dressed, glancing out the window watching Jason's car backing out of his driveway. On his way to Dublin, she supposed with a pang of sadness. She'd miss their night-time chats while he was gone and hoped the weather would clear when he came back.

But she had things to do and little time to daydream. First on the agenda was a visit to the vet's for Lucky's shot, then the library for a little research, followed by a trip to Sorcha's shop to buy something for dinner that would be easy to cook but healthy and nourishing for Sunny. Dressed in her Barbour and the green Aigle wellies she had worn on weekends at country houses in her earlier life, Lydia set off with Lucky on the lead. He seemed happy too, trotting obediently by her side as if he was performing at a dog show.

'He's such a well-behaved little dog,' Brian said a little later as he administered the shot.

'Yes,' Lydia agreed. 'He seems to have been well-trained. Perfectly clean in the house, too and sits when he's told. Maybe he is someone's much-loved dog after all.'

'Nobody has come forward so far,' Brian said. 'Which is strange considering how small the area is. But maybe he was dumped by someone who didn't want him. He's quite skinny so that could be because he's been on the road for a while. Could be that he was abandoned for some reason.'

'How strange.' Lydia lifted Lucky from the examining table and cuddled him before she put him on the floor. 'If he belongs to someone, I hope they'll tell us before we get too attached.'

Brian laughed. 'Looks like it's too late. You're already attached to him. And he to you.'

'I know. Sunny, my daughter, is worse. She'd be devastated if she had to give him up.'

'I'll delete the Facebook page tomorrow,' Brian offered. 'Two days is enough notice. After that, he's yours and I'll put in a microchip. After all, he didn't have one, or a collar and seemed to be abandoned, so I don't think he's owned by anyone.'

'That's very kind,' Lydia said.

'Wait till you get my bill,' Brian said, grinning.

'Oh.' Lydia stared at him. 'I didn't… I mean… How much do I owe you?'

'Don't worry, it's just five euros for the shot,' Brian said in a soothing tone. 'Then a tenner for the microchip. You'll need worming tablets and a flea treatment but those only cost a few euros. That'll be all and you can pay me when we do the microchipping. And then just fatten him up a bit and love him and you won't need me very often, if at all. I'll give you a brochure I hand out to all new dog owners free of charge about care and feeding and so on as well.'

'Brilliant,' Lydia said and clipped the lead onto Lucky's collar. 'Thank you so much, Brian.'

'Pleasure,' Brian said and held the door open for her. 'Easiest patient I've had for a long time. Much better than the horse I had to treat this morning. Tried to kick me to death when I had to pull a rusty bit of barbed wire out of his leg.'

'God, that sounds scary.'

Brian shrugged. 'Comes with the territory. See you soon, Lydia. Call back in a couple of days and we'll do the microchip.'

Lydia said goodbye and continued towards the library further up the street. She looked around as she walked, at the artistically painted shopfronts, the cute little cottages with neat front gardens and the old-fashioned lampposts. There was a feeling here that nothing had changed for a very long time and that it would continue to stay the same, which was somehow reassuring.

Once Lydia had reached the old Victorian building that housed the library she hesitated, looking at Lucky, wondering if he would be allowed in. But the door was open and as there was nobody inside, Lydia entered, carrying Lucky under her arm. A young woman sat at the counter checking through a pile of books.

'Hello,' Lydia said. 'Is it okay for my dog to be here?'

The woman looked up and smiled, pushing her glasses up her nose. 'I'm on my own so I don't see why not. He looks well behaved anyway.' She half rose and patted Lucky on the head.

'He is,' Lydia agreed. 'I won't stay long anyway. I'm looking for a book about the history of Sandy Cove. Or some kind of brochure or something. Would you have something like that?'

The young woman nodded. 'Yes, we have a tourist brochure about the village and its history from the eleventh century onwards.'

'Oh, that's a long time ago,' Lydia said. 'Anything about modern times?'

'It's all in the brochure. Haven't read it myself,' the woman said with a giggle and held out her hand. 'My name's Sinead, by the way.'

'I'm Lydia.'

'I know,' Sinead said as they shook hands. 'I heard you've moved into one of the Starlight Cottages.'

'How did you know who I was?'

Sinead looked Lydia up and down. 'The jacket and the boots. They say you're very classy.'

'Oh.' Lydia didn't know quite what to say. 'Thank you,' she added, not really knowing if it was meant as a compliment.

'You're welcome.' Sinead sat down again and turned on the computer on the counter. 'You'll find the brochures on a stand near the door, right under the notice board.'

'Great. Thank you. Nice to meet you, Sinead.'

'Lovely. Bye-ee,' Sinead chanted, her eyes on the computer screen.

Lydia walked back to the door and found the stand with all kinds of different brochures. She took the one about the history, flora and fauna of Sandy Cove and then glanced at the notice board that was crammed with flyers and advertisements about classes and courses, book clubs, flower arranging, bridge, yoga and walking groups. She was amazed that there was so much going on in this village. There were also offers of things for sale, all kinds of services but nothing that she needed. She was about to walk out when a note caught her eye. *Cleaner required*, it said. *Twelve euros per hour, 10 hours a week. Please call number attached if interested.*

Lydia looked at the note for a while, thinking hard. Twelve euros an hour. Ten hours a week… That would be a hundred and twenty euros cash in her hand every week. That could come in very handy and pay for some of her expenses. But cleaning…

Lydia stood there for a while, thinking about the idea. She'd never done much housework before she was forced to by circumstances, but she knew that it was both demanding and tiring. Then she mentally kicked herself, feeling all her Viking ancestors telling her it was hard, honest work and she was not too precious to do it. *Beggars can't be choosers*, she told herself, and she was definitively getting to the beggar stage right now. With a beating heart, Lydia typed the number into her phone. She'd call them as soon as she came home and had had a chance to think. She put Lucky down, put the tourist brochure in her pocket and walked out, trying to decide what to do. But there was no other option at the moment – no way to supplement their meagre funds – and she started to feel that perhaps it was meant to happen and that this was one of the challenges on the long road to her recovery.

Chapter Fourteen

The next morning, Lydia walked to the other end of the village for her job interview. She had left Lucky on his bed in front of the fire and then spent half an hour trying to find clothes that would make her look presentable but modest. She had finally settled for corduroy trousers and a denim shirt under her down jacket. Simple and discreet, she thought and nothing that shouted wealth in any way, except for perhaps the jacket. It was just a cleaning job, she told herself, as she walked, no need to be nervous. But her cleaning skills still left a lot to be desired even though she had had plenty of practice the past few months.

Looking after her own home had given her a growing respect for any cleaning lady or staff she had ever employed. Keeping a big house clean and tidy required a large measure of organisation and discipline, she realised; even the little cottage wasn't as easy to keep tidy as she had thought at first. But doing it professionally was another matter, and she hoped the woman she had spoken to wouldn't ask for references or proof of earlier employment. She had sounded rather demanding even if she had been coolly polite, speaking with an educated accent, rather like Lydia's own. Her name was Helen O'Dwyer and she had told Lydia on the phone that her husband was a doctor but now semi-retired.

Lydia walked on, the butterflies in her stomach fluttering and her mouth dry. She felt as if she was falling down the social ladder at speed and would never be able to climb to the top again. But she had to get this job if she was to survive. She just had to.

*

Five minutes later, Lydia stood in front of a starkly beautiful modern house with stunning views of the bay. It looked like the kind of architect-designed house in a house-and-gardens magazine. Lydia suddenly felt chilled to the bone despite the mild air. This would be no ordinary cleaning job and the employer no ordinary busy career woman needing a helping hand at home. Someone who had high standards and likely took no prisoners, Lydia thought as she stood in front of the chrome-and-glass front door trying to gather up enough courage to ring the fancy doorbell. But the door opened as she lifted her hand to press the button and, startled, she stared at a young woman about to leave the house.

'Are you looking for Helen?' the woman asked.

'Yes,' Lydia replied. 'I have an appointment.'

'I know.' The woman held the door open. 'She's in the living room. I've just put her through her exercise programme, so she's a little sore. But go in. She'll be delighted to see you. Go through the hall and down the corridor. First door on the left.'

'Thanks,' Lydia said and stepped inside, letting the woman pass on her way out. She found herself in a large bright hall with a huge flower arrangement on a round table in the middle of a black-and-white tiled floor. Shaking with nerves, she took off her jacket and hung it on a hallstand made of some kind of blond wood, then walked down the corridor and knocked on the door she had been told led to the living room.

'Come in,' a voice called.

Lydia pushed the door open and walked in, but came to a stop on the threshold, staring around in amazement. The room was huge, dazzlingly bright and possibly the most beautiful living room she had ever seen. The walls were white and bare, apart from a huge abstract oil painting opposite the plate glass windows that overlooked the bay and the ocean beyond. Oriental rugs were scattered across the parquet floor and the furniture consisted of a huge round white sofa, two unusual-looking easy chairs and a glass coffee table with stacks of art books. A faint floral scent emanated from a bowl with dried rose petals. Lydia breathed it in, feeling as if she had been transported to a garden in spring. How stunning it all was. All her senses were suddenly alive and she was so preoccupied by the effect the room had on her that she didn't notice the woman sitting in one of the chairs until she spoke.

'Hello? Have you come about the cleaning job?'

Lydia gave a start at the sound of the voice and noticed the person sitting in a chair by the window. She was a very attractive older woman with dark blonde hair pulled back in a bun, pale blue eyes and regular features. Dressed in a soft blue sweater and matching trousers, she looked a little wan and pale, as if she was recovering from an illness. But then Lydia noticed the crutches beside the chair.

'Hip replacement,' the woman said. 'So boring, but it had to be done.' She sighed. 'Old age is not for sissies, as the saying goes. Not that I'm old, but some things can't be avoided. Wear and tear and so on.' She held out her hand. 'I'm Helen O'Dwyer. I take it you're Lydia?'

Lydia came closer and shook Helen O'Dwyer's cool hand. 'Yes. Nice to meet you, Mrs O'Dwyer.'

'Please call me Helen,' she said and let her hand drop into her lap. She studied Lydia for a moment. 'You look familiar. Have we met?'

'No,' Lydia replied, thinking it was possible they might have moved in the same circles at some stage – before the disaster. 'I've only just moved here.'

'So I heard. You probably just look like someone I've seen somewhere. We all have a double, they say. I'm often told I look like Meryl Streep, which I take as a compliment, except my nose is better than hers. You're more of a Gwyneth Paltrow type. Pretty but not spectacular.'

'Uh, thanks,' Lydia said, trying not to laugh. Helen was obviously one of those women who spoke her mind without sugar-coating her words. Lydia had always found that funny.

'But I digress,' Helen said, sitting up straighter. 'Please sit down. You make me feel tired standing there looking young and fit. I've just been through a physiotherapy session which was exhausting. I think that woman enjoys making people suffer. But enough about me.' Helen's cool eyes swept over Lydia as she sat down on a padded stool opposite. 'You look a little, eh, upmarket for a cleaner, I have to say. That shirt... Armani?'

'Yes, well I buy a lot at TK Maxx,' Lydia said, cringing slightly at the lie.

Helen looked impressed. 'Gosh, you're good at finding a bargain.'

'Just lucky, I suppose.'

'Yes, but still,' Helen said. 'You don't look like the typical cleaning woman, if you don't mind my saying so. And I know you're old Nellie's great-niece, so that makes me wonder why you're here like this.'

Lydia twisted her hands in her lap, wondering what to say. Better to tell the truth than trying to invent a story. 'I'm very short of money,' she started. 'My husband died a few months ago. The only thing I had left was my great-aunt's cottage. I just arrived with my daughter for a bit of a break.'

'I see.' Helen's eyes softened. 'That's very hard. And I'm so sorry.'

'Thank you.'

'So you need this job?' Helen continued, the condolences out of the way.

'Yes, I do. Desperately.'

Helen nodded. 'And I need someone to help me. It's not easy to find anyone to do housework around here. I had a nice girl who came in three times a week but she got married and went to live in Clonakilty. And now I find myself like this, old and helpless.'

'But you're not old,' Lydia exclaimed. 'You're just weak after your surgery. I'm very willing to do housework and anything else you might need. I don't have any experience but I'll do my best,' she ended, looking pleadingly at Helen.

Helen sighed. 'That's not ideal, but I think you'll be all right. This house is big so I'll need a lot of help to keep it up to standards.' She grabbed the crutches and got to her feet. 'I've been told to move around a bit, so I'll show you the house.'

Lydia got up. 'If you're sure it's okay?' she asked.

'It's fine.' Helen made her way to the other side of the sofa, making a sweeping gesture with one of the crutches. 'This is the living room, as you can see.'

'It's a fantastic room. The views are amazing. And the furniture suits it perfectly. I love those chairs,' Lydia said, noticing how beautiful they were, made of unusual-looking wood and upholstered in blue-green velvet.

'Jason O'Callaghan originals,' Helen said proudly. 'He made those for us when the house was built. It's a mixture of driftwood and mountain ash.'

'Oh,' Lydia said, startled at hearing the name. 'Lovely wood,' she added, running her fingers over the silky-smooth ash.

'He's a very gifted designer. He has won several awards and every piece is handmade by him.'

'Oh yes, I know.'

'But of course.' Helen turned to Lydia with a smile. 'He's your neighbour, so you must have met him by now.'

'Yes, well, sort of,' Lydia said, wondering if talking across a hedge could be considered as having met him.

'Fascinating man,' Helen said with a glint in her eyes.

'Eh, I suppose he is,' Lydia mumbled, not wanting to commit herself.

'I've tried to get him to come to dinner but he's such a recluse. Doesn't go anywhere.' Helen walked slowly towards the door.

'But, come, I'll show you the rest and then we'll have to work out a schedule and sign an agreement.'

Lydia followed Helen as she made her way through the house on her crutches. There were three bedrooms, all with en-suite bathrooms, including the enormous master suite with a dressing room and a bathroom with a jacuzzi set into a bay window that seemed to hang over the edge of the cliff.

'Can't get into that right now,' Helen said with a sigh. 'But as soon as I have my stitches out, I'll be in there every day. It's a wonderful place to relax.'

'I can imagine,' Lydia said, remembering with a dart of longing her own gorgeous bathroom in Dublin, with a bathtub the size of a minor swimming pool. How lovely it had been to sink into that after a long, hectic day. She pushed the image away, reminding herself to live in the present. That was then – now she had to concentrate on this job and the fact that she'd have a bit of money to put food on the table for herself and Sunny.

They continued through the house that was on one level throughout, down a long corridor, passing a cosy study with two huge bookcases crammed with books, an oriental carpet and worn leather armchairs that Helen said was her husband's 'man-cave'. They emerged into a big state-of-the-art kitchen with not one but two stoves, a huge fridge-freezer and a big pine table in the middle of the tiled floor.

'My domain,' Helen said. 'This is where I get creative with food. I never cooked much before I retired, but now I'm really enjoying it.' She peered at Lydia. 'How about you? Do you like cooking?'

'Not really,' Lydia confessed. 'Sunny isn't too fussy, but I want her to eat healthy food, so I have to make an effort.'

'Sunny?' Helen asked. 'Is that your daughter?'

Lydia nodded. 'Yes. She's fourteen. Her name is short for Sunniva. Named after my Norwegian grandmother.'

'Unusual, but nice,' Helen said, leaning on her crutches.

'You look tired,' Lydia said, concerned.

'Yes, I am. I think I'll go and lie down and rest before my husband comes home. I don't have to cook. He's getting something from the restaurant in the village.' Helen started to walk out of the kitchen. 'I'll see you to the door.'

'Oh, but there's no need,' Lydia protested. 'I'll see myself out.'

'Thank you. We'll organise that agreement when you start working. I was thinking you'd come two hours a day, nine to eleven, Monday to Friday. Is that all right?'

'Perfect,' Lydia said, dying to ask when she'd be paid but didn't dare.

'Good,' Helen said over her shoulder. 'I'll see you on Monday morning, then.'

Lydia left the house, her legs wobbly, feeling both relieved and a little frightened. Helen had been nice enough but there was a steely look in those pale-blue eyes that told her she'd better do a perfect job or it would be over as fast as it had begun. But she decided there and then that this would never happen. *I'll be the best cleaner in Ireland*, Lydia told herself as she walked back. *Helen O'Dwyer will be amazed at how brilliant I am at cleaning a house from one end to the other…*

When she came home, she still felt slightly shell-shocked from her job interview so Lydia decided to go for a walk, as it had stopped raining. It was early afternoon and Lucky would probably love to come with her. She decided to try the path down to that beach just below the coastguard cottages, the one called Wild Rose Bay, where Nellie had walked with the German pilot who had written that sweet letter to her. The words in that letter echoed in her mind as she got ready. That pilot, the man called Hansi, had promised to come back to Nellie, his Irish rose, after the war. But why didn't he? Walking in their footsteps down on that beach might not tell her anything, of course, but she would think about Nellie and her lost love, who might now be together in another life. Lydia laughed at herself as she opened the door to her house. This place made her feel impossibly romantic.

*

Lucky greeted Lydia ecstatically, jumping and barking, wagging his tail furiously as she came into the living room. Laughing, she scooped him into her arms, twisting her face away from his frantically licking tongue. 'I'm happy to see you, too. And now we're going for a walk.' She put him on the floor and went to find her trainers. Then they left the house through the sunroom and walked across the small back garden and out through the gate set into the wall behind the woodshed. A ledge hung over the cliff face and Lydia stared down at the sea, feeling dizzy as she looked at the churning water about fifty feet below, but then she saw the steps cut into the rock further along, ending in a steep path that led to the beach. Not too dangerous once she had eased herself down the steps with Lucky in her arms.

She breathed a sigh of relief once she had made her way down the path and jumped down onto the sand, letting Lucky off for a run. She wandered slowly along the beach, picking up shells and enjoying the views of the ocean and the lighthouse on the headland far in the distance. Dark clouds chased each other across the sky and the colour of the sea shifted constantly from grey to dark blue and then green nearer the shore. Lucky, having sniffed among the seaweed and around rocks, trotted back as Lydia sat down on a rock to look at the waves. She put a few of the shells into her pocket and as she did, she found the folded tourist brochure she had picked up at the library and had forgotten to look at. She pulled it out and leafed through it, past flora and fauna and the early history through to modern times and the years during the war. And there, on the last page, she found it: the story of the German plane that crashed on the slopes of the mountain. Excited, she started to read about what had happened, trying to imagine Nellie's part in the story.

On 20 August 1940 a Luftwaffe Focke-Wulf 200 'Condor' aircraft took off from Nazi-occupied France with a crew of six. Its flightpath took it from Bordeaux to the west coast of Ireland for weather reconnaissance. Developing engine problems in the early morning, the four-engine plane lost altitude as it attempted to return along the Irish coast to western France. As is common in coastal areas there was dense fog waiting for the rising sun to burn it off.

The German captain headed for Tralee Bay to ditch the dying aircraft but with primitive navigation tools the aircraft had lost too much altitude. With a gap in the fog, Captain Hansi Mueller managed to react to the rising mountain above

*Sandy Cove village and the plane belly-landed on Faha Ridge
with a number of the crew injured.*

*They were relieved to have landed in Ireland, a neutral
country all through the war. The local Garda (police) met the
Germans as they carried their wounded off Mount Brandon on
the pilgrims' trail. They were given a glass of milk by a young
local woman by all accounts, and cared for at a nearby farm
for a few weeks before they were then taken by the Irish army,
the 5th Infantry Battalion, to Collins Barracks in Cork and
then transferred to the new internment camp at The Curragh
Army Camp in County Kildare, near Dublin.*

*It is a well-known fact that the internees were allowed to
sign out to attend horse racing at The Curragh, to attend public
dances and to visit the German Embassy. While visiting the
embassy, two German internees met their future Irish wives.*

Lydia read the piece twice. That young woman who gave the
crew glasses of milk might have been Nellie. And then they stayed
at a nearby farm for a while before they were taken to Cork…
During that time, Hansi, the captain, and Nellie fell in love. And
they walked together on this very beach. And then he was sent on,
first to the camp in Cork, and then to The Curragh. Was he one
of the internees who met their future Irish wives at the German
Embassy in Dublin? Did he forget all about Nellie when he set eyes
on some other Irish beauty?

Lydia stared across the beach, at the waves crashing in, thinking
of Nellie and her German pilot. She imagined that Nellie would
never have forgotten him and that she kept waiting for him to

return but he never did as he had married someone else. Poor Nellie, abandoned by the love of her life. So unlucky in love. How it must have hurt her that he didn't keep his promise. That bit of his uniform and the letter was all she had left. Lydia couldn't help feeling sad as she thought of what she imagined had happened. It brought home her own sorrow and Barry's betrayal and she felt a hard, painful lump in her chest, as she sat there looking out across the cold, dark water.

Lydia was jolted back to the present by Lucky suddenly sitting up with a yelp, staring at something at the far end of the beach. Something – or someone – was coming out of the waves. It looked at first like a seal sticking its head up from the water, but then a pair of shoulders appeared and Lydia saw that it was a man getting out after a swim. How could he possibly endure the cold water? He must be wearing a wetsuit, she thought as she kept staring at him. But as he waded into the shore, his body rising out of the waves, she saw his naked torso and that he wore only a pair of swimming trunks. Lucky was shivering in Lydia's arms and struggling to get away, but Lydia held him back while she stared incredulously at the man. Swimming in the sea in the middle of winter; how foolish.

He was too far away for her to see him clearly, but it was obvious, even from this distance, that he was tall and handsome. It suddenly dawned on her that this man must be Jason, which made her try to look at him more closely. His dark hair was slicked back from a face with strong features and his shoulders were wide and muscular. He picked up a towel from a rock and began to dry himself, looking around at the same time as he started to ease off his wet trunks.

In order to give him some privacy, Lydia slid off the rock she had been sitting on and walked slowly backwards, until she came to a big boulder she could hide behind. She waited there for a moment and then peeked out, but Jason was gone. She wondered if she had imagined it all, but Lucky was still shivering and whining. Then she saw a tall figure walking up the slope opposite the one she had come down. She realised he must have been walking along the edge of the cliffs from the main beach. So this was what Jason did to keep fit. But how on earth could he endure the freezing cold water?

It wasn't his courage that had impressed her the most, but his toned body and handsome face she had only glimpsed from afar. The image of Jason coming out of the waves stuck in her mind as she carefully climbed back up the path and made her way to the house, nearly slipping on the steps hewn into the rock.

Chapter Fifteen

Later that day, when they were cooking dinner together in the kitchen, Lydia told Sunny about her job.

'What?' Sunny exclaimed, nearly dropping the potato she was peeling at the kitchen sink. 'You're going to be a cleaning lady?'

'In a way.' Lydia shot Sunny a smile as she chopped carrots. 'I'm really just helping a lady who's recovering from surgery. But I'm being paid a salary and I thought it'd help us pay a few bills. Good idea, don't you think?'

'Oh, Mum, I think it's sad,' Sunny said, looking at Lydia with sorrow in her big dark eyes.

'It's a job and it's not forever,' Lydia declared. 'It'll get me out of the house and it's only two hours a day. And I'll be paid cash every week, which will help a lot. I'll even be able to give you some pocket money.'

'But I could earn that myself,' Sunny protested. 'A lot of the girls in school do babysitting. I'm sure I could get a job like that easily if I put up a notice at the library or something.'

'That's a very good idea, you know. But it should be as well as, not instead of me getting that cleaning job. Every little thing will help. And if you get some babysitting jobs or anything else, you can keep that for yourself. My pay will then go towards all the other costs. And…' She took a deep breath. 'I'm going to sell my handbags on eBay.'

Sunny actually dropped the potato this time and stared at Lydia. 'All of them?'

'Yes. Except the Birkin,' Lydia said. 'I couldn't bear to part with that one.'

'No, I couldn't either,' Sunny said. 'Dad bought it for you when you turned forty. I remember how happy you were when you found the parcel he had hidden under the stairs. And the party that night was fabulous.'

'You were nine,' Lydia said, looking at Sunny with tears in her eyes. 'And you wore a blue dress from Bonpoint that your grandmother bought for you.'

'Yes,' Sunny said looking into the sink. 'She was already very ill then, wasn't she?'

'She was.' Lydia sighed deeply, trying to blink away tears that welled up.

Sunny went to Lydia's side and gave her a tight hug. 'It's a happy memory, though, Mum. For me, anyway. That party and Dad and Granny and Grandad, and your friends and the lovely table and candles and music…'

'I know. It was a wonderful evening.' Lydia wiped her eyes on a piece of kitchen paper and hugged Sunny back. 'But now we're here in this house and we're trying to survive. And we have to look forward and…'

'And take the chicken out of the oven,' Sunny squealed as she bent to look at it. 'It looks a little burned, I'm afraid.'

'Oh God, I forgot about it.' Lydia grabbed two oven mitts and took the burned chicken out of the oven and put it on top of the cooker. 'Actually, it doesn't look too bad.'

'It looks great if you like black skin on a chicken,' Sunny said, laughing. 'But we can take the burned bits off and it'll be fine.'

'But we have to cook the potatoes and the carrots,' Lydia said. 'I don't think we got the timings right, somehow. How on earth did Margarita manage all this?'

'She was used to it. We're beginners,' Sunny said as she filled the saucepan with water and put it on the cooker. 'But we'll learn.'

'Of course we will,' Lydia said with a brave smile, reminding herself that they had a lot to be grateful for. They had met so many friendly people since they arrived, Lydia had found a way to make some extra money, they had a lovely little dog, but most of all they had a roof over their heads, all thanks to old Aunt Nellie. 'I meant to tell you,' she said to Sunny as she checked the potatoes. 'I found out what happened here during the war. I'll tell you when we're eating.'

'Great,' Sunny said. 'I'll just answer a text from Lizzie. She says her parents want her to go to this Irish-speaking boarding school, you see. It's called Coláiste Íde and it's a girls' school somewhere in Cork, I think.'

'I hope that won't stop the two of you seeing each other,' Lydia remarked.

'I don't think so. She'll be free most weekends. I'll find out anyway.'

They finally had dinner in the living room in front of the stove with Lucky sitting at their feet looking hopefully at every bite they took. But Lydia told Sunny not to give him anything as it would encourage him to beg. They would feed him later and then let him out into the garden before they settled down for the night.

'So tell me,' Sunny said as she chewed on a drumstick. 'What did you find out?'

'It was in this brochure I got at the library,' Lydia explained. 'All about this German plane that crash landed on the slopes of the mountain just above the village. Here,' she said, handing Sunny the brochure, 'it's all on the last page.'

Sunny put the chicken bone on her plate and wiped her hands on a piece of kitchen paper before she took the brochure and read the story. 'Wow,' she said, her eyes wide with excitement. 'Isn't that amazing? You could make a romantic movie about it.'

'Yes, only the ending is a little sad,' Lydia remarked. 'Hansi never came back to Nellie. I have a feeling he found someone else and married her instead.'

'Poor Nellie,' Sunny said with a sigh. 'But if he was that unreliable, maybe she was better off without him?'

'Oh, I don't think so,' Lydia argued. 'She spent the rest of her life alone. Is that better? Maybe she would have been happier if they had got together after the war, even if he proved to be unreliable in the end.'

'Hmm.' Sunny looked thoughtful. 'That's a good question. You might be right. I mean, it saved her from a man who might have made her unhappy, but she missed out on love and passion, even if it had lasted for just a short time.'

'Exactly. There might be something in that saying about it being better to have loved and lost and all that.'

'Maybe.' Sunny looked at Lydia and hesitated for a moment before she spoke. 'Is that what you think about you and Dad?'

'I think so,' Lydia said after a moment's reflection, suddenly reminded of Nellie and her romance. When she had married Barry, Lydia had given up her job and chosen to support Barry in his endeavours, working as a fundraiser partly in order to help raise his profile. She hadn't thought twice about it at the time, but now she realised she had given up her independence, which might not have been something Nellie had been prepared to do. But the good times they had had together were worth it, she had thought at the time. 'We were so happy together, especially when we were just married,' she said, nearly tempted to tell Sunny the whole truth about Barry. This would be a good opportunity, but… Lydia lost her nerve. She simply couldn't do it to Sunny. She took Sunny's hand. 'If I hadn't met your father, I might have had less pain and sorrow, that's true. But then I wouldn't have had all that excitement of falling in love and all those lovely times we just talked about. And I wouldn't have had you. I don't regret anything in my life. Not a single thing,' she said, thinking it wasn't quite true… Barry had done something she couldn't forgive and she was still trying to come to terms with it, to accept it and move on. But Sunny's question had made her dig deep inside. The problem was that Barry's crimes were still so fresh, they echoed through her with darts of pain that were nearly physical.

A sound woke her from her musings. 'What was that?' she asked, startled.

'Someone at the door,' Sunny said and shot up while Lucky jumped up and barked. 'I'll go and see.'

'Don't open the door before you've asked who it is,' Lydia warned, still in big-city mode.

Sunny rolled her eyes. 'Mum, this is Sandy Cove, not Dublin.'

'Yes, but still,' Lydia said and got to her feet to follow Sunny to the door.

But whoever was at the door had already opened it and Sorcha's freckly face came into view. 'Hi,' she said. 'Hope I'm not intruding. But Brian and I were at the pub and thought we'd call in with something you left at his surgery.'

'What did I leave?' Lydia asked.

'This,' Brian said, coming forward with something in his hand. 'Your scarf. I thought it was yours as nobody else would have a scarf from Hermès. With horses on it.'

'Oh,' Lydia said, taking the scarf. 'Yes, it's mine. I must have dropped it. Thank you.'

'But come in,' Sunny said, holding a squirming Lucky in her arms. 'I'll make you some tea and we can have a bit of that fruitcake Mum bought today.'

Sorcha glanced at Lydia. 'Thank you. We will, if that's all right with your mum.'

'Of course it is,' Lydia said, opening the door wider. 'We weren't doing anything much anyway. And it's Friday night, so no homework for Sunny. We'd love some company, actually.'

Sorcha and Brian walked inside and Sunny went into the kitchen to make tea. Within minutes she carried a tray into the living room with mugs and a plate with the promised fruitcake. They all settled around the coffee table, Sorcha and Lydia on the sofa and Brian on the rickety chair beside the stove with Sunny and Lucky on the rug in front of it.

Lydia put more logs into the stove. 'It's a wild night out there,' she said.

'Yes, but better weather is on the way,' Brian said, reaching out for another slice of fruitcake. 'Must say you're very cosy here with that stove.'

'Yes, but it has to be minded and fed all the time, like a baby,' Lydia said. 'It does keep the room warm, though.'

'You could do with some additional heating,' Brian remarked. 'I don't mean to be a busybody, but I have an old storage heater you could put up on the wall beside the door to the sunroom. It would heat up during the night, using the night rate which is very cheap and then release the heat during the day. I think it would provide great background heat in this room. And then you won't have to light the stove all the time.' He drew breath and looked at Lydia. 'What do you think?'

Lydia met his brown eyes and was touched by his kindness, even if the offer made her feel yet again like a pauper who had to accept charity. 'That would be wonderful, Brian,' she said, swallowing her pride and the instinct to refuse the offer. 'But how on earth will I install such a thing myself?'

'I could put it up for you,' he offered. 'Very easy to install. And I'll get my brother who's an electrician in Waterville to check it.'

'Brilliant,' Sunny cut in. 'Mum's not really that clued in when it comes to technical stuff. Or anything practical,' she prattled on. 'But now that she's going to be a cleaning lady, she'll have to learn.'

Sorcha stared at Lydia. 'Cleaning lady?'

'Yes,' Lydia said with a laugh. 'Well, it's really just helping someone out. I applied for a job with Helen O'Dwyer, the doctor's wife. She's recovering from hip replacement surgery and needs someone to help her.'

'She always needs someone to help her,' Sorcha said dryly as she put her tea mug on the table. 'She's a bit demanding, I have to tell you.'

Brian let out a snort. 'A bit? I'd say she takes no prisoners at all. You'll have to be on your toes with her, Lydia.'

'I can handle her,' Lydia said. 'It was the only job going, so I thought I'd apply. It's just two hours a day, after all.'

'Mum takes no prisoners either,' Sunny piped up. 'So I think she'll manage very well.'

Brian brushed crumbs off his white fisherman's sweater and shot Lydia a grin. 'I can imagine. Maybe Helen will finally have met her match?'

Sorcha shook her head and laughed. 'Yeah, I have a feeling it'll be very interesting.' She leaned forward. 'Helen has *notions*, you see. Comes from being wealthy. Her family owns a big pharmaceutical company. So she might be a touch bossy.'

'It's just a cleaning job, not brain surgery,' Lydia exclaimed. 'And I found Helen perfectly nice and correct.'

'Her husband is looovely,' Sorcha said dreamily. 'Dr Pat is everyone's favourite uncle in a way. And a wonderful doctor. I could never figure out their marriage though, but they seem happy the way they are.'

'They've been married a very long time,' Brian remarked, eyeing what was left of the fruitcake. 'Seems to be working whatever their arrangement. Would it be okay if I had another slice?'

'Of course, help yourself,' Lydia said absentmindedly while she took in what Sorcha had said. Helen might be a tough cookie and a bit snooty, but she understood where that came from.

She had herself been in that situation, trying to maintain her status which gave her a feeling of power and control. Running a house like hers and Barry's, entertaining clients and colleagues, maintaining a certain social standing all demanded a measure of aloofness. In Helen's case, being the head of a high-profile pharmaceutical company combined with the role of the wife of a country doctor carried certain responsibilities. Lydia felt a dart of envy as she thought of the stunning house with its tastefully decorated interior.

'It's just temporary,' she said. 'A job to tide us over until I can get us back on our feet.'

Sorcha looked confused. 'How do you mean?'

'I mean that I'll start looking at job opportunities online and see if I can get back into marketing,' Lydia said, trying to sound more positive than she felt. 'I've been a little too shell-shocked to do anything about it until now.'

'Great idea, Mum,' Sunny said. 'I think you'll be good at that. You marketed yourself and Dad so well before—' She stopped, looking suddenly sad. 'Well, you know,' she said and picked Lucky up, burying her face in his fur.

'So hard for you,' Sorcha murmured as she looked at Sunny. 'But you're managing very well, fighting your corner in school, I've heard.'

'Fighting?' Lydia asked, alarmed, looking from Sorcha to Sunny. 'What's going on?'

'It's nothing,' Sunny said and got up. 'I think Lucky needs to go outside for a bit. I'll take him.' Before Lydia had a chance to protest, Sunny walked out of the room with Lucky at her heels and closed the door behind her, leaving Lydia looking bewildered at Sorcha.

'What's going on at school?' she asked. 'Sunny always says everything is fine. I thought she was settling in.'

'She is,' Sorcha replied. 'But… well, she's being teased about being a "townie" and from Dublin by some of the kids, Fintan told us. He said he teased her a bit in the beginning but now he's trying to help. Some of the girls are a bit mean, he says. I think it might be that she's actually well ahead of the class in a lot of subjects, including maths and science.'

'Oh God,' Lydia said, her heart sinking. 'This was a problem in her last school too. She's always found it hard to make friends. She had one very good one in Dublin, but the girl moved to Cork and now I heard she's got a place in some Irish girls' boarding school called Coláiste Íde, so I think that's made her sad. They won't be able to meet up like they planned after that.'

'Coláiste Íde?' Brian said. 'But that's near Dingle town, only across the bay, on the other peninsula. I'm sure they could get together on weekends or something.'

'Really?' Lydia said, feeling more hopeful. 'I've heard of this school, but I thought it was somewhere on the other side of Cork.'

'It's only about an hour away,' Brian said.

'In fact,' Sorcha cut in, 'that school would be ideal for Sunny. One of those old-fashioned girls' schools where the academic standard is very high. Small classes and a great ethos of friendship and independence for women. My mother went there. And I think your great-aunt did too.'

'Did she?' Lydia asked. 'Sounds like a good school. But I could never afford it.'

'Ah, but they have all kinds of grants and scholarships,' Sorcha said. 'A good student like Sunny would have a strong chance. She'd have to be a fluent Irish speaker, though, to qualify.'

'That's out then,' Lydia said with a resigned sigh. 'Sunny's Irish is quite good but she is in no way fluent.'

'That's a pity,' Sorcha replied, looking disappointed. 'But maybe a good thing. Running away is not always the answer. Maybe better for her to stay and sort it out. You've only been here about a week, so I'm sure the kids will settle down given a little time.'

'I suppose,' Lydia said, still worried.

'I'm sure she'll be fine,' Brian soothed. He looked at Lydia. 'But what was that about you marketing your husband like Sunny said just now?'

'Oh that,' Lydia said, trying to come up with an explanation. 'It was just about me helping my husband raise the profile of his business.'

'I see,' Brian said. 'Like a lot of wives, I suppose.'

'Exactly,' Lydia said, happy she had managed to make it sound quite low-key.

Sorcha finished her piece of cake and got up. 'I think we'll get going now. Fintan has a match early tomorrow and I have to drive him there.'

'Yeah, I'd better be off too,' Brian said, jumping to his feet. 'I'm on call tonight so if a cow or a horse suddenly comes down with the flu or decides to have a baby, I'll have to get out of bed.'

'You sound like a doctor,' Lydia said, laughing.

'Well, that's what I am, really,' Brian replied. 'An animal doctor. Come on, Sorcha, we'd better leave these folks alone and get going. You have to be up early tomorrow anyway and then there's the weekend crowd.'

Sorcha put on her jacket. 'Yes. Even though it's still low season lots of walkers usually arrive here for the weekend. They stay at Riverside Farm, which is a great walking centre and hostel. It's run by Mick O'Dwyer's wife, Tara.'

'Mick O'Dwyer?' Lydia asked. 'The actor?'

'That's the one,' Sorcha said, picking up her bag. 'But now he's a councillor. He's also Pat and Helen's son as she might have told you.'

'No, she didn't say anything about that,' Lydia replied.

'Ah but she will,' Brian said with a grin. 'Never misses a chance to mention "my son the politician".'

'That's for sure,' Sorcha agreed. 'But now we'll say goodnight and get going. It's going to be a cold one with clear skies, so you'd better keep that stove going.'

'Clear skies?' Lydia said, her spirits lifting. That might mean…

'I see Jason's home again,' Brian remarked as if reading Lydia's thoughts. 'His old Land Rover is parked by his front door.'

'Land Rover?' Lydia asked, confused. 'But he has an Audi. It was in his driveway the other day.'

Sorcha shook her head. 'Nope. That must have been a client or something. Jason's Land Rover is well known. He drives it onto the main beach when he's looking for driftwood. He loves that old thing.' She sighed and looked dreamily at Lydia. 'You're so lucky to have him next door. Such a special man.'

'Special?' Lydia asked intrigued. 'How do you mean?'

'He's very attractive,' Sorcha whispered in Lydia's ear behind Brian's back. 'You must know that by now.'

'Eh, yes. I do,' Lydia admitted while Sorcha smiled and waved and followed Brian out the door.

'See you soon, Lydia.'

The door closed behind them and Lydia stood there thinking about Jason and what Sorcha had said about him. She couldn't help feeling a dart of something new as she thought of the man she had seen at the beach, who, of course, had to be Jason. His cold-water swimming made him even more interesting...

*

Lydia was still musing over what Sorcha had meant when the back door opened to let a shivering Sunny in, carrying Lucky in her arms. 'Mum? What's the matter? Why are you standing there like a statue?'

Lydia shook herself and laughed. 'Oh nothing. Sorcha told me a joke, that's all,' she said to cover her feelings. 'Kerry people are a little strange sometimes.'

'Tell me about it,' Sunny muttered as she put Lucky on his bed. 'The kids at school are weird. Always trying to trip me up.'

Lydia gave Sunny a hug. 'I know, sweetheart. It's very hard for you. But you have to be strong and stick it out. I'm sure they'll get used to you and you to them. They have probably never met a girl like you before.'

Sunny broke away. 'Stop it, Mum. I'm nothing special. There are kids in my class who are *awesome*. Some of them have medals in sports and debating and all kinds of other things. I'd rather be like them than any of the girls I know in Dublin. But they won't let me in.'

'Yet,' Lydia said, her heart breaking for Sunny. 'You just have to work at it, darling.'

'Yeah,' Sunny said bleakly. 'For like a hundred years.' She started to walk away. 'I'm going upstairs to talk to Lizzie.'

'Okay,' Lydia said. 'She'll be able to cheer you up. I'll be here looking up a bit more about the history of Sandy Cove. I want to see if I can find more about Nellie and her life here. Sorcha said she was a champion of women's rights and all kinds of other things, too.'

'Probably had a medal in Irish dancing and culture,' Sunny said dryly. 'They're big into medals around here.' She walked swiftly out of the room and Lydia could hear her stomp up the stairs and bang the door to her bedroom.

Lydia tided up the teacups and then put more logs into the stove, sinking down on the sofa with her laptop with the intention of looking up websites that might have more information about Kerry during the war years. She silently blessed Jason for letting them share his internet connection. Not only did it help Sunny with her homework, it also made it easier for her to connect with Lizzie through WhatsApp and Snapchat.

Lydia was about to start googling the history of Kerry when she heard a noise outside the front door, followed by a loud knock. Had Sorcha or Brian forgotten something? Lydia left the laptop on the table and got up to see who it was, as Sunny's voice could be heard from upstairs, obviously deep in conversation with Lizzie.

Lydia opened the door a crack and peered out. 'Hello?' she said into the darkness. 'Anyone there?'

The only answer was a little whine and then a bark and Lydia looked down to discover Lucky standing on the step, wagging his tail. 'What?' she said bewildered. 'Lucky? Did you sneak out again?'

'Yes, he did,' came the reply from a figure at Jason's open door. 'Then he snuck into my garden and ran around sniffing and whining. I think he was after a rabbit.'

Lydia picked Lucky up. 'The bold boy. I'm sorry if he disturbed you,' she said, peering through the darkness at Jason.

'Not really, I just thought you might want him back,' Jason said and retreated into the house before Lydia had a chance to reply or even get a good look at him. 'See you later under the stars perhaps,' he suggested before he closed the door.

A little shaken, Lydia stood on her doorstep with Lucky under her arm, staring from the Land Rover to Jason's door that had just banged shut, disappointed she hadn't got a chance to see him clearly. Lucky getting out through the back door and then running into Jason's garden had surprised her. And she felt disappointed he hadn't seemed to want to chat to her. She didn't need him to stay anonymous any more and just be a voice in the darkness, under the stars. Now he was real and she was dying to know more about him.

He really was a mysterious man.

Chapter Sixteen

The cleaning job started the following Monday and Lydia duly arrived at nine on the dot, being met by Helen's husband, who introduced himself as Pat. He was a tall man with grey hair and twinkly eyes behind his glasses and a lovely smile. He explained that Helen had taken a taxi to the golf club in Waterville to have morning coffee with some friends. He handed Lydia a list of chores and said to call him if there was a problem with anything.

'But I expect you'll breeze through all of this with gusto,' he said. 'Helen told me you were highly qualified.'

Then he left, as Lydia studied the long list wondering how on earth she was going to get through it all in only two hours. But she pushed up her sleeves and got stuck in, using her phone to google any of the cleaning jobs she didn't know how to do, which was hugely helpful, especially the YouTube clips on how best to clean a bathtub with baking soda and lemon juice, which she found fascinating. And it worked, she discovered, having followed the instructions. She looked at the sparkling clean jacuzzi feeling a huge sense of achievement. Who knew cleaning could be this interesting? On she went through the list, managing to finish most of the chores, except the pile of ironing as the silk shirts took a lot of time and trouble. She had to leave the rest for another day.

The morning had been more enjoyable than she had thought, as simply being here was a treat. The house had a familiar air of luxury and comfort. Lydia felt even the air was exclusive as she breathed in the scents from the expensive soaps and beauty products in the bathroom, remembering how it had felt to be pampered without a care in the world. She missed the comforts, but now as she walked around, she also remembered how superficial it had all been. Here, in this little village, she was meeting people who were more at peace with their lives even though they had to cope with normal everyday struggles.

Helen arrived home just as Lydia was putting away the rubber gloves and cleaning products into the cupboard in the utility room. She walked slowly into the kitchen on her crutches and smiled at Lydia. 'Hello there. Just finished?'

'Yes,' Lydia said. 'I managed nearly everything on the list.'

'Nearly?' Helen's eyebrows shot up.

'Yeah, well, I'm kind of new at this, so it was hard to get it all done and the silk shirts were a bit tricky. I'll do the rest tomorrow,' Lydia babbled, butterflies starting to flutter in her stomach under Helen's cool gaze.

'I see.' Helen looked around the kitchen. 'Well, this looks fine all the same. Did you change the filter in the extractor fan?'

'Uh, no. But I cleaned the hob and I'll do the oven tomorrow. And the fan if you tell me where the filters are.'

Helen nodded. 'I did tell you. It's on the list.'

'Oh. I'm sorry. I didn't…' Lydia took the list from her pocket. 'Must have missed that.'

'No real problem,' Helen said. 'I suppose you'll settle into the job in a little while.'

'Of course I will,' Lydia promised. 'I've never done this kind of thing before, so…'

'I forgot to ask you what your actual training is,' Helen replied as she pulled out a chair at the kitchen table and sat down.

'I'm… I have a degree in marketing,' Lydia replied. 'I worked at an advertising agency before I got married.'

'And after that?' Helen enquired.

'I had a baby and then I got into fundraising.'

'Fundraising?' Helen looked thoughtfully at Lydia. 'And… were you good at it?'

'I think so, yes. I managed to raise a lot of money for a number of good causes.'

'This is a bit of a change for you, then.'

'To put it mildly,' Lydia said with a laugh.

'Interesting.' Helen picked up her crutches and got up. 'I'll go and sit in the conservatory for a bit before Pat comes home for lunch.'

'The conservatory?' Lydia asked. 'I didn't know you had one.'

'It's around the corner from the living room and not visible from there,' Helen said. 'Come with me and I'll show you.'

Lydia followed Helen down the corridor from the kitchen, through the living room. Helen opened a door to a small lobby which had another door that led into the conservatory, built at the side of the house in order to catch as much sunlight as possible. 'Follow me,' she said and made her way inside.

Amazed, Lydia walked in after Helen, looking around at tropical plants, small palm trees and an abundance of flowers, including orchids and azaleas in full bloom. There was a round table and four wicker chairs at the far end, which had the same beautiful views of the ocean as the living room. Two parakeets squawked in a cage under a palm tree. Here, in the warmth and humidity, Lydia felt as if transported to an exotic place far away from the chill of the Irish west coast in winter. 'This is gorgeous,' she said, awestruck.

'Wonderful,' Helen said with a contented sigh as she settled in one of the wicker chairs.

'The parakeets are fun.'

'A bit noisy but I like them.'

'It's like another world in here,' Lydia said.

'I sometimes pretend I'm in Bali when I sit here. It took a lot of work to make it what it is, but it was worth it, don't you think?'

'Absolutely,' Lydia replied, looking up at the blue sky through the glass ceiling partly obscured by the fronds of the palm tree. 'It's kind of Victorian in a way. Like a conservatory I was in once when a friend had a party in her old house in Dublin. We all wore tropical outfits and drank cocktails out of coconuts.'

'Sounds like fun.'

'Oh yes, it was,' Lydia said, smiling at the memory of the grass skirt and flower garland she had worn, and Barry in a garish tropical shirt and pith helmet. 'Great fun.'

Helen nodded and took her phone out of her bag. 'I can imagine. But now I have a few calls to make. I know we haven't signed that agreement I talked about, but we can do that later. I'll see you tomorrow, then.'

Realising she had been dismissed, Lydia said goodbye and left the house, feeling satisfied with her morning's work, despite not quite measuring up to Helen O'Dwyer's expectations. She'd get the hang of it very soon, she felt, even though being under the spotlight of Helen's critical gaze was a little nerve-racking. But there was something about Helen that resonated with Lydia: a kind of restlessness that came from having all she could possibly want but still looking for a purpose in life.

As she walked home, Lydia wondered if she had been as demanding and cool towards her own staff in what felt like her previous life. She tried to remember, but all she could think of was how brilliantly they ran the house, like clockwork. The tables had certainly turned and now Lydia was finding out what it felt like to be on the other side of the spectrum. But she would stick it out and work hard, and try to get some kind of other job, whatever she could find. She just had to cast aside her pride and change her attitudes, which until now had been her biggest obstacle.

'How have you been?' Jason asked as they spoke that evening, this time on Lydia's deck, Jason sitting on the back step and Lydia on her deck chair wrapped in a blanket. 'Getting more settled?'

'Maybe,' Lydia said softly, staring at his profile illuminated by the light over the door. 'I'm still feeling a little lost. And Sunny seems to have problems fitting in with the rest of the class. They're from such different backgrounds, so it'll be hard for them to accept her.'

'I'm sure they will in time.'

'Time,' Lydia said with a sigh. 'I wish it would go faster and do all that healing it's supposed to do. I wish it was spring and the weather warm. It's such hard work keeping the house heated. I wish I could think of a way to make more money other than…' She stopped. She had been about to tell Jason about taking a job as a cleaner but then changed her mind. He didn't need to know that. 'Oh, I wish I could turn back time and undo some of my mistakes,' she ended. 'Then I wouldn't be here like this.'

'I'm sorry you feel like that,' Jason said, his voice soothing. 'But I do understand. Not that I think you ever did anything wrong, but guilt is part of grieving. Once you get past that, you've come a bit of the way and you'll find it easier to move forward.'

'I don't think I ever will.' Lydia looked up at the glimmering stars and the Milky Way that stretched across the dark sky like a diamond-studded belt. 'But I have to keep going for Sunny. She's all I have and I want her to be happy. So I put on a brave face and try to be cheerful, pretending I'm loving this place and enjoying meeting new people and telling her this new life is so wonderful despite us being as poor as church mice.'

'While deep down, you're miserable, angry and incredibly sad,' Jason said, turning to look at her.

'Yes.' Lydia sighed deeply. She looked up at the window to Sunny's bedroom above them, checking she could still see her gossiping with Lizzie on the phone. 'There is something I haven't told you about Barry. When he died, I found out that he had been cheating on his taxes and there was also some money laundering going on through his firm.'

'Oh,' Jason said. 'I see. I can imagine that it would have been a further shock piled on top of him dying so suddenly.'

'Yes. I found out about it a few months later. I've come a long way with my grief, even if I still miss him. But learning about his lies was like being hit by grief for a second time.'

'How did Sunny take that?'

'I haven't told her that part,' she whispered. 'I just can't bear for her to think badly of her father.'

'That's understandable. But maybe you should tell her eventually. She deserves to know the truth.'

'That's easy for you to say,' Lydia remarked, feeling he was being a little judgemental. 'Can we drop this? I don't want to talk about it right now.'

'Okay. Sorry if I stepped on a sore toe. You have a lot on your plate right now. But…' He paused. 'Try not to despair.'

'I'll do my best,' Lydia said with a sigh. 'The future doesn't look so bright right now, though. I doubt if it ever will.'

'But you have a lot to build on, you know. A lot more than you think.'

'How do you mean?'

'Once you start to accept what you can't change and delve into your own strengths, you'll get out of this. You just have to stop feeling sorry for yourself.'

Lydia sat up, the dreamy feel of the starlit night shattered by his words. 'What? I don't feel sorry for myself,' she protested, glaring at him in the dim light.

'Yes, I'm afraid you do,' Jason said. 'Quite understandable, but a little destructive. You're stuck in a groove, and that's what you need to fix.'

Lydia felt anger rise in her chest like hot lava. What right did he have to sit there and judge her? Accusing her of self-pity and telling her to snap out of it. But what about him? All that reclusiveness was suddenly irritating. 'What do you really know about me?' she asked, her voice cold. 'I have told you very little, just that... I lost...' She stopped.

'You lost all you had, including your husband,' he filled in, his voice calm. 'And he was guilty of fraud. That's what you told me. It doesn't take a lot of imagination to know how terrible that must have been for you. And you've been very brave. But you have to move forward now and maybe accept help from others. All the stiff upper lip and managing all by yourself isn't going to help you. Let it out, Lydia. Scream and cry and howl at the moon instead of locking it in. That's a good thing to do, believe me.'

'What do you know about how I feel or what I should do?' Lydia snapped. 'I don't want to talk to you any more. You can sit there and be *mysterious* all by yourself!' With angry tears coursing down her cheeks, she untangled herself from the blanket, struggled to her feet and walked inside, banging the door shut, making the windows rattle. She could see him move off and go through the hole in the hedge he had made further down the garden.

Lydia stood there for a while shivering with anger, mostly at herself. She had poured her heart out to a complete stranger, only because of his deep, warm voice and apparent wisdom and kindness. She had been in such need of empathy and understanding that she had trusted him simply because he had been there and appeared willing to listen. The fact that she couldn't see him had encouraged her to talk freely. And then, once they had met, he had turned on her and said she was feeling sorry for herself, as if he was holding up a mirror that showed a very ugly picture. Well, she wouldn't be that stupid again. She had been rude to him, but it felt truly justified.

Slightly calmer, Lydia dumped the blanket on the sofa and went upstairs. She could hear Sunny, still on the phone to Lizzie and knew there was a true friend who could help Sunny when she was down. And Sunny would probably settle down in school and slowly start enjoying life again. That was the most important thing right now.

Exhausted by her emotional outburst, Lydia went into her room and lay, still dressed, on her narrow bed, pulling the duvet over her. She put out the light and stared out the window at the starlit sky feeling a burning pain in her chest. Something told her it was some kind of delayed reaction to all that had happened to her. She had been working so hard to move from Dublin, selling everything she could, getting Sunny organised in school, settling into this cold, bare little house and trying to cope financially, that she had pushed away her grief and now it was hitting her with its full force.

So maybe I'm feeling sorry for myself, she thought. *But oh God, why shouldn't I? That man with his pop psychology couldn't possibly know what I'm going through.*

It all flashed through her mind like a film, every painful moment from Barry's sudden death to the discovery of having lost everything she owned, her whole privileged life from the moment she was born now gone, and she gave herself up to her grief and pain combined with her anger at Barry for abandoning her. She cried uncontrollably for a long time, holding the pillow over her face so Sunny wouldn't hear.

When she had no more tears left, she lay there, limp and exhausted, feeling as if she had been purged and cleansed. Jason's comments about self-pity had hurt her but he was right about letting it all out, she realised, completely spent. What he had said had opened the floodgates and made her let all her pain out after months of locking it in. The storm had passed but despite not feeling much happier or any less hurt and angry, the feelings were softer and less raw. And there was a glint of hope somehow, a promise of better things to come one day, even though they were far away. The struggle would continue, and she was stuck in this new existence where she had only her own resources to help her. But in an odd way she began to understand that this little village in the back of beyond was the right place to start this new sparkly clean life she hoped would come out of the ashes of the old one. If only she worked hard enough.

Chapter Seventeen

Everything seemed a little brighter and better when Lydia woke up the next morning, though she felt guilty about her outburst to Jason. She slipped a note saying, *Please forgive me*, under his door, but still feeling embarrassed. She didn't go outside that evening despite the beautiful night, spending the evening watching a movie on her laptop with Sunny and going to bed early.

The weather turned stormy and wet, and it lasted several weeks without any sign of a change, but then, suddenly it took a turn for the better. One sunny morning, Lydia couldn't help but look out the windows of Helen's house while she did the ironing hoping the rain would hold off so she could get out for a walk with Lucky. And to her delight it did. After a quick lunch, she set off along the cliffs and down to Wild Rose Bay. The sun was still shining from a pristine blue sky even though the north-west wind was biting. But dressed in her warm jacket, a blue cashmere beanie and her sturdy Timberland walking shoes, she felt warm and ready to face the cold.

Lucky trotted eagerly ahead of her, easily finding the steep path to the beach, while Lydia took it a little more cautiously, slowly making her way, holding on to clumps of heather and rocks as she slithered down the rough path, jumping onto the sand with a sigh of relief. Lucky ran ahead, sniffing at shells and the odd little crab, obviously enjoying himself until he suddenly stood stock-still, his ears pricked, his little tail wagging furiously. Lydia looked ahead, wondering why he was suddenly so excited and spotted the figure of a man far away among the rocks. It was Jason. She remembered when she had seen him swimming here before, when he had emerged out of the waves dressed only in a pair of swimming trunks. This time, however, he was standing on the beach, nearly fully dressed, pulling a thick black sweater over his head.

Lucky charged ahead while Lydia hung back, wondering if she should say hello or just turn around and leave. He might want to be alone. As Jason saw Lucky, he crouched down, patting the delighted little dog on the head. Lydia took a step closer and called Lucky, who didn't seem to have heard as he gave himself up to the stranger's patting and soft words in his ear.

'Lucky!' Lydia called again. 'Come here!' She smiled apologetically at Jason. 'I'm sorry. He isn't usually this forward with strangers.'

'But we aren't strangers, are we, Lucky?' Jason said to the dog. He got up. 'Hello, Lydia,' he said, smiling and holding out his hand. 'We meet in daylight at last.'

Feeling a little self-conscious, Lydia studied him, taking in every detail, his features clear in the daylight. He was tall and had dark hair with silver streaks, grey eyes under black brows, a long straight nose, a strong chin and a dimple beside his mouth. He smiled at her showing even, white teeth. She smiled back nervously. 'Hi, Jason. Strange to meet in daylight.'

'But very nice,' he said, taking her hand. 'Hello again, Lydia.'

'You know, when I first saw you I was a little surprised,' Lydia said with a nervous laugh as she shook his hand. 'I thought you were short, chubby and bald. And that you wore a lot of jewellery. I saw this man coming out of an Audi outside your house one evening, so I thought…'

Laughing, Jason let go of her hand. 'Ah, that was George, my business partner. He called in to tell me he had found a piece of timber for a table I'm making.'

'Oh,' Lydia said. 'How silly of me.' Her legs suddenly felt weak. She sat down on a boulder, still staring at Jason, wondering if, in fact, it was a good thing that they were finally seeing each other clearly. The anonymity of a voice over the hedge had made her lose her inhibitions, during the first week and when they had met in the evenings, she had still felt quite comfortable talking to him as she hadn't always been able to see him clearly. But now, in broad daylight, she tried to get used to him being more real instead of the shadowy figure in the dim light of the moon and the stars. He was no longer a voice in the darkness, which felt startling and new. She noticed his damp hair and the wet trunks thrown on a rock. 'I can't believe you're swimming in this cold weather,' she said, her voice shaking slightly.

'I wouldn't call it swimming exactly,' he said, smoothing his sweater over his slim torso. 'Just a little dip in cold water. It's incredibly invigorating and so good for the mind. Makes you feel awake and ready to tackle anything.'

'Must be excruciating,' Lydia remarked, shivering at the thought of going into that cold water.

'Yes, at first. But then a kind of calm comes over me as I slow my breathing and try to relax. Can't stay in long, though.'

'Of course not.'

Jason gathered up his wet trunks and towel. 'I meant to say sorry about what I said to you that night. I didn't mean to hurt you, just shake you up a little.'

'You certainly did,' Lydia said, getting up from the boulder. 'And maybe you were right, even if it was harsh. But I was rude to you, which wasn't nice.'

'But deserved?' he asked.

'I felt it was.'

'Sometimes you have to be cruel to be kind.'

'I'm not so sure that's necessary,' Lydia replied. Although she was glad that Jason had pushed her to face her feelings, she was sure that his delivery could have been a little better.

'Well, then I apologise again.' He stuck the rolled-up towel under his arm. 'But now I have to go. I have a meeting with a client this afternoon.'

'I have to go too.' Lydia clicked her fingers at Lucky. 'Come here, boy. We have to get back before Sunny gets home. And I have to think of something for dinner.'

'How about joining me?' Jason suggested. 'You and your daughter. And, of course, Lucky.'

'Oh,' Lydia said. 'Are you sure? I mean… I know you're not really into socialising much.'

'Says who?' he asked, looking confused.

'Just an impression I had.'

'Yeah, well… I'm not,' he said. 'But you're…'

'Not people?' she suggested with a laugh.

'Well, we're neighbours, so I can't avoid you, can I?' He shrugged and shot her a shy little smile. 'Don't come if you feel you don't want to. We could chat in the garden later if the skies stay clear, if you prefer.'

'No, I do want to come. I think Sunny would love it too. She could do with a break from my cooking. She's a very special girl.'

'I'm sure she is.' He stopped and studied her for a moment. 'You look a little shocked. I think I am too in a way. Seeing you so clearly feels good, but different. You're no longer a shadow in the dark.'

Lydia nodded. 'I know. It's like meeting someone you've been connecting with online. I knew kind of what you looked like, but not quite. And I think… I feel the chatting in the evening is going to be different now.' She didn't quite know how to say it, but seeing his face and his expressions so clearly as he spoke gave her a feeling of intimacy. Now there was a new vibe between them that was both exciting and a little nerve-racking.

'Now that you know I'm not George?' he enquired, his mouth twisting.

'I already knew that. But. Well, it feels a little strange right now,' she said, feeling the vibes coming from him were more than positive. He was no longer the avuncular confidant she had trusted with all her troubles, but a man she felt suddenly very drawn to. Was this good or bad? She didn't know, but something stirred in her heart while he kept fixing her with his grey eyes.

'Maybe it's just seeing each other clearly,' he said, moving away. 'But I think that's a good thing. So I'll see you later then. Seven o'clock?'

'Yes, that's fine. Bye for now.'

She watched him walk up the path opposite the one she had taken, feeling overwhelmed. Standing there, she suddenly felt as if the part of her that had been frozen for so long was slowly beginning to thaw. They wouldn't talk like they had the other week again, but she would never forget his depth of understanding and empathy during those first lonely evenings at the cottage. She realised that she didn't need to unburden herself to him any more. Now they could go forward and simply enjoy each other's company. This meeting had brought on a shift in their friendship. The prospect of dinner at his house seemed a lot more enjoyable than talking about her sorrows in the darkness.

Chapter Eighteen

Sunny arrived home later that day looking a lot brighter than she had when she had left that morning, worrying once again about the other children at school. Lydia could see that though Sunny was still nervous, things were improving.

'That Fintan guy,' Sunny said as she walked through the door. 'Sorcha's son. He was teasing me like mad in the beginning, but now he's sticking up for me and we're like on the same team. A team of two,' she added with a laugh. 'He's going to help me with my Irish homework because everyone is way ahead of me. And he says I should go to the after-school Irish dance class on Tuesdays and Thursdays because they're great craic. Only if you can pick us up afterwards, because the school bus will be gone and his mum will be working. Can I, please?' she added, looking pleadingly at Lydia.

'Of course you can,' Lydia promised, wondering how much the dance classes cost. And Irish dancing? She hadn't thought it was something Sunny would enjoy, but it might be a nice substitute for the ballet classes Sunny had loved so much when they lived in Dublin.

'Oh great. Thanks, Mum.' Sunny hung her jacket on the coat rack in the hall. 'And here's another thing. We've been asked to write a story about inspirational historical people in Kerry. So I thought

I'd write about old Aunt Nellie. I don't know if she's inspirational, but she seems to have had an interesting life, and I know you're keen to find out more about her too. I'm sure I could discover lots by interviewing old people in the village. And we could do it together.'

'That's a great idea,' Lydia said, feeling excited at the prospect. She also wanted to find out more about her great-aunt who seemed to have been so independent and courageous. 'I would love to help you with that.'

'Cool,' Sunny said. 'What's for dinner?'

'We're going out,' Lydia replied. 'Our neighbour has asked us to dinner.'

'Which one? That funny tall Dutch woman with black hair? She said hello to me just now when I walked home.'

'No, not her. The man next door. Jason O'Callaghan.'

'The mystery man?' Sunny said as she kicked off her shoes and picked Lucky up. 'That's what Fintan calls him. He's a hermit, or something.'

'He's an artist and he's a bit of a loner, I think, that's all. Not much for socialising,' Lydia said, thinking that being an introvert might have earned him a reputation for not being very friendly, which wouldn't go down well in a place where everyone knew each other. But she was eager to know him better and to find out what was behind that wall he had put up against the world. She took Sunny's shoes and put them on the mat beside the coat rack. 'Go and change out of your school uniform and get started on your homework. We're expected at seven.'

'Okay,' Sunny said. 'Oh, and give Sorcha a call. She said she had something to tell you when I met her outside the shop on my way home.'

'Like what?'

Sunny shrugged. 'No idea. Call her and find out.'

While Sunny skipped up the stairs, Lydia went to find her phone in the living room and called Sorcha to ask what she wanted.

'A job,' Sorcha said. 'For you.'

'I already have one,' Lydia replied.

'I know but this is another part-time job. Susie at the hairdresser's is looking for an assistant just for Friday afternoons and Saturday mornings. It's their busiest time of the week and Gerry, her partner, will be busy doing weddings. I said you'd do it, but you have to call her and confirm. Thought it would add a little extra cash in your wallet.'

'Hairdressing?' Lydia said and made a face.

'Yeah, just washing people's hair, sweeping the floor, tidying up and taking bookings,' Sorcha said. 'Easy stuff.'

'Oh.'

'I'll text you her number and you can give her a call.'

'Right. Thanks, Sorcha.'

'You're welcome. Got to go. Customers queuing up at the till. Bye for now.'

When she had hung up, Lydia sat down in the sofa waiting for Sorcha's message. *Hairdressing*, she thought. *Is there no end to the jobs I'll need to learn how to do in order to survive?* Lydia told the little voice in her head to be quiet as the text came through with the number. She punched it in and waited for a reply, telling herself to swallow her pride.

'Bizarre hair salon,' a voice replied. 'Susie speaking.'

Lydia suppressed a giggle at the name of the salon. 'Uh, hello. My name is Lydia Butler, and—'

'Ah, brilliant,' Susie said, interrupting her. 'Sorcha told me you were looking for a bit of part-time work. We just want someone to help out on Friday afternoons and Saturday mornings. Fridays we're open until nine, so we'd want you to start at three o'clock and work until we close. Saturday we'd need you from ten to lunchtime, to free up Gerry for the weddings. He does hair and make-up, so you can imagine how busy he is, the poor lad. But if he has someone to help out with the shampooing, that'd make it a lot easier. There are usually large parties with all the bridesmaids and mothers of the bride and groom and all kinds of sisters and aunties, too, who want to be tarted up for the occasion, if you see what I mean.' Susie drew breath.

'Yes, I can imagine,' Lydia said, smiling at Susie's choice of words.

'So you'd be slaving away while he's making everyone beautiful. We'll be dealing with all the girls going to parties or the disco in Waterville as well. Some just want to look pretty for a night out at the pub – they can be a bit of a handful, I have to tell you. But it's great craic too, of course. How about it?'

'Eh, but don't you want to meet me first before you decide?'

'Nah, that's not necessary. Sorcha says you'd be great. It's only shampooing and stuff anyway. Not brain surgery or anything.'

'In that case, I accept. I mean, I'll be happy to do it,' Lydia said, wondering if she could ask about her pay.

'Oh great. Welcome aboard,' Susie said, sounding relieved. 'It'll be great to have an extra pair of hands. Oh and I'll pay you eighteen an hour and double that on Saturday.'

'Euros?' Lydia asked, doing sums in her head.

'But of course. What did you think? Russian roubles?'

Lydia had to laugh. 'Well, that would be unusual.'

'Yeah. Hey, I have to hang up. Gerry just arrived in from his course in Dublin. He's been catching up on the latest trends in hair colours. Don't let him practise on you. He's big into pastel highlights at the moment. You might end up with green and pink streaks,' Susie warned. 'See you Friday, then?'

'Yes. See you then. Thanks, Susie. Bye for now.' Lydia hung up, smiling and shaking her head. Susie seemed like a bit of a character. But the job might be more fun than she had thought. And the salary was quite generous. A quick calculation told her she'd be able to add just over two hundred euros to her weekly salary from cleaning Helen's house. With that her weekly take would amount to over three hundred euros, an amount she'd spend on a morning's shopping without a second thought in her earlier life. Now it felt like a lifesaver which would pay for most of their expenses if she was careful, including Sunny's dance classes. And there was a nest egg left in her account, which she now wouldn't have to touch. They would survive until Lydia could find something better and more secure.

Feeling as if the dark cloud of despair was slowly drifting away, Lydia went upstairs to dress for dinner, something she hadn't done for months. It wouldn't be a fancy dressy-up party, but still, there was no harm in looking a little more polished. She grabbed her cream cashmere sweater, her black jeans and boots. She'd put on her gold hoop earrings, the only jewellery she hadn't sold because they had belonged to her mother. A good, casual look that wouldn't seem as if she'd tried too hard. She hoped.

Chapter Nineteen

Jason's house was not at all what Lydia had expected. Instead of the spartan, bare look that she had imagined, judging by his furniture designs, the living room was furnished in a tasteful contemporary New England style with a large green sofa facing the fireplace, flanked by two deep matching armchairs and a padded bench serving as coffee table. The pale-yellow walls were hung with exquisite landscapes and the odd still life. Rugs in rich colours were scattered over the polished wooden floor and at the far side, a round mahogany table was laid for three with place mats, silver cutlery and crystal glassware. Lydia saw a large work table in the sunroom with a stack of drawings and bits of wood beside a huge computer monitor. Jason's work space, she deduced; like hers, it would have glorious views of the bay.

'Welcome to my house,' Jason said as he led the way into the room. Dressed in brown corduroys and a black polo neck, his hair brushed back from his face, he looked less wild and windblown than when Lydia had met him earlier that day. His eyes on her revealed he was happy to see her again. Then he turned to Sunny and held out his hand. 'Hi, I'm Jason. Nice to meet you, Sunny.'

'Hi.' Sunny shook his hand while she held Lucky in her arms. 'Thanks for inviting us.'

'Lovely room.' Lydia looked around, unable to hide her surprise.

'Looks like the White House,' Sunny piped up. 'I mean that house the president lives in. Old-fashioned and kind of posh.'

'I hope that was a compliment,' Jason said, smiling at Sunny.

'It was an observation,' Sunny said, still holding a squirming Lucky under her arm. 'Can I let him down?'

'Of course,' Jason replied. 'This is a living room. Meant to be lived in. And I like dogs, especially Lucky. He's so friendly.'

'He seems to like you right back,' Sunny said as Lucky trotted over to Jason, looking up at him adoringly.

Jason crouched down and patted Lucky on the head. 'We're becoming friends, aren't we, Lucky?'

Lucky barked in agreement and then proceeded to trot around the room, sniffing at everything.

Jason rose and rubbed his hands together. 'So, how about dinner then? Or do you want to have a drink first?'

'We're starving,' Sunny said. 'And something smells yummy.'

'I think that decides it.' Jason gestured at the table. 'Everything's ready, I made Boston clam chowder,' he said, pronouncing it 'chow-dah'.

'Fish soup?' Lydia asked.

'No, not at all,' Jason protested, laughing. 'Well, maybe a little. It's a creamy concoction of shellfish, fish, bacon and potatoes. Us Bostonians were raised on it. I got all the ingredients except for the bacon from the fish shop in Waterville. Hope you'll like it.'

'We'll love it,' Sunny promised, walking to the table. 'Better than fish fingers and spaghetti hoops from a tin, I bet. Mum isn't really into that cuisine thing,' she added in a conspiratorial whisper.

'I'm trying,' Lydia said, embarrassed at Sunny's revelations. 'I never learned really, you see.'

'We had a housekeeper before we came here,' Sunny explained. 'So Mum never got a chance to have a go at cooking.'

Lydia made a face. 'I just didn't have the time,' she said, worried Sunny's words would make her seem spoiled.

'But I'm sure it won't take long before you learn the basics.' Jason handed Lydia a bread basket. 'Help yourself to rolls while I get the chowder.' He walked out of the room only to return seconds later with a steaming pot of chowder that he ladled into bowls and handed to Lydia and Sunny before he helped himself. When he had poured the wine, he sat down at the head of the table, Lydia and Sunny on either side.

'Yummy,' Sunny declared after her first mouthfuls. 'Is it hard to make?'

'No, really easy.' Jason took a bread roll from the basket and broke it in two. 'I'll give you the recipe if you like.'

'Please,' Lydia said. 'It's time I tried some real cooking.'

They ate in silence for a moment, exchanging smiles and concentrating on the food which was indeed delicious. Sunny gobbled hers up in record time and nibbled on the bread while she studied Jason. 'What's your story, then?' she said.

'How do you mean?' Jason asked, looking taken aback.

'I mean, why do you live here and not in Boston?' Sunny replied.

'Oh…' Jason looked suddenly awkward. 'Well, it's a little complicated.'

'Sunny,' Lydia chided. 'You shouldn't grill people like that.'

'I'm not grilling him, I'm asking,' Sunny argued. 'I mean, he seems to know our story, so why can't we know his?' She looked at Jason. 'Is it some kind of secret? Are you hiding from the Mafia? Like in a witness protection thing and your name isn't really Jason O'Callaghan but Marco Pugliani or something like that?'

Jason burst out laughing. 'Yeah, wouldn't that be more exciting than the real story?' He shook his head, still smiling. 'It's not a secret, really.' His expression sobered. 'I came here after a very hard time in my life. Painful break-up of my marriage and a very bitter custody battle about Annie and Lauren, my two daughters, you see. Which I lost – or gave up, to be more precise.'

'Why?' Sunny asked, ignoring Lydia's stern look.

'Because I didn't want them to suffer,' Jason said to Sunny. 'Bad enough that their mother and I divorced but to ask two young girls to choose between their parents was very unfair.' He leaned forward and looked at Sunny. 'I did want to fight really hard for custody, but then I saw what the divorce was doing to them and I just couldn't continue. They were so close to their mother and I didn't want them to lose that, you see. So I gave in, because I knew they needed us to get on as a family, even though we would be living apart. It seemed the right thing to do at the time. Still does.'

'I agree,' Sunny said. 'That was very brave of you. So did you stick around and see the girls when you could?'

'I think that's enough questions,' Lydia said, noticing the pain in Jason's eyes.

Jason turned to look at Lydia. 'No, it's all right. I don't mind telling Sunny.' He turned to look at Sunny. 'Yes, I did. I saw them as often as I could. I gave up my share of the house so they wouldn't have to move. I don't know if I did the right thing by giving up the custody case, but I just wanted all the hurt to stop for them.'

'You did the right thing,' Sunny stated. 'Fighting about them would have been such torture for those girls, I've seen friends from school deal with that. How long ago was it?'

'Ten years. And now they have grown up and have their own lives. They seem to be happy and well adjusted. And I see them now that it's their choice, of course.' Jason lifted the bottle of wine and looked at Lydia. 'More wine?'

'Yes, please. It's very good,' Lydia replied, feeling that Jason wanted to close the subject.

'Mâcon-Villages. Nice and crisp. Goes well with fish,' Jason said. 'So, Sunny, that's what happened in a nutshell.'

'You don't have to say any more,' Lydia cut in. 'We can imagine how difficult it must have been.'

Jason nodded and topped up Lydia's glass. 'Yes, I'm sure you can. But I think that'll be it for now. It's not easy to go back to a hard place, as you probably know.'

'Yes, I do,' Sunny said, looking chastened.

After a slightly awkward silence, Lydia turned the conversation to Aunt Nellie and the letter she had found and what it said. She was glad to see Jason's eyes light up at her discoveries, and to get to share it with someone else. 'It seems to me they had a romance and then he left, promising to come back after the war. I keep wondering why he didn't.'

'Maybe he fell in love with someone else,' Jason suggested. 'They probably couldn't communicate much during the war years, so they might have lost touch. And then, as the saying goes, out of sight out of mind.'

'Men are unreliable,' Sunny cut in, sounding astonishingly grown up. 'Women are better at keeping in touch and we are way more loyal,' she added, a new sharp tone in her voice.

Lydia glanced at her, wondering if Sunny was referring to the bad atmosphere between her parents, as she might have overheard their many heated arguments and felt the negative vibes of a marriage in trouble. She must have been disappointed that Barry had been so absent as he spent more and more time either at the golf club or at work. She had never understood why Barry was on his way to London when he had the heart attack. Jason's suggestion that Sunny deserved to know the truth suddenly popped into Lydia's mind, but she pushed it away. Sunny wasn't ready for that yet.

'I'm not sure you're right about that,' Jason said. 'It depends on each individual. In that case it could have been Nellie who didn't keep in touch.'

'We don't know what happened or whose fault it was,' Lydia said.

'I'd say it was his and that Aunt Nellie was very sad about it,' Sunny insisted.

'Maybe not,' Lydia interrupted. 'You don't know that. She might not have wanted to marry him and move to Germany. Maybe she didn't want to get married at all? She was a very independent woman, I've heard.'

Lucky suddenly whined under the table and ran to the back door. 'He wants to go out for a bit,' Sunny said. 'Can I let him out into your garden?'

'Of course. Go out through the sunroom and let him have a run outside.'

Jason turned to Lydia when Sunny had left. 'She's a lovely girl. You must be so proud of her.'

'I am. But…' Lydia hesitated. 'She's a little too inquisitive. I'm sorry she forced you to talk about your divorce. I think it reminded her of what happened with her father. She didn't mean any harm.'

'I know she didn't. And I only told her part of my story anyway.'

'I thought there might be more,' Lydia admitted.

'Yes,' Jason said, his eyes full of pain. He smiled suddenly. 'But one thing was a little eerie. Sunny is right. Jason O'Callaghan isn't my real name.'

Taken aback, Lydia stared at him, but Sunny's figure through the back window stopped her from asking what he meant.

When Sunny and Lucky came back in, they all cleared the table and then moved to the sofa where Jason served them brownies with ice cream. 'Not my own, I'm afraid,' he confessed. 'The bakery in the village is a hard act to follow, so I don't bother.'

'Their stuff is really good,' Sunny agreed as she scoffed the lot in a few seconds. 'I love their cupcakes that Mum buys for an after-school treat sometimes.' She put her plate on the tray and leaned back in the sofa with a contented sigh. 'I'm stuffed. Dinner was awesome. Mum, you have to get the recipe for that fish thing.'

'I will,' Lydia promised, handing Jason her plate. 'Thank you so much for this delicious dinner, Jason.'

'Thank you for coming,' he replied as he took their plates and put them on the table. 'It's nice to have company sometimes. I don't socialise much, but tonight, I felt I should meet the neighbours and get to know them a little better.'

'Why don't you?' Sunny asked. 'Socialise, I mean?'

'Oh, well, I…' Jason started.

Lydia sat up. 'Sunny, I think we'll have to say goodnight now. It's getting late. You have school tomorrow and I have to go to work.'

Sunny nodded, looking contrite. 'All right, Mum. I get it.' She stood up and held out her hand. 'Goodnight, Jason. Thank you so much for inviting me and Mum.'

Jason smiled and shook Sunny's hand. 'You're very welcome, young lady.'

Lydia rose and picked Lucky up. 'Lovely evening, Jason. We'll invite you to our house soon, if you're brave enough to try my cooking.'

'And our furniture,' Sunny mumbled. 'Especially the saggy sofa.'

Lydia looked at Sunny and burst out laughing. 'Oh yeah. Our furniture. Not for the faint-hearted.'

'No faint hearts here,' Jason said, leading the way to the front door. 'I'd love to come for dinner some day when you feel ready.' He opened the door. 'See you soon in one way or the other.'

They stepped out into the cold, crisp night and hurried into their own house, Lydia feeling a nice afterglow from the evening that had just passed. Jason had been a lovely host and treated Sunny with kindness and understanding. Then, as she prepared for bed, she remembered what he had said about his name. How strange that Sunny should have guessed that part. But what *was* his real name, and why had he changed it?

Chapter Twenty

Lydia quickly adjusted to her new routine. She was handling two jobs, collecting Sunny and Fintan from Irish dancing twice a week and also camogie practice that Sunny had added to her after-school activities, as Fintan had hurling the same day. He was a friendly, fun boy with Sorcha's red hair and freckly face and Lydia had liked him immediately. Working late at the salon on Fridays was no problem as Sunny could go to Sorcha's and help out in the shop with Fintan, stacking shelves and tidying up and then have dinner with them. Then Sunny was asked to babysit Dr Kate's little girl on Saturday nights, which became a regular occurrence as Kate and her husband liked to go out for a meal together at that time. Dr Kate was the other GP in the village, working in tandem with Dr Pat and the two made a wonderful team. This babysitting job meant that Sunny was earning pocket money, easing their financial burden even more.

The weeks suddenly seemed to whizz by and even though St Patrick's Day was a wash-out, they managed to have a good time joining Sorcha and Fintan for an Irish musical evening at the pub in the main street, enjoying some good food and laughs. After that the evenings were brighter and the weather a little warmer even if the spring storms were a regular occurrence. And suddenly, it was

April and the shops and restaurants in the village started to prepare for the start of the season.

Lydia hadn't seen Jason since that evening in his house, but she knew he was very busy with different projects – he'd mentioned an exhibition in London when they'd had dinner together. Although she missed their starlit chats, she felt that she didn't need them as much as she had when she'd first arrived, even if she found herself longing to see him again.

Brian arrived one afternoon to take a look at the storage heater. Lydia had to admit that the heater, although big and ugly, had delivered a lot of heat and made the cottage a lot more comfortable even half an hour after it had been switched on. But now it was acting up, so she had called Brian to see if he could help her. It didn't take long for it to be working perfectly again.

When she thanked him profusely, Brian lingered at the door and put his hand on hers, his kind brown eyes full of admiration. 'I'd do anything for you, Lydia. You just have to ask.'

'That's very sweet of you,' Lydia said, at the same time moved by his kindness and slightly alarmed by the adoring look in his eyes. 'And you've been so helpful with Lucky. I'd be happy to repay you in any way I can as well, of course.'

He smiled and squeezed her hand. 'Maybe you'd come out for a drink one evening? Just down to the pub in the village. Saturday night is always good craic there. Or—' He moved closer. 'We could go out to dinner, just the two of us. There's a nice little restaurant that's opening for the season soon.'

Lydia eased her hand out of his grip. 'Oh, that would be fun, but... I'm not sure I'm ready to go out on dates. Yet,' she added to soften the blow, slightly alarmed at his forwardness. Brian was a nice, good-looking man and he had been extraordinarily kind, but she had thought he just wanted to be friends. His eyes told her he was hoping for more, however and that, she knew, would never be on the cards for her. Even if she had been in a better place, she wouldn't be attracted to him in that way. She didn't really have a 'type' when it came to men, but if she had, he wouldn't be it.

'I understand,' Brian said, looking both contrite and disappointed. 'I'm sorry. I shouldn't have rushed you like that. It's too soon after all you've been through. We'll just be friends for now,' he said, sounding like a teenager. 'And my offer of help stands, of course. I didn't mean…' His voice trailed away as he moved away from her.

'I know,' Lydia soothed. 'And I might come to the pub on Saturday night with you and Sorcha soon,' she said, hoping he understood what she meant. 'We could even invite Saskia. She's good fun.'

'Yes, that would be great,' Brian said, looking as if he thought there might be hope for him after all.

They said goodbye and Lydia went back into the house to enjoy the now warm and cosy living room. She blessed Brian for his kindness, even though she felt a little guilty to have dashed his hopes of a romantic evening for two.

Lydia stood at the window and stared out over the bay, where the sun shone through the clouds on the dark choppy water. The weather had changed again after a brief spell of spring sunshine. Would it ever be warm? she wondered. And would she ever get out of the gloom she had been in for so long? The people she had met since she arrived had been so kind and so welcoming, but despite this, and her hopes of starting a new life here, she still felt a pull towards the bright lights of Dublin. Maybe that's where she really belonged?

'Are you beginning to feel more settled?' Helen asked one morning as Lydia put away the cleaning products in the utility room.

Lydia closed the door to the broom cupboard and shrugged. 'Not really. Well, of course everyone's very nice and everything, but to the life I'm leading now is not exactly the one I always thought I'd lead.'

'I can imagine,' Helen said. 'But I mean…' She paused, looking confused. 'Why are you doing these jobs? Why don't you try to find something better, something that would fit your qualifications, whatever they are?'

'My qualifications are slightly out of date,' Lydia said as she untied her apron. 'I worked as copywriter at an advertising agency before I was married, but that was over twenty years ago. I tried reaching out to my old firm but they didn't have any vacancies. The fundraising was more recent, but neither of those careers are exactly thriving in Sandy Cove. And this is the only place that I can live right now.'

'I suppose that's true.' Helen looked thoughtful. 'But fund-raising… I have been thinking about that. Pat will be turning seventy-five soon and he wants to organise a birthday fund for Doctors Without Borders. I thought we could do a big dinner at the golf club and charge people, but that seems so last year. I'd like to do something fun and different that would involve everyone here, not all the boring golf people. Would you have any ideas?'

Lydia looked at Helen and as their eyes met, had a flash of inspiration. 'I might,' she said. 'But I need to think about it. And...' She paused, wondering if she could say what had occurred to her. 'I would have to charge for my services if you want me to work on this.' The words were out before she could stop them and she stared at Helen, waiting for the scathing comments she knew would come.

Helen met Lydia's eyes without speaking. 'Oh,' she said after a moment's loaded silence. 'I didn't think of that. But of course, if you are, as you say, a professional fundraiser, then I would be prepared to pay you. But I need to see a plan first.'

'I'll draw it up and give it to you tomorrow,' Lydia promised. 'Then, if you like it, we can go ahead.'

'Go ahead?' Helen asked. 'What does that mean?'

'It means I'll be in charge and you don't really have to do anything, except look elegant and be the formal head of the whole programme.'

'And you'll handle the donations and all the tedious bank details?'

'Of course,' Lydia promised. 'I have done it before so that's no problem at all.'

'Oh,' Helen said, her eyes lighting up. 'That sounds excellent. And I will call my son, the councillor, at once and ask him to be patron of this fund. A very famous man,' she added.

'I know,' Lydia replied. 'Mick O'Dwyer. Former Abbey Theatre actor and now a high-profile politician,' she added, deciding to lay it on as thickly as she could.

'That's right,' Helen said, a gleam of pride in her eyes. 'And he will be running for a seat in the Irish parliament in the next election.'

'Wonderful,' Lydia said. 'And I believe he has a lovely wife and a new baby, too.'

'That's true. They made me a granny in October. He's a little boy called Daniel.' Helen touched her hair. 'It feels strange to take on that role as I'm quite young.'

'You certainly don't look like a grandmother,' Lydia soothed. 'But grannies are getting younger and younger these days, of course.'

'We are,' Helen agreed. 'Becoming a granny is quite wonderful, really.' She started to move towards the door, walking much better now than just after her surgery. 'So, before we say goodbye, we'll agree that you will present your plan tomorrow and we'll start work on it. Pat's birthday is on the twenty-second of April, only three weeks away. Just after Easter, as a matter of fact.'

'Good time to run the campaign,' Lydia said, picking up her bag and her jacket. 'The weather should be a little warmer by then.'

They said goodbye and Lydia left the house feeling for the first time since she arrived in the village that she could find a career. This project would be just what she needed. A challenge and maybe the start of something she could build on. *Maybe*, she thought, *Helen's friends or contacts might notice me and hire me. And then I can slowly get back on my feet and we can return to Dublin…*

Chapter Twenty-One

Despite the cold wind and steady drizzle, Lydia took Lucky for a walk on the beach just after lunch. She hadn't thought she'd see Jason in such inclement weather, but there he was in the distance, putting on a waterproof jacket and stuffing his swimming trunks and towel into a plastic bag. She waved and called his name and he waved back and started to walk towards her.

'Hello,' he said. 'Didn't expect to see you here today.'

'Nor me,' she said, trying to catch her breath as she looked up at him, an odd sensation starting deep inside that spread slowly like a warm wave through her body. 'It's so nice to see you.'

'Very nice,' he agreed, a smile suddenly lighting up his face.

'You've been swimming?'

'Just a dip really.'

'Must be excruciating.' Lydia tried to imagine getting into such ice-cold water but found she couldn't. 'You're very brave.'

'Or mad,' he said, grinning. 'Hey, how are you? I haven't seen you for a while.'

'I've been busy. I got another job and then Sunny decided to do all these after-school activities so I've been playing chauffeur.'

'Another job?' he said, impressed.

'You're looking at the new shampoo girl at the Bizarre hair salon.'

Jason laughed. 'I can see that you'd be very busy.'

'Yes. Sunny and I have been trying to find out more about Aunt Nellie on the internet, too, without much luck. So we're going to try to find older people in the village who might know more. And I've just been asked to propose a fundraising event for Helen O'Dwyer.' She stopped and laughed. 'Sorry. That was all me, me, me, wasn't it? What have you been up to since that lovely evening at your place?'

He swept his wet hair back from his face, 'Oh, just the usual. We got some wonderful Arbutus wood from Killarney and I'm working on a very large table for a client in France. It's quite tricky to fit it to the design but I'm getting there.'

'Oh. Good.' She was suddenly stuck for words standing there in the fine drizzle. As Lucky looked up at her and whined, she moved away. 'Well, nice to see you. It's getting a little too wet for me and Lucky, so we'd better head home.'

He pointed up the slope on the other side. 'My Land Rover is parked up there. I was on my way to the workshop, but...' He paused, looking at her with a strange expression. 'I want to talk to you. I meant to call in, but then I didn't want to disturb you. Could we talk in the car? I have a thermos with coffee we could share.'

'And I have a wet dog,' Lydia said with a laugh. 'But yes, why not? If you need to talk, I'm here. God knows you've listened to me like a hundred times. I think I owe you.'

'You don't owe me anything,' Jason replied. 'Let's get out of this drizzle, anyway.' He bundled the bag with the trunks and towel under his arm and started to jog up the steep slope, his long legs taking big strides.

Lydia followed in his wake and Lucky made up the rear, trotting behind them, panting and letting out the odd whine. Near the top of the slope, Lydia took pity on him and lifted him up. 'A bit of a challenge for short legs, is it?' she said, tucking him under her arm. When they got to the top, she let him down and they walked along the path on the edge of the cliff until they reached the Land Rover parked outside a café called The Two Marys'.

Jason had already arrived and he was drying his hair on a towel before he spread it on the back seat. 'Here, put Lucky on this and he'll dry in no time.' He opened the passenger door. 'Sit here and I'll get the thermos. I even have an extra mug.'

Lydia took off her wet jacket and put it on the floor before she sat down and closed the door against the now pelting rain. 'Phew, we missed that heavy shower,' she said, relieved to be dry and relatively warm.

Jason followed her example and tossed his wet jacket on the back seat beside Lucky, who had settled happily on the towel. Then he took the thermos from a bag on the floor, poured Lydia a nearly full plastic mug and handed it to her. 'No buns or cookies, I'm afraid. The Two Marys' isn't open yet.'

'That's fine,' Lydia said, sipping the hot coffee, feeling content and strangely happy to sit with him here in the confined space of his car. 'This is great after the walk in the rain. But I don't know how you get into that cold sea.' She met his eyes and smiled as she saw something in his expression that mirrored her own pleasure in this moment of intimacy.

'It was hard in the beginning,' Jason said, pouring coffee into the cap of the thermos. 'But then you get used to it and once you start to feel the positive effects you get hooked. Cold water swimming is good for mental health and can help lift your mood, I read somewhere. So I tried it and it truly works. It gives me a huge energy boost and helps me focus on my work. You should try it.'

'No thanks,' Lydia said with a shiver. 'I admire your courage, but that kind of shock would probably kill me.'

'Maybe later on, in the spring,' Jason suggested. He drained the cup and put it on the dashboard.

'So,' Lydia said after a while. 'What was that about your real name and the other reason you left Boston that you hinted at when we had dinner at your house?'

He was quiet for a long time; Lydia nearly regretted her question. 'My story, as your daughter called it,' he said with a flicker of pain in his eyes, 'is long and tedious and hard to talk about.'

'You don't have to,' Lydia soothed, worried she had upset him by reminding him of something that was obviously very painful.

'I think I need to,' Jason said, turning to Lydia. 'For me, not for you, if you don't think that's too selfish.'

'Of course not,' Lydia said, the look in his eyes making her heart ache. It had to be something awful. Something that would be as hard to hear as to tell. But she was ready to listen as he seemed suddenly in desperate need for a sympathetic ear. 'Go on,' she urged. 'Tell me what happened to you.'

'Right.' He cleared his throat and stared out over the misty ocean. 'It all happened just after the divorce. You see, I wasn't a designer then, I was an architect. I ran a firm with a friend, designing houses and apartment blocks. We were quite successful and had built up a good reputation in the Boston area. We had just finished an apartment block that took a long time to complete – quite a controversial project with new designs and concepts and so on. I was so proud of it and we were featured in several national architectural magazines. I thought we had it made. It was such a great boost for me after all the pain of the divorce and the custody battle. But then…' He paused.

'Then—?' she whispered. 'What happened?

'Something terrible. Shortly after the building was completed and some of the new owners had moved in, part of the building collapsed.'

'Oh my God,' Lydia gasped. 'Did anyone die?'

'No. Nobody was even seriously hurt, but a lot of property like expensive furniture and carpets were damaged. Pipes burst and there was water damage everywhere. It appeared that sub-standard building materials had been used instead of what we had agreed. I got the blame as my name was on all the designs, but it was in fact my friend and business partner who had changed the orders to the builders and pocketed the money he saved by not using top-grade material. Then he ran off and couldn't be found, so I was on my own, having to deal with a court case that went on for months with all the owners suing us. Not only had my business partner cheated on the materials, he had also not paid the insurance, so I was left not being paid for my work. My name and career were ruined.' Jason sighed deeply, running his hand through his hair. 'You can imagine how that was, right after the divorce and that whole painful period.'

'God, yes.' Lydia put her hand on Jason's shoulder. 'How terrible it must have been.'

He bowed his head. 'Yes. It was.' Then he looked at her with a strange expression and put his hand over hers. 'I haven't talked to anyone about this, but I felt ever since we first met that you were the kind of person I could really talk to. I feel we connect in a very special way. Don't you?'

'Yes,' Lydia said, her hand warm under his. 'I do.' She had felt the same about him, that he was somehow a kindred spirit – a twin soul – and that their meeting was meant to happen somehow. It could have been those starlit chats, the magical moments under the immense star-studded black sky, or simply a yearning for someone to comfort her, but it all felt so right just now. 'Go on,' she urged. 'Tell me the rest.'

Jason nodded. 'At that same time, my ex-wife announced she and the girls were moving to California. She was getting married again and had to move to where her new husband lived and worked. The girls were in their late teens at that time, so it was only a matter of a year or two before they were adult enough to make their own decisions. I didn't want to create more tension, so they left, with the promise they'd spend their summer vacation with me, which I accepted. A long vacation is better than short weekend breaks, I thought. At that time I was so low, I wanted to just crawl into bed and stay there. Forever.'

'Of course you did,' Lydia whispered.

He lifted his head and looked at her. 'I knew you'd understand.'

'I think you did exactly the right thing with your daughters. It must have been such a tough time. But why did you decide to come to Ireland?'

He sighed. 'I was a little lost and thought a break would be good. In any case I needed to disappear and escape all the rumours and gossip. I had been to Ireland many times before. My great-great grandfather came from Tralee. His name was Jason O'Callaghan, so I took his name and then I went to Connemara and studied furniture design at the design college there. In a place called Letterfrack.'

'I know. I've heard of it.' Lydia looked at Jason's pale face with concern. 'Are you all right?'

He smiled weakly. 'I'm fine. Telling you is both hard and comforting. Hard, because it forces me to go back to a very sad time. But comforting because you're here, listening and not judging.'

'Why would I judge you?'

'You might think I had something to do with the disaster of that building.'

'I don't think that at all,' Lydia protested.

'Thank you.'

'So then you came here?'

He nodded. 'Yes. I had just finished the course at Letterfrack and George, who had seen one of my designs that had been featured in a magazine, contacted me. He was setting up a workshop in Waterville and needed a partner. He's a master upholsterer and specialises in chairs and sofas. We complement each other. To cut a long story short, once the workshop started to make money, we went into partnership together. Then I bought the house next to yours.'

'Oh, I see. That's a good ending to your story.'

'Or the beginning of a new one,' he said, smiling warmly as he looked at her.

Lydia couldn't help smiling back. 'Yes. A good beginning, I think.'

'Time will tell if that's true.'

'I'm sure it is,' Lydia replied. 'But now I'm curious,' she continued, 'what is your real name?'

'It's Jack,' he said. 'Jack Chapman.'

'Oh,' Lydia said, trying to think of him as Jack instead of Jason. 'So do I call you Jack, then?'

'Not unless you want to.'

'You'll always be Jason to me,' Lydia declared. 'And you'll be chubby and short and bald in my mind,' she added with a grin. 'I mean, that's how I first saw you. Sorry,' she added quickly.

He relaxed his shoulders and smiled at her. 'You don't need to apologise. Now I feel oddly calm. It was good to talk, even if it was hard.'

'It must be hard every day. I mean, your friend… Such a horrible thing to do. Has he ever been in touch to say sorry?'

'No. I don't think he will. He was never a real, true friend, even though I thought he was. We were friends in college and we had a lot of fun together. But he let me down. Didn't go that extra mile, you know?'

'Oh, yes. I know exactly what you mean,' Lydia said, thinking of those people in Dublin who she had thought were her friends but who had abandoned her when she had lost everything. 'A fair-weather friend,' she said, sadly.

'Exactly.' Jason shifted in his seat. 'I trusted him, but that turned out to be the biggest mistake of my life. He'd been going from job to job ever since he left college. Then he wanted to get into construction and start his own company, so I thought I'd help him out and we became business partners. It worked for a while, until this happened.'

'That must have been such a blow for you. I can't understand how anyone could act like that man did.'

'Me neither,' Jason agreed. 'It's been gnawing at me ever since it happened. But I'm beginning to think it's better to leave all those things alone and not keep going around in circles. Some chapters just have to remain closed.'

Just like the chapter of how Barry left us, Lydia thought. *I should close it and never open it again.* 'I think you're right,' she said. 'Trying to understand some people is like banging your head against the wall. It's painful and it serves no purpose.'

Jason glanced at her. 'But it's very difficult to get it out of your head, isn't it?'

'Nearly impossible.' Lydia looked behind her to check on Lucky, but he was fast asleep on the towel.

Jason's phoned pinged. He picked it up. 'George wondering where I am. I'd better get back to the workshop. I'll drop you off outside your house.' He started the car and drove carefully down the rough track.

'Thanks,' Lydia said, her mind whirling with what she had just learned. She looked at him, as he drove, the clean lines of his profile, his strong hands on the wheel, his thick silver-streaked hair and felt a sudden pull towards this complex, interesting man who had been through so much but come out the other side better and stronger – and free. No wonder he kept away from people after what had happened. She realised like her, he didn't want everyone to start talking and digging into his past and somehow finding out his real name and what had happened to him.

But Lydia didn't have to dig anywhere. She had, during the past hour, found out who he truly was. And it filled her with joy. There was only one thing that gnawed at her right now. And that was the dilemma of telling Sunny the truth about her father. She still couldn't bring herself to do it, but perhaps it would help them both to go forward?

Chapter Twenty-Two

'You should go and chat to a nice old lady called Noreen Scally,' Brian said later that day when Lydia called in to his practice to get more worming tablets for Lucky. 'I mean, for Sunny's Aunt Nellie project,' he explained. 'I've been thinking about it since you told me she was doing it. Noreen would have known your aunt despite their age difference. She's younger, of course, so she would only have been a child during the war, but she'll probably remember her.'

'Oh, thanks,' Lydia said, feeling a little awkward. They hadn't met since that day he had tried to ask her out and she still felt guilty about giving him the brush-off. 'That's a great tip, Brian. Where does she live?'

'Only a short distance away, up a side road and then down a boreen, in a little house called Primrose Cottage. You can't miss it.'

'I'm sure I can,' Lydia said, attempting a joke to hide the slight tension between them. 'I've been down more boreens than you can shake a stick at while trying to find people's houses. It appears I can miss places nobody else can.'

He laughed. 'I suppose it's more difficult if you don't know the area well.'

'And there are no signposts,' Lydia complained. 'So for someone who hasn't spent all her life here, it can be a little tricky.'

'Yes, but if I give you a few landmarks, it should be easy enough.' He tore a page off his notebook, scribbled on it and then handed it to her. 'There. Just follow that and you'll find it easy enough.'

'*Up the road with the broken fence, then left at the old pump, carry on until you get to a field with two cows and then take a right at the ruin of the O'Briens' old house,*' Lydia read. 'That should help. I think. But what if there's only one cow in that field?'

'There are always two,' Brian said.

'Okay,' Lydia said, trying not to laugh. 'I'll have to believe you. Thanks, Brian, I'll do my best to follow all this. But are you sure she'll want visitors? Shouldn't we call her first?'

'Not at all,' Brian said with a laugh. 'Noreen loves people calling in. She'll put on the kettle the minute she sees you. Any time at all will be fine. Maybe even today when Sunny comes home from school?'

Lydia thanked Brian, relieved that he didn't seem annoyed at her in the slightest, even if there was a sad look in his eyes as he looked at her. 'Hey, why don't we get a few people together on Saturday night and go for that drink?' she suggested on a sudden impulse. 'I'll ask Saskia if she wants to come and you get a hold of Sorcha and we could meet up at the little pub right here on the main street.'

His eyes brightened. 'Great idea. I'm not on duty, so that would be grand. See you there at eight?'

'Perfect,' Lydia said. 'Sunny's going to Cork for the weekend to visit her best friend, so I don't have to worry about her. See you then, Brian.'

'Looking forward to it,' he said and waved as she left.

Lydia walked away with Lucky on the lead, happy she had made that suggestion. She hadn't been out socially since before Barry's death and now it felt like the right time to start. Nearly six months had passed since that terrible day and so much had happened that Lydia felt as if her life had a whole new dimension. Her look on life and what was important had shifted and she was beginning to heal. She was getting over the worst pain and there was now only a lingering sadness.

Lizzie's mother had called to invite Sunny to spend the weekend and Sunny had been so excited to go. This would be the first time they were apart since they arrived. Lydia felt it would be good to have a little time to herself, even if she would miss Sunny, who was now very settled in her school. She only wished she could find that kind of peace herself. But it was impossible to feel down in this place on such a nice day.

There was something about seeing the sun shining on the blue ocean that made you feel like it was the only thing that mattered in the world. She was glad to be able to look forward to a night out with a few friends at a little village pub. She shook her head as she reached the cottage and laughed. *You're becoming a real softie*, she told herself. But deep down she knew that she was getting more and more content to live the simple life, even if earning a basic income was a struggle. She glanced at Jason's house and thought about what he had told her. He had found peace here and was now living a quiet life. But was that what she wanted? She didn't know. Even asking the question disturbed her. It was better not to analyse everything and just keep on living, for now at least.

*

'Oh, that Nellie was a tough cookie,' Noreen Scally told Lydia and Sunny when they visited her in her little house down a country lane lined with early spring flowers. The primroses that gave the cottage its name were just unfurling their blooms and the birdsong was nearly deafening as they got out of the car. Lydia had found it easily following Brian's descriptions. And just as Brian had predicted, the kettle went on and they were soon sitting in front of a roaring fire with a tray of tea and biscuits on the coffee table.

'A tough cookie?' Sunny asked, looking at Noreen with big eyes. 'What did she do?'

'She was always protesting and sending letters to politicians,' Nellie continued. 'Mostly about the fact that women teachers and civil servants had to give up their jobs when they got married. It was called "the marriage ban" and it wasn't abolished until 1973, would you believe. Nellie organised a march in Dublin against it sometime in the nineteen fifties. I didn't go because I had just had a baby, but a lot of the women in this village went. Not that it made any difference. Those men up in Dublin didn't give a tinker's curse about what women wanted in those days. I wouldn't say that has changed much, except now they have to take notice because it's politically correct.' Noreen made a disapproving face as she sipped tea from her china cup.

'Do you think that's why she didn't marry?' Sunny asked, sitting on a stool beside Noreen. 'Because then she wouldn't be able to work?'

Noreen shrugged. 'I really don't know. I was only a child in those days, so I don't remember much about it. But I heard she had a little romance with one of the pilots who were stranded here during the war, but nothing came of it. He never came back like he promised. But I couldn't swear it was all his fault. Nellie was headstrong and determined. Loved her job at the library and was very inspirational to a lot of the young girls around here. But during the war...' Noreen paused, her pale blue eyes thoughtful. 'I was much younger than her, only around ten, so I didn't talk to her much. But I know she was busy doing translations for the British Government. Some texts in German that arrived regularly.'

'How did you know about that?' Sunny asked.

'Good question, young lady,' Noreen said with a twinkle in her eyes. 'I knew because my father was the postmaster here, when there was a proper post office. I used to help sort the letters after school. So, these letters with an English stamp arrived for Nellie regularly by registered mail. I asked her once if she had a sweetheart in England and she laughed and said no, she was just helping out as best she could, doing translations. She told me years afterwards that they were German government documents that English agents had come across. They didn't contain much but had to be translated and filed anyway. And then, when that plane crashed on the mountain, she was asked to be interpreter. Those pilots didn't speak English, you see. I'm guessing that's how she fell for that handsome captain.'

'That's so romantic,' Lydia said, her heart warming to her late great-aunt. 'She was a pretty girl then. I know from photos.'

'Very pretty,' Noreen agreed. 'And he was a handsome man. I think his name was Hans. Tall and blond, I seem to remember.'

'How amazing that you saw them both,' Sunny said, looking at Noreen as if she was some kind of legend. 'But...' she continued, 'you don't know why the romance ended?'

'I don't.' Noreen shook her head. 'But I can tell you that Nellie didn't mope about it. She was incredibly active and filled her life with other things than romance and men.'

'Yeah, and that's what I'm going to do,' Sunny declared. 'No men for me.'

Noreen looked at Sunny and laughed. 'Well, girl, you'll have a job fighting them off.'

Lydia joined in the laughter. 'We'll see how you feel in a year or two, darling.'

'Oh, I'll feel the same,' Sunny stated. 'I'm going to go to university and then I'll travel the world like Aunt Nellie.'

Lydia smiled. 'I hope you will, darling.'

The subject changed to other things and then Lydia and Sunny got up to leave while Noreen remained in her easy chair, waving at them and making them promise to come back very soon.

'That was lovely,' Sunny said as they drove off. 'And it has given me some ideas about how to find out the rest of the story. I got a bit stuck trying to google things but nothing much came up.'

'What kind of ideas?' Lydia asked, staring ahead at the winding road.

'I'll tell you after the weekend.' Sunny sighed happily and stretched her arms over her head. 'Oh God, I'm so looking forward to seeing Lizzie again. A whole weekend together!' She glanced at Lydia. 'You'll be okay, won't you, Mum?'

'I'll be fine,' Lydia assured her. But in her heart she knew she'd be miserable until Sunny came back. They hadn't been apart since that awful day when Barry died, and now Lydia wondered how on earth she would survive the weekend on her own. But it wasn't just the weekend. One day in the not-too-distant future, Lydia knew, Sunny would leave for good to live her own life and Lydia would be all alone. And the thought terrified her.

They were still talking about Aunt Nellie as they drove home in the late-afternoon sunshine. The evenings were brighter now and the sun didn't set until nearly eight o'clock, a huge change from the dark winter evenings when they arrived.

'That was a nice visit,' Lydia said. 'Noreen seemed to enjoy it anyway.'

'So did I,' Sunny said. 'She's really cute. I was trying to imagine what it would have been like in this village when she was young. Must have been so hard.'

'I'm sure they didn't think so at the time,' Lydia countered as she turned into the main road. 'But it was a different world, that's for sure.'

'I can't imagine what it would have been like without the internet or mobiles or TV,' Sunny mused. 'Must have been so boring.'

'I don't think they would have been the slightest bit bored,' Lydia said, laughing. 'In those days, life was a struggle and they had to work hard. Boredom wasn't on their agenda, I'm sure. Even though Ireland wasn't in the war, there were food shortages and practically everything was scarce. And they were always under the threat of attack despite being a neutral country. It would have been a hard life for everyone in those days.'

'I suppose,' Sunny said. 'But it's difficult to imagine what they did for fun.'

'I'm sure they did have fun in some way, though. Like dancing at the crossroads in the summer and music and singing and sports like hurling, Gaelic football and swimming and that kind of thing. You should ask Noreen next time we visit her.' Lydia indicated to turn down their lane.

'I will,' Sunny said and went quiet for a moment. 'What's for dinner?' she eventually continued.

'Lamb chops and baked potatoes,' Lydia replied. 'But it's not dinnertime yet. I have some stuff to do on the computer before I even think of cooking. Make yourself some toast if you're hungry.'

They arrived at the cottage within minutes and Sunny disappeared into the kitchen while Lydia turned on her laptop in the living room. She wanted to find out how to run a fundraising campaign on Facebook for Pat's birthday fund. She had noted down a few ideas which she would show Helen tomorrow and this would form part of the campaign she planned to run. She stared at the screen while she waited for it connect to the internet, but after a while she realised something was wrong. An error message saying 'no internet' appeared on the screen. She tried the connection again, but it was no use. The internet was down. Had Jason changed the password? she wondered, thinking she should call him and ask. She suddenly remembered that they hadn't exchanged phone numbers, but she had seen that his Land Rover was parked in front of his house so he had to be at home.

'The internet isn't working, so I'm just calling in to Jason to see what's wrong,' Lydia called to Sunny, who was still making herself a snack in the kitchen. 'Back in a minute.'

'Okay, Mum,' Sunny shouted back.

Lydia swiftly walked out the door and stepped over the small fence that separated the front gardens, skirting the Land Rover and pressing the doorbell. She could hear it ring inside and smiled, waiting for Jason to come out.

The door opened slowly. But it wasn't Jason who stood there staring at Lydia. It was a woman – drying her wet hair with a towel.

Chapter Twenty-Three

Lydia's smile died on her lips as she blinked and stared, her breath caught in her throat. The woman in front of her was strikingly attractive, with dark hair and large hazel eyes under her wet fringe. She peered at Lydia, who couldn't help sweeping her eyes over her stunning figure encased in a tight black polo neck and leggings.

'Uh,' Lydia started. 'Sorry, but…'

'You're looking for Jason?' the woman said, still towelling her hair.

Lydia nodded. 'Y… yes.'

The woman glanced behind her. 'He's… busy.' Then she smiled and held out her hand. 'I'm Ella. Ella Caron. I live next door to Saskia. I just arrived back from Paris.'

Lydia shook the woman's hand automatically. 'Hi, I'm Lydia.'

'Thought so,' Ella said and flashed Lydia a grin. 'Tall, blonde, classically beautiful. Fits the description perfectly.'

'Whose description?' Lydia asked, beginning to feel irritated.

'His. Jason's, I mean.' Ella shivered. 'I'm getting cold here. I'm just out of the shower. I'll tell Jason you called in. What was it about?'

'The internet,' Lydia said. 'It's not working. We're sharing his connection, and…'

'I'll tell him. See you around. Bye,' Ella said and closed the door in Lydia's face.

Lydia stood there for a moment before she was able to move, all kinds of scenarios whirling around in her mind. Jason and this Ella were in a relationship? Or... was this just a spur-of-the-moment thing? Jason had seemed to be such a lone wolf, someone who shied away from people. He obviously didn't shy away from Ella. But what man would? The pretty face and that body... Lydia shivered despite the warm spring breeze and hurried back inside.

'What did he say?' Sunny asked as she came out of the kitchen with a plate of buttered toast.

'He wasn't there, so I left a message.'

'Okay.' Sunny nodded and continued out to the sunroom where she sat down to enjoy her toast while checking messages on her phone. 'I hope it'll be fixed soon, though. I want to look up some stuff on the internet for my project.'

'I'm sure it will be,' Lydia replied.

She didn't have to wait long. Jason arrived only minutes later, smiling at Lydia as she opened the door. 'Hi,' he said, sounding breathless. 'Sorry about the internet. I turned off the router by mistake and then I went out. I meant to turn it back on but I got distracted by a phone call. Should have told you, but I don't have your number. I meant to call in to tell you, but things got in the way.'

'That's okay,' Lydia said, the idea of what kind of 'things' had got in the way popping into her mind.

Jason handed her a piece of paper. 'Here's my number. Call me if there's a problem.'

'I will. Thanks,' Lydia said, her tone curt.

'Everything okay?' Jason asked, looking confused.

'Absolutely fine,' Lydia replied. 'Thanks for calling in.'

'You're welcome.' He hesitated. 'Uh… So everything's fine then?'

'Perfect.'

'How about a walk on the beach later on? Lovely evening.'

Lydia looked away, to hide how upset she was at the thought of Jason with that woman. It had surprised her that she felt so strongly about it and now she didn't quite know how to react. 'I'm rather busy, actually,' she said awkwardly.

'Really?' Jason looked at her curiously. 'Okay. Maybe another time, then?'

'Yeah. Maybe,' Lydia said airily.

'Great. Give me a shout when you feel like company.' Jason started to walk away. 'See you around.'

'Yes. Bye and thanks.' Lydia nodded and closed the door, feeling unreasonable anger rise inside. A walk on the beach? Did he mean the three of them? Well, he could forget about that. She wasn't going to join in a cosy threesome with him and his girlfriend. Then she shook her head at those feelings. What was that all about? They were just friends, very close, but still no more than that, surely?

Lydia pushed those strange thoughts away and walked into the living room. 'All fixed,' she said to Sunny. 'The router was accidentally turned off. It's back on now.'

'Oh great.' Sunny turned on Lydia's laptop. 'There you go. All ready. What was it you wanted to look up?'

Lydia sat down beside Sunny on the sofa. 'I was going to find out how to run a fundraising campaign on Facebook. It's Dr Pat's seventy-fifth birthday in a fortnight and Helen wants me to organise a campaign to raise money for Doctors Without Borders. She had ideas based on her experience of running high-profile campaigns, but maybe something a little less ambitious would be better for the village? I thought I might do a whole series of things,' she told Sunny. 'Starting with a Facebook ad.'

'Oh, cool. That's a great idea. But you know what? It should be running all week. That's the best way to do it. And I'll help and share it too and get people in my class to do that.'

'Wonderful,' Lydia said, putting her arm around Sunny, the vison of the woman on Jason's doorstep fading. 'Any other ideas?'

'Loads,' Sunny said, turning to Lydia. 'There so much you could do to raise money.'

'Like what?' Lydia asked, amused by Sunny's sudden interest.

'Why not do a local run too and have a big party on his actual birthday?' Sunny suggested. 'Or... maybe a picnic on the beach with games and stands and a huge barbecue? A lottery too, with amazing prizes.'

'How do we get amazing prices? That costs money.'

'We get people to donate stuff, of course,' Sunny said. 'Like... like you could donate your handbags.'

'I was going to sell them on eBay and get a bit of money for them, remember.'

'Just donate one, then,' Sunny argued. 'The Prada one, for example. It's very glam and nearly brand new. It would be a great prize. And then you could ask Saskia to donate a piece of her jewellery as well. It would be good marketing for her brand, wouldn't it? And maybe Jason could—'

'Hold on,' Lydia said, laughing. 'That's aiming a little too high. His pieces take a long time to make and cost a fortune.' And she didn't want to ask him anything, after what just happened, anyway, she silently told herself.

'Maybe not him, then,' Sunny agreed. 'But the Wild Atlantic Gourmet could donate a dinner for two. And the Wellness Centre could offer a massage or a couple of yoga classes for free. Sure, this whole village is full of businesses that could help out.' Sunny drew breath and looked at Lydia with excitement.

'You're a genius,' Lydia said and placed a kiss on Sunny's head, thinking that Sunny had inherited her head for marketing. 'Will you help me draw up a plan that I can present to Helen?' she asked, cheered by them doing something like this together. 'I'll call on these people and ask if they'd like to help. And then we'll check the forecast and see if that beach picnic is possible.'

'We could have horse racing on the main beach,' Sunny suggested. 'They do that in Rossbeigh every August, so why not here? That's what Fintan told me.'

'Let's not get too ambitious,' Lydia said, laughing. 'Let me get a pen and paper and then we'll write down your ideas, and some of mine, too. And then I'll look into the Facebook fundraiser thing.'

'Okay, Mum. We should have all this done before tomorrow when I leave to spend the weekend with Lizzie. Her mum is picking me up from school. We're planning to do a lot of fun things in Cork.'

'Lovely, darling.'

'Sure you don't want to come?' Sunny asked. 'Lizzie's mum did invite you.'

'Yes, but I have to work tomorrow evening. It's very busy then with everyone getting ready for the weekend,' Lydia said, feeling a dart of dread. She had momentarily forgotten about Sunny's weekend away. She didn't like the thought of being on her own even more now that she couldn't spend time with Jason, as he would have someone else on his mind. She had to get used to the idea of being alone in the house when she came home from her outing at the pub. Sunny needed time away from the cocoon Lydia had created, she had felt when she had declined the invitation to join them. Sunny needed to be free to do other things, be with other people. *And maybe*, Lydia thought, *I need some space and a little me time as well?* But as she looked at Sunny, Lydia knew she would be counting the hours until her daughter came back.

Chapter Twenty-Four

Lydia arrived at Helen's house the next morning with the plan she and Sunny had drawn up for the fundraiser. She looked into the living room, but found it empty, so she went down the corridor to the kitchen, where Helen was sitting at the table with a magazine in front of her.

'Hello,' Lydia said, taking the papers with the plan and suggestions out of her handbag. 'I have some great ideas here for the campaign. My daughter helped me and I have to say her suggestions are really good.'

Helen looked at Lydia, her eyes cold. 'I can't let you do it,' she said. 'And I'm thinking I might have to fire you.'

Lydia blinked stared at her. 'Fire me? Why?'

Helen thrust the magazine at Lydia. 'Because I have just found out who you are.'

Her hands shaking, Lydia took the magazine and stared at the open page. There were a series of photos from a social event and as her eyes focused, she saw herself in her previous life, her hair swept up, wearing a black strapless dress and several rows of pearls. 'The Christmas party at The Shelbourne,' she whispered.

'Hosted by the Chamber of Commerce,' Helen filled in. 'You're wearing a dress by Chanel, if I'm not mistaken.'

'You're not,' Lydia said, her voice hoarse. She stared at the photo, feeling the woman in it was someone else, someone from another world, a world she had left and had longed to get back to.

'You're Lydia Harrington,' Helen said in an accusatory tone. 'Wife of Barry Harrington, the property developer and business-man, among other things, who, it is said, was guilty of fraud and tax evasion. Offshore accounts, money laundering…' She paused. 'I read about it in some of the newspapers a few months ago.'

'I only found out myself just before I came here,' Lydia cut in. 'I had no idea what he was up to. It was like being hit with a sledgehammer.'

Helen didn't appear to have heard. 'When you came here for the cleaning job,' she continued, 'I didn't know who you were, but I had a feeling I had seen you somewhere. Of course, I see now that it was in the society pages of the magazines I read at the hairdresser's. You were voted the best-dressed woman in Ireland last year, weren't you? It was in *Image* magazine.'

'Yes, I was. Not that it's something I thought was that important,' Lydia said.

'Nice to be picked, though.' Helen folded her arms, still sitting at the table. 'But that's beside the point. What's important here is what I have just found out about you.'

'About me?' Lydia said. 'What are you implying?' She looked at Helen quizzically and then realised what she was inferring. 'Do you think that I had something to do with what my husband was involved with?'

'Well, you must have been aware of what was going on at his firm.'

'I wasn't,' Lydia said. 'I had no idea until my solicitor told me. He also explained that I had nothing left except for my aunt's house and a few thousand euros in an account in my maiden name. The rest was repossessed by the bank. That's why I needed this job…'

Helen looked a little shaken. 'Oh. I thought… well, as you can imagine, when I found out about your background, I felt very nervous about letting you run the campaign. I mean, you'd be in charge of a bank account and would handle what I would hope would be large sums of money.'

Lydia stared at Helen, suddenly very angry. 'If I had had anything to do with whatever Barry was involved with, don't you think I would have found a way to siphon off some money for myself? Wouldn't I be in the Bahamas right now, instead of here, cleaning your house and washing people's hair at the Bizarre hair salon? Would I be in a cold little house accepting charity from some very kind people and trying to make ends meet to support myself and my daughter?'

Helen looked a little shaken. 'I suppose not.'

'Damn right I wouldn't,' Lydia snapped. Seething with anger, she stepped away. 'I think the right thing for me to do now is to quit both the job and the fundraising project. You'll have to find someone else to iron your silk shirts and feed those stupid parakeets in the conservatory.'

'Oh,' Helen said, looking shocked. 'You quit?'

'What else can I do?'

Helen didn't reply as the thought of having to clean her own house seemed to flit through her mind. 'Oh, but…' she started.

'No buts,' Lydia snapped. 'I'm leaving. Goodbye.' Lydia walked out of the room, marching down the corridor to the front door. She stopped and turned when she heard footsteps behind her.

'Wait,' Helen panted and put her hand on Lydia's arm. 'Don't go, Lydia. I'm sorry about what I said. That was very unfair. Please come back and we'll sort this out. I don't know what came over me. I was so shocked to see your photo in that magazine that I didn't think straight.'

Lydia was going to shake Helen's arm off but the genuine remorse in Helen's eyes was oddly moving. There was a hint of sorrow and loneliness in them where they were normally cool and appraising. Did she regret what she'd said? Did she seem ashamed?

'Okay,' Lydia said, her anger dissipating. 'I'm willing to listen.'

'Let's have a cup of coffee in the kitchen,' Helen suggested, looking relieved. 'I'll make it. You sit down and get your plan ready and we'll talk.'

They walked back to the kitchen, where Lydia sat down at the table while Helen busied herself at the Nespresso machine. 'How do you take your coffee?' she asked.

'Black, please.'

'Long or short?'

'Long. I love the Vivalto Lungo one from Nespresso.'

'Me too,' Helen said, smiling at Lydia. 'And how about a choco-late praline? Pat got me some from the Ballinskelligs chocolate place.'

'Lovely,' Lydia said. Her emotions were still in turmoil after what had happened. She had been so angry she didn't know what she was saying and now she went over it in her mind. She might have been rude, but it was certainly justified, she felt. 'I didn't mean to say your parakeets are stupid, by the way,' she confessed as Helen brought the coffees to the table.

'But they are,' Helen said with a giggle. 'Really stupid. They don't have any opinions on as much as the weather. I've tried to have a conversation but all they can do is tweet and screech. A bit like the women at the golf club.'

Lydia had to laugh, delighted at Helen's sudden flash of humour. 'But they're very pretty.'

'That's true.' Helen put a small box of chocolates on the table and sat down opposite Lydia. 'So,' she said, picking up her cup and taking a breath, 'here we are. I've been horrible to you and you got angry and stalked off in a huff. I apologise for what I assumed about you. I can see I was wrong. How do we get over that, then?'

'We forget about it,' Lydia said. 'I understand how you must have felt when you discovered who I was back then… In another life or something. I would probably have reacted the same way. Now I don't think I would, but I'm a different person.'

'You used to be like me, you mean?' Helen said. 'Someone who seems to have everything but in a way has less than people with nothing.'

'Uh, well, I wouldn't be that dramatic.' Lydia sipped her coffee. 'But yeah, something like that. A life of luxury but without real, true friends because everyone around you is competing about who's the most successful and who has the best life. Not a very healthy environment, really, is it?' Lydia realised that Helen had suspected her of being involved in Barry's fraud because she moved in circles where this kind of thing happened. Not being able to trust anyone even if they appeared to be friends could have been what triggered Helen's first reaction.

'But some of it had to be fun, though,' Helen argued. 'My life when I was in business wasn't on your level at all. But I did enjoy the perks. Didn't you?'

Lydia picked a chocolate praline from the box. 'This is where I should say that it was all horribly shallow and that my new life is much more fulfilled and wonderful and I have learned the true values in life and all that. But this isn't one of those feel-good movies, so I'm going to say that yes, I did enjoy a lot of it. And I miss it. The money, the carefree existence and the glitz and glamour. And, of course, the comfort of a big, warm house. I was good at the representative part. I loved to shine and to be the best-dressed woman in Ireland. But in the end… All that money… I think it destroyed my marriage.'

Helen nodded. 'I know the feeling. I'm lucky, because my husband never wanted any of that. I tried to make him come and live that life with me, but he only lasted a few weeks. Then he came back to the practice and all the people he loved so much. So I decided to join him and that way, I have a good marriage and still have a substantial income from my family's business.'

'We could have had that too,' Lydia said. 'The last few years were hectic and I tried to slow down and make my husband spend more time with me and our daughter. But Barry wouldn't listen. He always wanted more. And that was his undoing.'

'Like Icarus,' Helen said with a sigh as she picked another praline from the box.

'Exactly.' Lydia sipped her coffee. 'Barry tried to fly too close to the sun and his wings fell off.' She felt a sudden pang of grief and she blinked back tears that threatened to well up. 'He was a nice man behind it all. I should have got him off that train we were on, but it was running too fast. So I just went along with it until the wheels came off and I was forced to leave everything behind. And here I am, in this village surrounded by people who have been so extraordinarily kind to me.' Lydia took a deep breath and sat up straighter. 'I just have to learn to count my blessings, you know?'

Helen studied Lydia for a moment. 'You're a very strong woman. You'll be fine.'

'Oh, I know. I'll just have to pull myself together.' Lydia pushed the cup away from her. She looked at Helen. 'Maybe I was little too hasty to quit my job.'

'You never lost it,' Helen said. She reached across the table and touched Lydia's arm. 'You know, the moment you walked in here looking for the job, there was something about you that resonated with me. I felt as if a kindred spirit had just arrived. I have a feeling we're quite alike, and I think we'll get on very well from now on.'

'I'm sure we will,' Lydia agreed.

'Excellent. Let's just look at your plan for the campaign and then, perhaps… you and your lovely daughter would like to come for dinner some evening?'

'That would be lovely,' Lydia said, feeling she had not only made peace, but also, despite the age difference, that she had found a friend. She took the notes out of her handbag and handed them to Helen. 'Here are my ideas and a time plan. I thought the campaign should run for a week and then at the end of that week, we should have a picnic at the beach with a barbecue and all kinds of competitions and stalls and so on. Weather permitting, of course.' Lydia drew breath while Helen studied the plan.

'And if the weather doesn't permit?' Helen said, looking up from the notes. 'Do you have a plan B?'

Lydia squirmed on her chair. 'Eh, uh, well I haven't really thought that far.'

Helen raised an eyebrow, seemingly back in employer mode. 'Well, we'd better have one then. And we'll have to ask these people on your list if they want to donate something for the lottery.'

'Oh, that won't be too difficult,' Lydia said. 'I'm sure they'll agree. And I'll donate something too.'

'Like what?'

'My Prada handbag. I was going to sell it on eBay to get a bit of cash, but I thought this is such a good cause, so…'

'That's extremely generous,' Helen said, her tone warmer. 'But such a thing might not be that popular around here. I mean, what would a sheep farmer's wife do with a Prada handbag?'

Lydia had to laugh. 'You're right. Maybe I'll just sell that one and donate the money instead.'

'Yes, that might be the best option. We have to have a few prizes, though. Have you asked Saskia for a piece? Her jewellery is lovely. That sea glass is very pretty and not at all expensive.'

'I'll ask her. And then, perhaps your firm could donate some kind of basket with products from your cosmetics range?'

'Good idea,' Helen said, writing it down on the list. 'And I heard Ella Caron is back from Paris. How about asking her for one of her smaller paintings? And Jason might…' She stopped and shook her head. 'No. Perhaps not. His furniture is usually very expensive. And he spends a lot of time making each item. I ordered a small table over a month ago and he hasn't delivered it yet, even though he promised to have it ready this week. Wouldn't be fair to ask him to donate anything.'

'No,' Lydia agreed, the mere mention of Jason making her face hot.

'I suppose not.' Helen shot Lydia a glance and then got up. 'Right, then I think we have a few ideas to work on. Will you…' She paused for a moment, clearing her throat. 'Could you take care of everything, including the accounts?'

'If you trust me to do that, of course I will,' Lydia said, meeting Helen's gaze levelly.

'I do,' Helen replied without hesitation. 'I'm sorry if I implied earlier that you weren't to be trusted.'

'No problem,' Lydia said. 'I think we closed that chapter. So,' she breezed on, 'when I have the fundraiser up, I'll send you the link by text message so you can share it around. I've made a list of local organisations and groups who have a large audience. I'll be in touch with them to help drum up publicity for the campaign. I'm keeping a low profile on Facebook, so I won't be able to do it myself. I hope you understand.'

'Of course,' Helen said. 'And just to reassure you, I won't tell a soul about your identity.'

'Thank you,' Lydia said, relieved. The story would go no further this time, but she realised that the time might have come to finally tell Sunny the truth about her father before someone else found out about her connection to Barry.

Helen got up from the table. 'That's it for now, I think. I have a few errands in Killarney, so I'll be home late. Maybe you could get started on the bathrooms today, and then the living room needs dusting, some of the plants in the conservatory need water and the parakeets – well, you know what to do.'

'Of course.' Lydia got up. 'I'll get started straight away.'

'Brilliant,' Helen said with a broad smile. 'And you know what? Next week I'll tell you about an idea I have for us to work together.'

'What idea?' Lydia asked, intrigued by the glint in Helen's eyes.

'I'll tell you when we've finished this campaign. Bye for now.'

When Helen had left, Lydia started on the cleaning: dusting and hoovering the living room, watering the plants in the conservatory and feeding the parakeets before she got started on the bathrooms. She laughed as she remembered Helen's joke about the birds.

The previous conversation was still fresh in her mind, including Helen's first reaction to her true identity. She had been suspicious and quite hostile, implying that Lydia was somehow implicated in what Barry had done, before she had backed down after Lydia's angry tirade. Was that what other people thought, too? That she had been in on the money laundering and tax fraud? Would she get the same reaction if she revealed her married name to anyone? And what did the people in her former social circle believe? She had been so set on returning to Dublin but now she wasn't sure this would be a good idea. She had made some good friends since she came to Sandy Cove and that was a huge help, making her life here a lot more tolerable.

Tired and hot as the sun streamed through all the big windows, Lydia went into the master bedroom to clean the en-suite bathroom.

When she had finished, she longingly eyed the gleaming jacuzzi in front of the huge window with stunning views of the bay. It would be lovely to sink into that with the waterjets massaging her aching back and look at the view. Just to lie there for a while and relax… In her imagination, she turned the taps and as the water gushed into the tub, poured in a generous amount of bubble bath. She stood there, dreaming of slipping into the warm foaming water and imagined the feeling of total relaxation. It would be heaven. It reminded her of the good times, of her own bathroom that had been like a mini spa, where she had relaxed and pampered herself before a big evening out. Oh, those halcyon days when everything had seemed so easy. Would she ever have that level of comfort again?

Lydia's daydream didn't last long as she was jolted out of her thoughts by a noise coming from the living room. Somebody walking around. She blinked and froze. Who was there? Not Helen, the footsteps were too heavy. Dr Pat? But he was far away visiting a patient on the mountain road.

'Hello?' a voice called. A voice she knew so well.

Chapter Twenty-Five

The footsteps were coming closer and Lydia walked out of the bathroom, and straight into Jason coming down the corridor.

'Hi,' she said, slightly out of breath.

'Hi,' he replied, his eyes full of laughter. 'Nice to see you."

Lydia tried to tidy her hair. 'Yes. Very nice,' she said, suddenly at a loss for words. 'But what are you doing here?' she asked.

'Delivering a table. Helen ordered it a while ago and told me to put it in the living room if she wasn't in. There is a spare key hidden in the garage.'

'Oh.'

'Yeah.' He looked at her for a moment. 'I didn't mean to disturb you. It was just that I heard the jacuzzi going and…'

'I was cleaning it.' She looked up at him as he towered above her and quickly put her shoes on.

He cleared his throat. 'I put the table in the living room, so I'm leaving,' he said, sounding as awkward as she felt.

'Me too,' Lydia replied. 'I finished the chores, so I'll go home.' She looked behind him, desperate to get away. The woman who had opened the door of his house loomed into her mind as she looked at him.

'Do you want a lift?' he asked.

'No thanks. It's a nice day and only a short distance to walk.'

'How about lunch?' he asked. 'The Two Marys' have just opened for the season. It's a really nice place.'

'Well, I'm not sure I have the time.'

'Sunny said she was going away for the weekend. Doesn't that mean you have a little extra time?' he asked, frowning.

'Yes, but I'm working this afternoon,' Lydia replied. She didn't want to be short with him, but things had changed between them and lunch with him was the last thing she wanted to do.

'At three o'clock, right? It's only coming up to twelve, so you have plenty of time.'

'I'm not hungry.' Lydia went to find her bag that she had left in the kitchen, but Jason followed her.

'What's wrong?' he asked.

Lydia met his gaze. 'Wrong? What do you mean?'

'You're being very evasive and stand-offish for some reason.'

'Yeah, well…' Lydia picked up her bag from the kitchen chair. 'I thought you didn't like socialising.'

'Having a sandwich with you in a nearly empty café would hardly qualify as socialising,' he said, looking amused.

'People might talk.'

'What would they say? That we were having a chicken and stuffing sandwich in a public place?'

Lydia faced him. 'But maybe your girlfriend wouldn't like it?' she said, trying to sound casual.

Jason looked confused. 'What girlfriend?'

'Ella Caron. I met her at your door with wet hair. I mean *her* hair, not mine.'

Jason burst out laughing. 'That would have been a little…
eh, strange.' He shook his head, still smiling. 'But Ella is not my
girlfriend. She had just arrived back on a flight from Paris and found
when she came home her shower wasn't working. She knocked on
my door and asked if she could use my bathroom while she waited
for the plumber. I said yes as I was going to Sorcha's shop to buy
milk and bread. When I came back, she was gone but had left a
note to say you had called in and why.'

'But she said…' Lydia stammered, 'that you were busy. She made
me believe that you were there, that you and she had… you know,'
Lydia ended lamely, her face on fire. 'Not in so many words, but
that's the way she acted.'

'Oh, I see,' Jason said, his eyes full of laughter. 'She was teasing
you, I think. Typical of her. Having a little fun at your expense.
She might have thought you and I are involved in some way and
wanted to make a little mischief.'

'Oh,' was all Lydia managed, feeling an odd sense of relief.

'Don't you realise that if I was involved with anyone, I would
have told you the other day when I was telling you the story of my
life?' he said, taking a step towards her.

'I suppose you would,' Lydia replied, feeling stupid.

'So now that we have that out of the way, I'll ask you again: will
you have lunch with me?' Jason said, looking exasperated.

Lydia sighed and laughed. 'Oh, okay. Why not?'

Jason sighed. 'Finally. Let's get going then. The carriage awaits
you, my lady.'

Lydia followed Jason out the door with an odd feeling that in
the last few minutes, there had been a shift in their relationship. He

now knew that she cared who he was spending time with, and he seemed eager to make sure she understood he was single. Were they stepping away from their friendship into something new? Whatever it was, Lydia wondered if she was ready for it.

Lydia and Jason's lunch in the little café above the main beach was tense and awkward, despite Lydia's attempts to stay cool. She looked around the quaint little café and remarked on how the interior was just like a traditional cottage from the old days, with the original fireplace and whitewashed walls. But it was no use, there was still an awkward atmosphere between them which was hard to break. Jason kept giving Lydia admiring glances, his eyes full of laughter while he bit into the chicken sandwich.

Lydia turned away from him while she toyed with her sandwich. 'Nice view,' she said, looking out across the water and the islands in the distance.

'Wonderful,' he said between bites, not taking his eyes off her. 'Best view in Ireland.'

Lydia met his gaze. 'Stop it,' she ordered.

'What?'

'That. Looking at me like that.'

'What other way is there?' he asked with mock innocence.

Lydia rolled her eyes. 'You know what I mean. You look at me as if I'm on the menu.'

He laughed. 'I'm just admiring you,' he said and put what was left of his sandwich on his plate. 'I'm enjoying having lunch with you, that's all. What's wrong with that?'

'Everything.' Unable to eat, Lydia pushed away the plate with her nearly uneaten sandwich.

'So if I asked you out for a date, you'd say no?'

'At this time, yes.' She looked at him, trying to explain without putting him off completely. 'I still need time. There is so much to cope with right now.'

Jason's eyes were suddenly serious. 'I know. I'm sorry. It was just that I felt something happening between us earlier. Not sure what it was, but it felt nice. Do you know what I mean?'

Lydia looked away for a moment. 'Yes, I do. And the reason I'm being a bit stand-offish is not because I'm still grieving for Barry. I've come through the worst of that and I've accepted what happened. I have even been able to deal with what he did to a certain extent. But I still need time to feel settled and to talk to Sunny about it all. That's why I have to wait a bit longer before I get into something that has to do with you and me.'

Jason nodded. 'I understand. I just felt suddenly so carefree and happy. I like being with you.'

'Me too,' Lydia had to admit. 'You have helped me so much, especially the first few weeks when I was so raw and hurt. And now after these months, I feel so much better. I can look forward and start to enjoy life again. Partly thanks to you.'

His hand moved on the table, nearly touching hers. 'And you helped me. It was good to talk and tell you everything. It was… cathartic for me. I've only told my girls about what happened, but nobody else. Telling you felt like a huge burden lifting off my shoulders. You listened without judging. It released me from all the anger I've felt ever since it happened.' He looked at her with great affection in his grey eyes. 'You're good listener, Lydia. I could feel your empathy and understanding while I talked about what happened to me.' He smiled and touched her cheek. 'It felt like angel's wings carrying all my troubles away.'

Lydia returned his smile. 'That's a lovely thing to say.'

'Maybe a tad over the top, but that's how I felt.' He laughed, his eyes suddenly flirtatious again. 'Can I tell you how beautiful you looked in your apron, all flustered and your hair mussed up when we bumped into each other in the house earlier?'

'No,' Lydia said, a tiny frisson making her shiver as their eyes met. 'Absolutely not.'

'Okay, I won't then.'

'Can we talk about something else now?' Lydia pleaded, longing for the tension between them to ease. It was oddly exciting, but she didn't know if she could handle any more.

'What do you want to talk about?' he asked. 'I was enjoying this conversation. But before we move on, I just want to thank you for being such a huge help.'

'In what way?' she asked, puzzled.

He finally took her hand. 'Just by listening the other day. And being the way you are, making me smile. And your sweet, smart daughter and the dog and you just being yourself, struggling but not complaining.'

'Oh, I complain,' Lydia protested, knowing she should pull her hand out of his light grip. But the feel of his warm hand on hers was so comforting. 'But only to myself. I cry in the shower sometimes, so Sunny won't hear. And I often rage against what happened and the unfairness of it all. And sometimes I hate Barry for what he did to us. So I'm not that brave, you know. I don't like living this hand-to-mouth existence, but that's all I can do for the moment.'

'Yes, but you're still brave,' he insisted. 'Raging and crying are very normal reactions and probably good for you. Letting it all out from time to time. Of course it must be hard to try to make ends meet as well. But I feel more positive vibes from you today. As if you had a lovely morning. And I don't mean cleaning Helen's house,' he added with the hint of a smile.

Lydia laughed. 'You're right. I did have a nice morning with Helen. But it didn't start so well. She had found a photo of me in an old magazine and then, of course, she realised who I am. Then she hinted that she couldn't trust me because I might have been involved in what Barry was doing. We had a heated discussion where I told her off.'

'You told Helen O'Dwyer off?' he asked, an amused glint in his eyes. 'That must have been a first for her.'

'Yeah, she was a little surprised when the worm turned.' Lydia let out a giggle. 'But then we talked for a bit and she backed down very quickly. And now we get on even better than before. And we're doing this fundraising thing together, which I'll enjoy.'

'What's that all about?' he asked, still holding her hand.

Lydia told him what they were planning to do the week after Easter and how they hoped to raise a lot of money for Pat's birthday fund. 'We'll end with a beach picnic if the weather is good.'

'Sounds like fun.' He looked at her thoughtfully for a moment, letting go of her hand. 'I think I might have a piece to donate. I have a small side table I made for a client who cancelled his order just before I was going to ship it. Not much, but it might raise a bit of money.'

'That would be wonderful,' Lydia said, touched by his generosity. 'We could make that the top prize. Your pieces are beautiful. I've seen them on the internet.'

'Thank you,' he said, looking at her plate. 'Maybe, if you're going to finish the sandwich, we'll have a cup of coffee and a slice of the wonderful carrot cake?'

Lydia picked up what was left of her sandwich. 'Sounds perfect.'

While Jason got up to order, Lydia turned to the view while she ate her sandwich, trying to gauge her feelings. But she couldn't quite get a grip on anything, least of all her relationship with Jason and how it was turning into a lot more than friends sharing their life stories. Jason was the compete opposite to Barry. With him, she had felt that they were like a couple in a movie, performing at social events, all eyes on this glamorous couple. But when the lights went out and they stripped off their finery, they didn't have much to talk about. They had been madly in love in the beginning, but after Sunny was born and took up a lot of Lydia's time, the flame seemed to have gone out. Had it been simply some kind of infatuation that didn't last? Barry had been loving and caring at the beginning, wanting Lydia by his side at all times. Was that because he needed her as some kind of trophy wife? Or because he was unsure of himself? But asking those questions was futile. She would never know.

Jason arriving back with the coffees and cake on a tray jolted Lydia out of her thoughts. 'This looks yummy,' she said and took a bite of the cake.

'It's truly delicious,' he agreed as he dug in.

They smiled at each other as they ate and talked about trivial things, while tiny sparks flew between them. But it felt very sweet to Lydia and she enjoyed basking in his admiring glances, even if she felt she needed to keep her distance.

'It's okay,' he suddenly said. 'I know how you feel. And I understand.' He leaned forward and looked into her eyes. 'I just want to say this: don't feel bad about whatever this is between us. Being attracted to someone else is not a betrayal of the man you loved. There is a whole different landscape when you meet someone new, and it has nothing to do with whoever you used to love – and maybe still do.'

'I'm not sure if I do,' Lydia said quietly. 'The first horrible grief is gone, but I still feel sad sometimes. It's all so confusing.'

He sat back. 'I know. Let's just leave it alone and be friends like before, eh?'

'Okay,' Lydia said. But in her heart, she knew that was impossible. It would never be like before again.

*

Declining Jason's offer of a lift home, Lydia walked along the lane and up the main street, taking a shortcut along the cliffs to her house. She needed to be alone and think about what had happened between them. It wasn't anything dramatic or something that could be explained – it was just there, and she wanted to put it in perspective. Sitting in the car with Jason would be too much right now; she needed to put a little distance between them and sort out her own feelings without being distracted by his eyes on her.

As she walked away from the café, Lydia's phone rang. She glanced at the caller ID and saw it was a Dublin number. Intrigued, she stopped walking and answered it.

'Lydia?' a woman's voice asked.

'Yes?'

'Hi. This is Clare at Dynamic Advertising.'

'Oh,' Lydia said, her heart beating faster at the name of her old firm. 'Hi, Clare.'

'How are you?' Clare asked.

'I'm fine, thanks,' Lydia replied, impatient to hear why this woman was calling.

'Good. Okay, I'll get to the reason I'm calling you. We've lost one of our copywriters and need someone to take her place. As you called a while back to ask if we were hiring, we thought we'd see if you'd be interested. We have a vacancy for a copywriter and someone you used to work with recommended you. Now, before you reply, I have to tell you that the starting salary is very basic, but it might increase in a year or two, depending on your performance.'

'What kind of figure were you thinking of?' Lydia asked.

'I can only give you a ballpark figure. This would be your yearly salary after tax.' The woman paused and then mentioned a sum that made Lydia's heart sink.

'Oh.' She sat down on a low stone wall. 'Well… I'm not sure,' she said, her voice weak with disappointment. That salary wouldn't be enough to pay the rent on a flat, let alone buy food or pay Sunny's school fees.

'I'm sorry I can't offer you more,' Clare said. 'But we were hit badly by the recent recession and we're only getting back on our feet, so to speak. But we're hoping with talented copywriters, we might return to where we were when you worked here. Which was twenty years ago, so you have a bit of catching up to do, of course. Much has changed since then.'

'I understand,' Lydia said. 'But…'

'Don't say anything yet,' Clare urged. 'I'll email you the details and then you could think about it for a while and get back to me.'

'Okay,' Lydia said, even though she knew she couldn't accept that offer with such a low starting salary. 'Thanks for calling.'

'Talk to you soon,' Clare said and hung up.

Lydia sat on the wall, still shaken by that phone call. It could have been a lifesaver had the salary been better. But as it was, she couldn't accept it. She knew rents were high in Dublin and even a small studio apartment in the wrong part of town would cost most of what Clare had offered. And in any case, Sunny might not want to move, now that she was beginning to settle into her new school and seemed to truly enjoy life here in Sandy Cove. Unlike Lydia, who had been pining for her old life in Dublin.

She slowly got up and resumed walking back to the cottage, suddenly noticing what a heavenly spring day it was, with a soft breeze and the dark blue of the ocean meeting the light blue sky at the horizon. Tiny clouds sailed across the sun from time to time and the air was full of birdsong. A delicious smell of newly baked bread floated in the air from the bakery, and Lydia felt her spirits soar as she breathed it in.

Life here wasn't that bad, really, and there didn't seem to be a better place to be on this lovely April day. She thought of the weekend ahead, with Sunny gone until late Sunday evening. But she had Saturday night at the pub to look forward to and decided to call in to Saskia before she headed to the salon to ask if she wanted to join them. But first, Lucky needed a walk. A good opportunity to gather her thoughts and consider her options.

Lydia walked to her front door and opened it, nearly stepping on a large envelope on the doormat. She picked it up and looked at it. The postmark said Dublin and as she turned the envelope, she saw the address of her solicitor. Intrigued, she tore it open and read the short note. She nearly stopped breathing as she came to the end, then read it again before she fully grasped what it meant.

'Oh my God,' she whispered as Lucky trotted into the hall to greet her. She hardly noticed him, as she stared at the note again, her knees suddenly like jelly, her heart beating. Then she looked at the little dog standing there, furiously wagging his tail. 'Do you know what this is?' she asked, waving the letter at him.

Lucky barked.

Lydia laughed and picked him up, hugging him tight. 'That's right. It's a bloody miracle, that's what it is.'

Chapter Twenty-Six

Lydia sat down on the edge of the sofa with Lucky beside her and read the letter again very slowly, relishing every word.

Dear Lydia,

I hope this message finds you well. I was going to call you, but thought a letter would be the best option in this case. As you can see from the attached, a life insurance policy was found while we went through Barry's files. We had overlooked it during the probate, but then, when we had to do another check to see if there might be some funds in his many accounts that could be a help to you, we came across payments made by direct debit to the insurance company from a personal account that had nothing to do with his business dealings. I suspect the money came from the amount you transferred when your parents passed away to invest in Barry's company. But he seemed to have used it to pay for this life insurance. It is not a huge fortune but it will still help you to start afresh, or maybe just improve your living standards. In any case, I was happy to find it and made sure it was lodged into your bank account as soon as possible.

Let me know if there is anything I can do should you need help
with this or other things.

With kind regards,
Jonathan

She looked at the piece of paper he had attached with the letter and counted the zeros, in case she had got it wrong. But no, it was there, in writing. Three hundred thousand euros had been lodged into her account three days ago. Not a fortune, as Jonathan had said, but a lot of money all the same. She could go back to Dublin, rent a small flat, put Sunny into a good school and above all, accept that job offer, the kind of job she would never find here. The possibilities suddenly felt endless, and yet as Lydia lay back in the sofa and stared out the window across the sea, she didn't feel as excited as she should have, daydreaming about returning to her old life. Did she really want to go back to all that she had left behind? When it wasn't possible, it had seemed like a mirage, but now the thought of leaving the little village and this quiet way of life made her feel sad.

As she looked at the sum of money, Lydia's thoughts drifted to Barry, remembering his handsome face, his expressive dark eyes, his melodious voice and the way he used to look at her in the early days. All the anger she had built for him disappeared as she realised that he had left a kind of message in this windfall – a message that said he cared and wanted her and Sunny to be safe if something should happen. Her grief and anger dissipated into a softer, more loving sorrow that would be with her for the rest of her life.

Lucky barking at the door jolted Lydia out of her thoughts. He needed a walk, and then she had to go to the salon for the evening shift. Right now she had to stick to the present and keep working while she decided what to do – she didn't want to let anyone down. But one thing was certain: she wouldn't tell anyone about the money. Except Sunny. She had to be told. This was the perfect time to also tell her that her father had been guilty of a crime. With this money arriving, Sunny might find it easier to forgive Barry as he had made sure they would be taken care of if anything should happen to him.

Lydia spent nearly half an hour getting ready for the evening at the pub on Saturday night. It was her first night out since that terrible day nearly six months ago. She felt a spark of excitement as she gazed at herself in the bathroom mirror. She was looking forward to the evening now she felt she had reached a calm acceptance of what had happened. She had grieved enough and, although the sorrow was still there in her heart, she felt she was ready to enjoy herself a little bit. After all, it wasn't a party, just a drink with friends in a country pub.

Lydia applied an extra layer of mascara and a touch of blusher and stepped back, checking her appearance in the mirror. Her skin glowed as a result of her daily walks in the spring sunshine with Lucky. Her hair that she normally tied back fell to her shoulders in glossy blonde curls, framing her face, and the blue sweater intensified the sapphire hue of her eyes. When the doorbell rang, she was ready and she grabbed her bag and ran down the stairs to meet Saskia.

'Hi,' Lydia panted as she opened the door. 'Isn't it a beautiful evening?'

'Gorgeous,' Saskia agreed. 'And you look amazing.'

'Thank you,' Lydia said. 'You look pretty amazing yourself,' she remarked, looking at Saskia's deep red velvet trousers and white sweater that she had teamed with pale-green sea glass earrings set in gold. Her hair was swept up on top of her head and she wore high-heeled boots, making her even taller, which added to her willowy look.

'I look like a flagpole,' Saskia replied. 'But I don't care. I like scaring people.'

Lydia laughed. 'You don't scare me. Hang on, I'm just going to settle Lucky and we'll be off.' She left the door open while she went to make sure Lucky had water and that the back windows were closed. Then she joined Saskia and they walked together up the lane in the light of the evening sun that was sinking behind the Skellig Islands far away in the distance.

The quaint little pub was already quite crowded, but Brian had managed to get a table near the open window, a good move as the pub got increasingly hot when more people started to arrive. But there was a good atmosphere and Lydia enjoyed watching people step inside the door, greeting each other. She waved and smiled back as the people she knew spotted her. A breathless Sorcha ran inside as they sat down and Brian ordered their drinks: white wine for Sorcha and Lydia, a pint of Guinness for both Saskia and himself and a plate of grilled sausages and chips for them all to share.

'I've already had my tea,' Sorcha announced. 'But I can't resist a sausage and a few chips.'

'Dig in,' Brian said and heaped his plate. 'I didn't have time to eat as I had to rush out and deliver a calf. And I've been on night duty with the lambing season kicking in.'

'When do you ever get some sleep?' Saskia asked as she picked up a chip and popped it into her mouth.

'In the winter,' Brian replied. 'Ah, here's our drinks,' he said as a waitress arrived with a loaded tray. He grabbed his pint and held it up. 'Here's to a great night out with friends,' he said and took a deep gulp of his Guinness.

'Cheers,' Saskia said and downed a considerable amount of her glass. 'Ah,' she sighed when she had swallowed, 'that has washed the dust from my throat.'

Sorcha sipped her wine and laughed. 'You two could star in an ad for the black stuff. You look as if it's the nectar of the Gods.'

'A fine Kerry woman you are with the white wine,' Brian retorted. 'Too fancy for a pint then, are we?'

Sorcha made a face at Brian. 'So what? I never took to stout. Too bitter for me.'

'Some women put lemonade in it to sweeten it,' Saskia remarked, setting her glass on the table. 'But that turns it into mush, I think.'

'Totally agree,' Brian said, taking another deep swallow.

'Lydia?' a voice said beside them.

Lydia looked up and blinked as she recognised the woman. 'Yes? Ella, isn't it?'

'Yes.' Ella, looking even prettier in a tight black top, large dangly earrings and black jeans was standing before them. She held out her hand. 'We weren't properly introduced the other day. I'm Ella Caron. So nice to meet you, Lydia.'

Her lovely voice with just a touch of an English accent was charming and her wide smile contagious. Despite her earlier suspicion, Lydia immediately liked this exotic-looking woman. 'Lovely to meet you too, Ella. But... I thought you were French?'

Ella let out a throaty laugh. 'Nah, that was my last husband. I'm half-German, half-Irish with a little bit of French Canadian somewhere. Went to school both in England and Switzerland. But the French name is useful for my career.' She winked. 'Gives me a leeetle bit of, how do you say, allure?' she added with a fake French accent.

Lydia laughed. 'I see. It's all about marketing, isn't it?'

'Yup,' Ella agreed. 'You have to create a brand in all art forms.'

'Will you join us, Ella?' Brian asked, moving his chair closer to Saskia.

'No, well... I'm not alone, you see.' Ella gestured at a fair-haired man at the other end of the pub. 'I'm with that tall man at the bar ordering drinks. But he actually wanted to meet Lydia. That's why I'm here. So...' She hesitated, looking at Lydia. 'Could you join us for a moment? I think Conor has something to tell you.'

'Oh?' Lydia asked, intrigued. 'Why? Who is he?'

'I'll let him tell you himself,' Ella said, looking at the man coming towards them. 'Hi, Conor. This is Lydia.'

'Hello,' the man said. 'You're Lydia Butler? Nellie Butler's grandniece?'

'Yes,' Lydia said, mystified.

'My name is Conor M—' The rest of his name was drowned in a burst of laughter from a neighbouring table.

'Moloney?' Lydia asked when the noise subsided.

'No, Mueller,' he corrected.

'Oh…' Lydia frowned. 'Oh!' she exclaimed, her hand to her mouth when she realised what that name meant. 'Your name,' she said. 'I know that name so well.'

Chapter Twenty-Seven

Conor Mueller nodded and smiled. 'I thought that might ring a bell, somehow.'

'Of course it does,' Lydia said, trying to recover from the shock of hearing the name. 'You must be related to Hans Mueller, the pilot who crashed his plane on the mountain during the war.'

'That's right,' Conor Mueller said, his smile widening. 'I'm his grandson.'

'Oh my God,' Lydia said, her heart racing. 'That's amazing. We – my daughter and I – have been trying to find out more about what happened between him and my great-aunt Nellie. We've been all over the internet trying to find anyone who knew them. But we weren't very successful. And now, here you are.' She studied him for a moment and returned his smile, charmed by the friendly look in his eyes. 'I just can't believe it.'

'I know,' Conor said. 'I'm pretty amazed too. It's so strange to meet someone related to the woman my grandad used to talk about. Hey, could we sit somewhere quiet and talk?'

'Of course,' Lydia said, her heart still beating like a hammer. 'But where?'

'The snug seems to be quite empty,' Ella declared. 'That little room just off the main pub area. Through the archway,' she said, pointing.

'Great.' Conor looked at Lydia. 'Okay with you?'

'Yes,' Lydia said, getting up, taking her glass. 'I'll be back in a minute,' she said to the others.

'I'll mind your seat,' Ella said and sat down on Lydia's chair. 'I need to catch up with everybody anyway. I'll get them to serve your drink over there, Conor. See you later, guys.'

When they were seated on a bench in the little snug, Lydia looked at Conor. 'Tell me, first of all, how did you find me?'

'Your daughter,' he said. 'She contacted me through my business website. Sunny Butler. Is that her name?'

'Yes,' Lydia replied. 'Of course. That's what's going on. She just wouldn't give up. She must have been googling like mad to find you.'

'I suppose,' Conor agreed. 'We exchanged a few emails and she told me who she was and that she lived in Nellie's cottage and asked me all sorts of questions. So I thought I'd come down and meet you both and see the cottage where this Nellie lived. I knocked on your door but there was no reply. I tried the other houses until Ella answered her doorbell. When I explained I wanted to get in touch with you, she said you were at this pub and she came with me to help me find you.'

'I see,' Lydia said. She drank the last of her wine and put the glass on the table. 'Sunny didn't tell me about this, but she's staying with her best friend for the weekend. She is doing a project on Aunt Nellie and the story of her romance with…' Lydia stopped. 'Sorry for blathering on like this.' She studied him for a moment, not knowing what Sunny had told him. 'So you're Hansi's grandson?' She paused and smiled, shaking her head. 'Sorry, I'm a bit confused here.'

Conor laughed. 'I don't blame you. I'm a little confused myself. But let me tell you the part of the story I know, and then you can tell me yours.'

Lydia nodded. 'Go ahead.'

A waiter arrived with a glass of Guinness while Conor dug in his pocket, producing a small photograph that he handed to Lydia. 'My late grandfather, Hans Mueller, also known as Hansi. He died seven years ago.'

Lydia looked at the black-and-white photo of a blond young man in uniform. She noticed that with his high cheekbones and strong chin Conor closely resembled the young man in the picture. 'There's a great family likeness,' she remarked.

'Oh yes, so I'm told,' Conor agreed. 'As you know, my grandfather crash landed here on the mountain in 1940. And he and the crew were taken care of by the locals and stayed here for the summer. During the time he was here, he met a young woman called Nellie Butler.'

'My great-aunt,' Lydia filled in, her heart beating faster.

Conor nodded. 'That's right. They had a romance that lasted until the German crew were sent first to Cork and then to The Curragh Army Camp. They stayed there until the end of the war.'

'Yes, we've read that in the tourist brochure. But that's all we know. Your grandfather then wrote to Nellie and promised to come back when the war was over. But he never did. Do you know why?'

'I think so,' Conor replied. 'We found a letter to him from Nellie that was written during his time at The Curragh. Could be the reply to the letter you found. In it she says that although she fell in love with him, she couldn't possibly marry him and move to Germany. She had her mother to think of and she wanted to finish her degree at Cork University. But if he was prepared to wait, she would write to him again when she was ready.'

'But he didn't wait, did he?'

Conor shrugged. 'I have a feeling he did for a while. But a year after he arrived at The Curragh camp, he met a girl called Kathleen who later became my grandmother. They married just after the war when my grandfather came back from Germany.'

'Not very patient, was he?' Lydia couldn't help remarking.

Conor smiled. 'Or maybe he felt it wasn't meant to be,' he suggested. 'I have a feeling he waited to hear from Nellie, but then gave up. The war made it difficult to communicate. But he stayed in Ireland when the war ended and got a job at Board na Móna in Portarlington, cutting turf and then setting up the first mechanical turf-cutting machine. He was an engineer by trade. Hans and Kathleen had three children, one of whom was my father, who started a metal recycling plant that I now run, and we recycle most of Ireland's metal and electronic waste.'

'That's amazing,' Lydia said. 'Maybe Nellie wasn't keen to marry as she thought she'd have to move to Germany? I was trying to find out about that. I wonder if she would have changed her mind had she known Hans would be happy to live in Ireland.'

'Maybe. We'll never know.'

'No, I suppose not.'

'But my grandfather never forgot her. He often spoke of the lovely girl who gave him a glass of milk just after the crew were taken off the mountain. He called her his Irish rose. And he told us all about the beautiful beach he used to walk on with her during that summer. I've seen the main beach but there must be another, hidden one somewhere that would fit the description better.'

'Yes, there is,' Lydia said. 'Wild Rose Bay, just below the cottages. That's where Hans and Nellie used to walk on warm summer days. They must have had such a bittersweet romance in the middle of that awful war. I'm sure neither of them ever forgot it, whatever happened afterwards.'

Conor smiled. 'Just like every first romance we all had when we were very young. A beautiful episode that stays in your memory forever.' He drained his glass. 'I'm so glad I came here and talked to you. It closed the chapter on that part of my grandfather's life. We don't quite know why their romance didn't last, but that's not important."

'No,' Lydia said, her voice gentle. 'Now they can rest in peace.'

'That's a lovely thought.'

'Yes.' Lydia silently thought of her own sorrow and the peace she had found yesterday when that letter arrived.

Conor looked into the main pub. 'But I'm sure you want to join your friends. They seem to be having a great time over there.'

Lydia looked across the room at the group, who were laughing and talking, Ella being the centre of attention. She got up. 'Yes, let's join them. Do you want another drink?'

'No thanks, I'm driving. I'm staying in Killarney tonight. But I'll get you another white wine if you like.'

'Thanks,' Lydia said. 'See you over there.'

Ella looked up when Lydia arrived. 'Hi. You want your chair back?'

'I'll pull one up for you,' Brian offered and got another chair from a neighbouring table.

Lydia sat down between Brian and Ella. 'Thanks for bringing Conor to meet me. We had a very interesting conversation.'

'About Nellie and his grandfather?' Ella asked. 'He filled me in on the way here. Sad story.'

'Not as sad as it seems,' Lydia countered. 'Nellie was the independent type. Didn't want to marry, which is understandable given the rule for married women in those days.'

'Yes, but if you love someone passionately, you'd put up with anything to be with them, wouldn't you?'

'I suppose,' Lydia said. 'But they were separated for such a long time during the war, so maybe the fire went out.'

'Not real, true love then,' Ella stated. She looked at Lydia for a moment. 'I meant to say I'm sorry for the other day when I led you to believe Jason and I were… well, you know. I didn't mean to play a trick on you when you stood there on the doorstep looking so shocked.'

Lydia felt the heat rise in her cheeks. 'Well, I…'

'Jason was quite annoyed. He didn't tell me off, he just gave me one of his cold stares. I didn't mean any harm, so if it caused problems between you, I'm sorry. I have a feeling he likes you a lot, so maybe there's something going on between you two?'

Conor handing Lydia a glass of wine saved her from having to reply. She turned back to Ella. 'No, there's nothing like that at all. We're just friends.'

'Friends, eh?' Ella said, raising one of her eyebrows. 'You've managed to speak to him more than anyone and you've only been here a few months. Well done.' She leaned closer. 'He's quite a dish, isn't he?' she whispered into Lydia's ear.

'Quite attractive, I suppose,' Lydia said, trying her best to hide her real feelings.

'Not your type?' Ella asked.

Brian came to Lydia's rescue, emboldened by two pints of Guinness. 'Hey, you two, what are you cooking up?' he shouted above the din in the now packed pub.

'Nothing at all, darling,' Ella said, winking at him. 'Just discussing dishy men. And you'd be one of them, of course.'

'Oh shucks,' Brian said, his face turning bright red. 'You're having me on.'

'No, we're not,' Ella said. 'You're a real looker, too, you know.'

Brian laughed and shook his head. 'Yeah right, you just want me to buy you a drink, you brazen hussy. What'll it be?'

'I'll have a Bailey's, thanks,' Ella said. 'With ice.'

'Coming up,' Brian said, waving at a waiter. 'How about you, Lydia?'

'I'm fine, thanks,' Lydia said. 'I've had enough for tonight. And I think I'll go home, actually. Sunny said she'd call me before going to bed and I can't talk to her with all this noise. But please don't break up the party.'

'Can't you stay for a little while?' Brian asked, looking disappointed.

'Just another minute,' Lydia said, remembering what she had promised Helen. 'I do want to tell you all about Dr Pat's birthday fundraiser actually,' she said, getting everyone's attention. 'Helen and I are going to run this campaign during the week before his birthday and then the weekend after that there'll be a barbecue on the main beach to celebrate and surprise Pat with what we've managed to raise.' She went to explain how the campaign would run. 'And we were wondering if any of you would be willing to donate something for the raffle. Jason has already promised to donate a small side table.'

'Has he?' Ella said, looking impressed. 'That's very generous. Okay, in that case, I can donate a framed watercolour.'

'And I'll raise you one with a pendant and matching earrings,' Saskia cut in.

'How about a hamper of goodies from my shop?' Sorcha suggested.

'Fantastic,' Lydia said, taking notes on her phone.

'We'll tell everyone about the event – it will spread like wildfire,' Conor offered.

'Wonderful.' Lydia smiled at everyone. 'Thank you all so much.'

Conor got to his feet. 'I'll be heading off to Killarney now. I parked my car outside your house, Lydia, so I'll walk with you.'

'Oh great.' Lydia smiled at the others as she got up. 'We'll be off so. See you soon, everyone. Thanks again for your donations. Have a nice weekend.'

'Bye for now,' Ella said. 'See you around, Lydia. Let's grab a coffee at the Two Marys' when you have the time.'

'That'd be fun,' Lydia said and waved as she walked away. She and Conor pushed through the crowd and were soon standing on the street, the cool air a relief after the stuffy pub.

'This feels good,' Conor said, breathing in deeply.

'Oh yes,' Lydia said and fanned her face. 'Lovely to be out in the fresh air.'

'It was a fun evening, though,' Conor said as they started to walk down the street. 'This is a great little village. I'm sorry I didn't come here sooner. We've talked about it long enough in the family. And we've been wondering about this girl our grandad used to talk about with such affection.'

'How did your granny feel about that?' Lydia asked.

'Oh, she didn't mind. She said we all have lovely memories of our youthful romances. Which is true. And everyone has a past, another life they led. Especially true during the war.'

'Yes,' Lydia said. 'And maybe they are meant to prepare us for the real, lasting relationships when we're more mature. Young love can be so unrealistic – you tend to cast yourself in some kind of movie, expecting that happily ever after of fairy tales.'

'You're very wise,' Conor remarked, giving her an appreciative glance.

'Wise and a little worn by life,' Lydia replied.

'Aren't we all a little dented and scarred by life? Nobody escapes pain and sadness, really,' Conor said, his voice suddenly hoarse.

'You're right,' Lydia said, glancing at him, wondering what hard times he'd been through. He looked so bright and cheerful, as if he had been successful in his life. But it was true that nobody really went through life unscathed.

When they reached his car, parked in front of Lydia's house, Conor smiled at Lydia. 'Well, I'll be off then. I can't tell you how great it was to meet you and talk about my grandfather and your great-aunt. She seems to have been a very special lady. Just like you.'

'I have a suspicion your grandad was pretty special, too,' Lydia said, returning his warm smile. She stood on tiptoe and kissed his cheek. 'Come back and see us soon, Conor. I'd like you to meet Sunny.'

'I'd love to come back to explore this wonderful place. Or maybe you'll come to Dublin? Give me a shout if you do.' He dug in the inside pocket of his jacket and pulled out a card. 'Here. All my details. If you find anything about my grandad, let me know. A letter, postcard or a photo.'

'Of course,' Lydia said. 'Goodnight and have a good drive back.'

'Goodnight, Lydia. See you soon, I hope.'

When Conor had left Lydia went inside, turning on the lights, the silence in the house reminding her that Sunny was away and she was all alone.

Lydia went out to the deck to look at the stars before calling Sunny. The sky was dark with a strip of golden light at the horizon. A lone star appeared above the still water of the bay and Lydia looked at it and sent it a wish, hoping she would one day find love and peace and finally settle down somewhere she could call home. Sunny would be off to try her wings and Lydia needed to be secure and independent and not lean on her only child.

'Hello?' a voice whispered in the still night. 'Lydia?'

'Yes, Jason. It's me. Who else would it be?'

'Well, you never know. Life is strange. I saw you with a man just now, outside your house.'

'Did you now?' Lydia smiled into the darkness. Was that a touch of jealousy in his voice? Had he been as shocked to see her with a strange man as she had been when Ella appeared on his doorstep? 'A very nice man I just met,' she continued. 'He lives in Dublin.'

'Oh.' Jason walked closer to the hedge and peered over it. 'And…' He paused and cleared his throat. 'I was going to ask if you were free tomorrow. But if you're not, I understand.'

'I'm free,' she said, her heart beating a little faster. 'Why do you ask?'

'I thought we might take a trip to Garnish Island. Have you ever been there?'

'No,' Lydia had to admit, although she had often wanted to go to this subtropical island just off the coast of west Cork. 'That would be fabulous. I've heard so much about it.'

'It's the best time of year to go,' Jason said, sounding happier. 'And tomorrow's forecast is good. A little rain in the morning and then sunshine the rest of the day. We can have lunch at the café there. It's also just before the real tourist season starts, so it'll be reasonably quiet. We'll set off around eleven, if that's okay with you?'

'Perfect,' Lydia said. 'I'm looking forward to it already.'

'Me too.'

'I have to take this,' Lydia said as her phone rang in her pocket. 'It must be Sunny. See you tomorrow, Jason.' She pulled out her phone and answered it as she heard him go inside and close the door.

'Hi, Mum,' Sunny chanted. 'I'm having a fabulous time here with Lizzie. How are you?'

'Great, darling. I just came from an evening with Sorcha and Brian and Saskia at the pub. And do you know who I met?'

'No?'

'A man called Conor Mueller. Does that name ring a bell in any way?' Lydia enquired.

'Uh, oh. Yeah. I was going to tell you about him but I forgot. What did he say?'

'I have a feeling you know his part of the story already, so I won't go into that until you come back. But we had a nice chat anyway. Not that I approve of you looking up strangers on the internet like that, though.'

'It was research,' Sunny argued. 'And it didn't do any harm. I found out a lot, as you know, and I can put that into my essay.'

'Well, that's good, I suppose,' Lydia said.

'Yeah. Hey, Mum, did you see that report about my school in *The Irish Times*?'

'No? What about it?'

'We're only at the very top of the league table,' Sunny announced. 'Nearly the best result in the Leaving Cert last year in the whole country. Isn't that great?'

'Wonderful,' Lydia agreed. 'I must have missed that article. But that's amazing for a country school.'

'It's awesome,' Sunny declared. 'And what's even better is that Lizzie's parents are looking into her going there for fifth and sixth year, so she can do her final exams there and get top results for university.'

'I thought she was going to this Irish boarding school?'

'Yeah, she was, but she doesn't want to go there, so her parents have changed their minds and now she might be going to my school. She might even be in my class. Her mum's cousin lives in the town, too, which is ideal for her. And me. Isn't it just amazing?'

'Yes, but I thought… you said you hated the school a couple of weeks ago.'

'Did I? Maybe that was just because I got a bad result in my last Irish exam. But I love it now.'

'Oh God,' Lydia said, not knowing whether to sigh or laugh. Sunny's mood swings made her dizzy sometimes. 'I wish I could keep up with all the drama in your life.'

'Drama?' Sunny said. 'What drama? I'm a teenager, Mum. There'll be lots more drama to come.'

'I'm sure there will be. But before it starts, I just want to tell you I love you very much, whatever happens and whatever you do or say.'

'Love you too, Mum. Oh, Lizzie is calling me downstairs. She made popcorn and we're going to watch a scary movie on Netflix. See you tomorrow night, Mummy.' Sunny hung up without saying goodbye, leaving Lydia shaking her head, laughing. She put away her phone and picked Lucky up in her lap, squeezing him tight.

'What are we going to do when she leaves us, Lucky?'

Lydia sat there with the dog in her lap, looking out at the night sky. The windfall she had learned about yesterday had seemed like a lucky break, a chance to get out of the poverty trap they were in and get back to a new life in Dublin. But what Sunny had said just now had made her suddenly realise that Sunny may not want to leave. *But what about me*, Lydia thought, *I need to get back to my big city roots and my true identity. A flat, a job, a better standard of living, they're all possible now.* She sighed and let Lucky down on the floor. No more thinking and fretting. Time to go to bed. Tomorrow was another day. A day with Jason.

Chapter Twenty-Eight

Sunday morning started with brilliant sunshine and a light, warm breeze. The water glinted invitingly below the cliffs and Lydia almost felt tempted to go for a swim. But as it was only April, she knew it would be too cold. For her, but not for Jason, who she spotted coming up the path, a towel around his neck and a pair of wet swimming trunks in his hand. He waved at her as she sat on the back deck with her tea and toast, shouting to be ready for their drive at eleven. Lydia waved back and put her thumb up to signal she would be on time and quickly finished her breakfast. Then she ran inside to shower and dress, her beige chinos, navy polo shirt and a white sweater to put over her shoulders already laid out on the bed. She quickly blow-dried her hair and applied mascara, a dash of blusher the only other enhancement to her light tan. She put on her trainers in the hall and grabbed a rainproof jacket on her way out, just in case of a shower or two as the weather was unreliable this time of year. She settled a sad-looking Lucky on his cushion in the living room. 'I know. You'd like to come, but dogs aren't allowed on Garnish Island. We'll go for a long walk when I get back,' she promised, patting the little dog on his head before she ran out the door.

Jason was waiting in his car, the engine running. He opened the passenger door as soon as Lydia appeared. 'Hop in,' he said. 'We need to get going. The boat leaves in two hours. There are only a few running until the season starts, so we have to get to Glengarriff and the pier in time.'

'Grand,' Lydia said as she settled on the passenger seat. 'I'm really looking forward to this outing. I would have had to spend Sunday on my own if you hadn't invited me.'

'No you wouldn't,' Jason argued as he slowly drove down the lane and turned into the main road. Then they drove up the street and took the road that led around the southern part of the Ring of Kerry towards Kenmare. 'I knew Sunny was away so I thought it would be a nice trip as the weather is so good. But had it been raining, I'd have invited you to the cinema in Killarney, or even just a game of Scrabble in my house. I know how it feels when your children start having their own life and go off on trips and weekends away. Not a good time to be on your own and contemplate your old age.'

Lydia laughed. 'I'm lucky to live next door to my own personal psychologist. I hope I can afford your fees.'

'The only payment I require is your beautiful smile.'

'Oh,' Lydia said, not quite knowing how to reply. She had felt comfortable in his company and thought their relationship had reached a kind of plateau of warm friendship, but now she felt a strange flutter in her heart. He wasn't being flippant or flirtatious, and she knew he meant what he said. 'Thank you,' she whispered, more to herself than to him.

He glanced at her and then turned his attention back to the road, leaving Lydia studying his handsome profile and his silver-streaked dark hair. They settled into a companiable silence, in their own thoughts, giving each other space and time to reflect. Lydia was astounded by Jason's amazing ability to read her feelings, always doing and saying the right things to comfort her. She wasn't ready for any kind of romance, but she knew he understood and that maybe, he even felt the same. That was more than enough for now.

They drove through Waterville and on to Caherdaniel, where the road took them along the coast towards Sneem, a charming village with colourful cottages lining the town square. They stopped briefly for coffee in the beautiful town of Kenmare but as Jason wanted to press on, didn't linger to explore. They continued towards the inland road and the Cork/Kerry border.

'We are now leaving Kerry and entering enemy territory,' Jason joked. 'But as neither of us are real Kerrymen, we won't worry about it. Cork is a beautiful county too, you know, especially west Cork.'

'So I've heard,' Lydia replied. 'But I've only been as far as Kinsale. Never been to Bantry and beyond.'

'How strange. But maybe you're just a true-blue Dubliner?'

'Not really. It's more that my family liked the east coast better. We had a summer house in Wicklow. And then, when we married, Barry and I used to go to the south of France mainly for our holidays. We never explored Ireland, which is a pity. I think this stay in Kerry has been great for Sunny.'

'Stay?' Jason said with a quick look at Lydia. 'You mean your move here is not permanent?'

'Oh, no,' Lydia exclaimed. 'It never was, really. Except we would have had to live here for a long time if…' Lydia stopped, realising she had nearly told Jason about the insurance money.

'If?' Jason asked.

'If things hadn't started to look much better quite recently,' Lydia said, suppressing a sudden urge to tell Jason her news. But she stopped herself. It had only just happened and she needed to digest it and try to figure out what to do next. 'I can't tell you any more at the moment, sorry.'

'No need to apologise,' he reassured her. 'You don't owe me any explanations. And look ahead at the view, will you? Isn't it incredible?'

Lydia looked ahead, forgetting everything as the most beautiful vista came into view. Green hills and mountains circled a small harbour, its blue waters glimmering in the sunshine. Small boats lay at anchor, swaying slowly on the gentle swell of the waves. 'How beautiful,' she said, her breath caught in her throat, as she spotted the green island just off the coast. 'That looks like something from a fairy tale. Is it Garnish Island in the distance?'

'That's right.' Jason slowed the car and drove down a steep lane. 'We'll park at the harbour and get on the boat. I think it's that one waiting for us at the quay.'

It was. As they got out of the car, the man standing on the quay, where a small motor launch was tied up, waved and shouted Jason's name.

'Hello there,' he said when they came closer, lifting his captain's hat. 'Paddy Murphy at your service. Skipper of this here fine vessel. You're just in time for high tide. We can take off straight away, if you're ready. Maybe you, sir, could get on board first and then help the lady?' With that, he undid the ropes, leaped across the gangplank and started the engine, while Jason got on board and held out his hand to Lydia. 'Careful, that gangplank is a bit slippery.'

'I'm used to boats,' Lydia said, ignoring his helping hand. She stepped aboard with two easy strides, jumping onto the deck and down into the covered little saloon lined with seats. 'Are we all alone?' she asked, looking around.

'Yes,' Paddy shouted over the rumble of the engine. 'Private taxi for you today, missus. You're from Dublin, aren't you?' he added.

'Yes, but I live in Kerry,' Lydia shouted back. 'And my friend here is American but a Kerryman through his grandad.'

'Ah sure we won't hold that against him,' Paddy shouted back.

The boat slowly left the quay and glided down the narrow channel and out onto the bay where Paddy increased the speed and they swept out toward the island far in the distance. Lydia looked at the headland and the rocks where seals basked in the spring sunshine with delight. The seascape here was slightly different from the dramatic coastline of Kerry, the smooth rocks sloping gently into the sea and the green hills above more rounded with lush vegetation. She knew that Garnish Island had a microclimate that was nearly subtropical because of its proximity to the Gulf Stream that curved close to these shores and that the gardens had been planted over a hundred years ago.

The noise of the engine changed and the boat slowed as they neared the island and its landing place at a small quay, where they soon docked, Lydia eagerly jumping ashore before the boat had stopped moving. The small landing dock was flanked by a cute little café with a deck over the water and planters full of geraniums already in bloom. The path up the hill was lined with rhododendron and azalea bushes in in all shades and hues. After jumping ashore and telling the skipper they'd call him when they wanted to get back,

Jason joined Lydia at the start of the path. 'It's lunchtime. Maybe we should have something to eat before we explore the island?'

'Good idea,' Lydia agreed, taking off her jacket. 'And it's warm enough to sit on that lovely deck with all the flowers.'

'I think so. Let's go inside and see what they have. Or maybe you trust me to pick something for you?'

'If they have a tuna sandwich, I'd be happy with that,' Lydia replied, touched by his caring for her. 'And a big mug of tea.'

'I'm sure they'll have that,' Jason said. 'You go and sit down and enjoy the view. I won't be long.'

Lydia went to sit at a table on the deck, idly looking at the planters full of flowers and then down into the clear blue-green water where a shoal of fish darted in and out of the rocks. A flock of seabirds rode on the gentle swell a little further away, flapping their wings, then settling down again. There was such peace here, a feeling of being far away from the troubles of life, the modern world receding into the distance. The smell of flowers mingled with newly baked bread and a salty tang from the water, an odd mixture but wonderful to Lydia, who breathed in the soft air and closed her eyes to the sun.

'Here you are,' Jason said, jolting Lydia out of her reverie. He held up a paper bag. 'No tray, but a picnic, would you believe. The lovely woman at the café said we should have our lunch at the Martello tower instead of here, so we can enjoy the views out to sea at the same time. Tuna sandwiches made with her own newly baked bread, cinnamon rolls and tea in two small thermos flasks that we have to bring back when we return to catch the boat.'

Lydia got up from the seat. 'That sounds great.'

'Let's go then,' Jason said and led the way up the slope.

Lydia followed and they walked slowly through the maze of paths and lanes lined with subtropical plants and trees, most of them in full bloom. The warm air was thick with their scent and a recent shower had sprayed the leaves and petals with water that dripped onto Lydia's head and face. She knew her carefully blow-dried hair would be frizzy and her shirt damp, but she didn't care. She felt as if she was walking in an enchanted forest and when Jason took her hand and smiled at her, she was carried away by the romantic atmosphere of this beautiful little island. 'Is this a dream?' she asked when they came to a clearing with a more formal garden at the end of which was a pavilion in front of a square pool.

'No dream,' Jason reassured her as they walked around the pool towards the pavilion. 'But a very nice excursion on a beautiful day. This is the Italian garden.'

'It's wonderful.' Lydia thought for a moment, stopping by a huge azalea covered in pink blooms. 'I read about Garnish Island, but I've forgotten how it came about.'

Jason took a leaflet from his pocket. 'I picked this up at the café. It tells the whole story. Why don't we go and sit on the little terrace behind the pavilion? There are seats and we can look at the view of the mainland and the mountains while we eat our lunch. I'll read what it says here to you.'

'Perfect,' Lydia said, smiling at him. 'Lunch and entertainment. Is there no end to your efforts to give someone a special day?'

'A special day for a very special woman,' Jason said, the look in his eyes making her blush.

'You're pretty special too,' she said, feeling it was true. He had been so thoughtful all through their trip, thinking of everything to give her a magical day.

They sat down on a stone bench on the little terrace where they could gaze across the water to the green hills on the mainland, the sun warming their backs. Lydia munched on her sandwich while Jason read the story of the island from the brochure.

'*The gardens of Ilnacullin – that's the Gaelic name for the island – owe their existence to the creative partnership, around a hundred years ago, of John Annan Bryce, then owner of the island and Harold Peto, architect and garden designer. Once shelter belts made up of evergreen trees had been established, it was possible to implement Peto's designs to create the distinctive gardens of Ilnacullin. After the death of John Annan Bryce in 1923, the development of the gardens was continued by his widow, Violet. In 1932, their son, Roland Bryce, took over this work, continuing to add interesting plants from many parts of the world. He was ably assisted by Murdo Mackenzie, an outstanding Scottish gardener. On the death of Roland Bryce in 1953, the island was bequeathed to the Irish people.*'

'What a wonderful gift,' Lydia said as she ate the cinnamon bun, washing it down with tea from the thermos. 'But you must eat, Jason. No more reading,' she ordered.

Jason laughed and picked up his sandwich, devouring it with a few bites. Then he started on the cinnamon bun and quickly finished that too, while Lydia sipped the last of her tea. 'That was a delicious sandwich. And the bun wasn't bad either.'

'It was divine,' Lydia said, wiping her mouth with a paper napkin. She sighed happily and looked at the view. 'How wonderful it would be to have a house here. Did the Bryces never think of living here?'

'They did. Their planned mansion didn't happen, but they built a cottage and lived there for a few years.'

'That must have been gorgeous. Pity about the mansion, but I'm sure a cottage was better than nothing. If I lived here, I wouldn't care if I was in a mud hut,' Lydia stated.

'Oh yeah,' Jason said with an amused smile. 'I can see you in a mud hut.'

'That was meant as a metaphor,' Lydia retorted. 'I meant that if you live in a beautiful place, you don't worry too much about comfort and style.'

'Much like Sandy Cove, don't you think?' Jason asked in a casual tone.

Lydia didn't know how to reply. She knew he was asking her a question that she didn't know the answer to. 'Well,' she started, 'if I had come there by choice – choosing to live there because it's a beautiful place – I would feel differently. But I came there in a state of shock and grief, my whole life having been turned upside down. There was so much to cope with, and there still is. But I agree that it's a blessed place and I don't think I'd leave my cottage completely when…' She stopped.

'When…?' Jason filled in. 'When your boat comes in and you can go back to a more fashionable life?'

Lydia stiffened at his slightly scathing tone, which threatened to break the spell of the magical day. 'Please,' she pleaded, her hand on his arm. 'Let's not talk about my plans or what I'm going to do next. Let's just enjoy this day in this wonderful place.'

'And each other,' he said, his hand covering hers. 'I'm happy when I'm with you, Lydia. Apart from the worry that you might one day up sticks and leave, your company lights up my days.'

'Oh,' Lydia said, afraid to meet his eyes. Not because of his feelings, but because of hers. The strong pull towards him that she had felt ever since they met in person became stronger each time they were together. She kept telling herself it was just a warm friendship, but her heart had different ideas. She finally looked at him. 'I don't know what to say.'

His arm slid behind her back and he pulled her so close their lips nearly touched. 'Don't say anything,' he murmured while his mouth hovered over hers for an instant. Then he placed a kiss as light as a butterfly on her lips and drew back, his eyes so tender Lydia felt tears well up. 'Sorry,' he said, looking guilty. 'I swore I wouldn't do that, but I couldn't help myself.'

She grabbed his shirt. 'Kiss me again,' she whispered, pulling him back against her. Their kiss this time was stronger, deeper, with a touch of mutual longing for more. The feel of his lips and his warm hand through the fabric of her shirt were nearly making her dizzy and all she wanted was that this moment would never end. The beautiful surroundings, the soft breeze in her hair, the scent of flowers all added to the magic. She sank into his arms wanting to kiss him again and again.

But Jason finally pulled away, taking Lydia's hands, bringing them to his lips. 'Darling Lydia. I know it's all so hard and confusing for you. And I have a feeling you're on the cusp of something that'll take you away from here – from me. So, if you are planning to leave, I don't know how I could bear it. During these past months, you have managed to get in under my carefully constructed armour and walked straight into my heart.'

Lydia took a deep breath. 'Jason, I…'

But he put his finger on her mouth. 'Let me finish. I know you feel it's too soon and it wouldn't be right to start a relationship, or even a romance after all that has happened to you. But, my darling, life is so very short and neither of us are teenagers. Do we really have the time to wait a year or two so that we can act according to conventions? Do you want to wait and see what happens and all that – and then risk for it to never become something real?'

'Like leaving Christmas presents under the tree until Easter, you mean?' Lydia said with a laugh.

Jason smiled. 'Something like that.'

'And then you might have grown out of Granny's Christmas sweater she knitted for you,' Lydia continued.

Jason laughed. 'Brilliant metaphor.'

Lydia looked at him, knowing he was leaving it up to her to say either yes or no. She felt a strong urge to call a halt to her feelings, to tell him that she was leaving and they couldn't embark on a relationship that was doomed to end. But the look in his eyes pushed those arguments away and all she could do was put her arms around him. She suddenly thought of Nellie and how she sacrificed love for independence. 'Let's not put life on hold.' The words were out before she could stop them, but as she said it, she knew it was what she wanted with all her heart. 'Whatever happens, I want to be with you.'

'Are you sure?' he said, his expression telling her he didn't dare believe her.

'Yes, I'm sure.' She hugged him tight, breathing in the scent of his newly ironed shirt mixed with a spicy aftershave. 'I want to be with you so much.' She pulled back and looked at him. 'You must have guessed that something has happened that might change things for me, but I haven't decided anything yet.'

'Can you tell me what this thing was?'

Lydia nodded. 'Yes, I will. I haven't even told Sunny. But it's only fair to tell you.' She paused for a moment. 'It's quite incredible, like a lottery ticket I had forgotten I had bought. The other day, I got a letter from an insurance company, you see. It appears that Barry took out a life insurance with me as beneficiary. Quite a large sum in case he died. Three hundred thousand euros.'

'Oh.' Jason looked shocked.

'And just before that happened, the ad agency I used to work for called to offer me a job. But I didn't think I could accept it because the salary isn't enough to cover my expenses. But then with the money, everything seemed to fall into place. A job and enough for a down payment on a small flat. I can go back to Dublin and start again. Sunny can go back to her old school—'

'That she hated,' Jason filled in.

'Yeah, well she can go to another school. Plenty to choose from in Dublin.'

'And you can keep your cottage as a summer house or something – or let it again,' Jason cut in. 'Seems like the perfect scenario for a new start to me.'

'Yes,' Lydia said, looking at Jason. 'But it isn't,' she said as a tear ran down her face. 'I don't know what to do now that you and I have these feelings for each other,' she said, feeling increasingly sad. She lifted her tear-stained face and looked at him. 'But we can work it out, can't we? You could come to Dublin from time to time, or I could get down to Kerry for weekends. That'd be all right, wouldn't it?'

'No,' Jason said, moving away from her on the bench. 'I don't think so. I'm not sure that would work in the long run. We need to be together all the time. I do, anyway. I could never agree to some kind of long-distance relationship. I know how painful it is to be separated from someone I love, and I can't do that to myself again.'

'I suppose you're right.' Lydia sat up and groped in her pocket. 'And now I can't find a tissue,' she said and started to cry again. 'What a mess I am.'

Jason produced a handkerchief from the pocket of his jeans and started to gently pat her face. 'Don't cry, Lydia. It's all right. I understand how you feel, I really do.'

Lydia took the handkerchief from him and blew her nose. 'There you go understanding again. It drives me nuts. Can't you just for once *not* understand and get mad or something? Shout at me, tell me to get a grip. I feel like such a fool, such a spoiled brat sitting here crying when everything I was wishing for is coming true.'

'Was being able to move from here what you wished for?' Jason asked, his voice gentle.

'No. I was just wishing to be happy.'

'But you're not,' Jason stated.

'I am,' Lydia said. 'I mean, I'm happy sitting here in this beautiful place with you and you telling me how much you care for me and me feeling the same and… But then that makes me sad at the same time.' She dabbed her eyes. 'Oh God, I'm so confused.' She looked at him pleadingly. 'Tell me what to do.'

He shook his head. 'I can't. You must decide for yourself. I can't tell you how to run your life.'

'I suppose you're right,' Lydia said. 'I can't expect you to make up my mind for me.'

'No.' His gaze drifted as voices could be heard from the garden. 'I think we should continue our walk. I see a group of people over there. Another boat must have arrived.'

Lydia pulled herself together. 'Good idea. I can't sit here and cry all day.'

Jason put the thermos flasks and wrappings into the bag and got up. 'Come on then. Let's keep walking. Think of other things for a little while.'

'I'll try,' Lydia said with a weak smile.

They walked away from the Italian garden and up a path that led to the Martello tower rising above them. Lydia looked up at the brilliant blue sky, at the seagulls gliding around, the little clouds drifting across the sun and breathed in the soft air. It seemed churlish not to enjoy all of this and ruin an outing Jason had gone to so much trouble to organise for her.

Jason walked ahead with an easy stride, his wide shoulders and straight back a reassuring sight. *A true rock*, Lydia thought. *And he could be my rock if I wanted. If I chose the right way at the crossroads I'm at. But then I'd be giving up some of my freedom.* Aunt Nellie suddenly popped into her mind again. A strong woman who had chosen independence above a life full of love and perhaps a family. Had she regretted it? There was no way of knowing. But she must have been lonely at times, especially in later years. *Independence is a good thing for a woman*, Lydia thought. *But not loneliness. Could I live without someone to love me?*

Jason turned and smiled at her as they reached the tower. 'Feeling better?' he asked.

Lydia smiled back. 'Yes. It seems wrong to be sad in such a place.'

They stood together on the hill looking out over the ocean, not talking, both deep in thought. When their eyes met, Lydia felt a strange current running through her. She knew in a flash of insight that she could never give up love, especially the love of this man who understood her so completely. She took his hand. When he turned his head to look at her, she knew what she wanted to do. Even if her Aunt Nellie may not have approved.

Chapter Twenty-Nine

Sunny had already arrived home when Lydia and Jason came back. Lydia was still in a daze after what had happened between them and their ensuing conversation in the car. She knew now that she had to tell Sunny about her father, which was the hardest task of all. Lydia's feelings were in such tumult, she found it hard to be sensible and take any kind of decision, but Jason told her there was no rush to change anything about their relationship and things could just remain as they were.

'We're here now,' he said, when they pulled up outside the cottages. 'We know how we feel. Let's leave it at that for a while. The first step has been taken. But a new relationship is a fragile thing. You need to feel more secure, and to be absolutely sure that staying here is best for you. I didn't mean to put pressure on you when I said that a long-distance relationship is not possible for me. It wasn't a way to sway your decision, I was only telling you how I feel.'

'And you're probably right,' Lydia agreed. 'It might not work for me either. I'd be constantly worried about your feelings for me if I hadn't heard from you, wondering where you were and who you were seeing. I'm not sure I could live with that kind of stress.'

Jason nodded. 'Exactly. Let's be sensible. In any case, you have a lot to do next week with Helen's campaign and the beach picnic next Sunday.'

'Yes. I'm looking forward to that. But here's Sunny in the kitchen window, staring at us. I'd better go in.'

'Then I can't kiss you goodbye.' Jason took her hand and squeezed it. 'But we have plenty of opportunities to be together during the week. We'll steal an hour or two here and there.'

Lydia laughed. 'A secret romance. How exciting.'

'I like it,' Jason said, his eyes full of laughter. 'See you soon, my secret girlfriend.'

'Thank you for a heavenly, magical day,' Lydia said with a last look at him before she got out. She tried to adopt a bland look while she walked to the door and opened it, hoping Sunny wouldn't notice the stars in her eyes or her pink cheeks.

But Sunny was too preoccupied with her own news to notice anything about Lydia. She could have grown a moustache and dyed her hair green and her daughter wouldn't have seen anything different. 'Mummy!' she exclaimed as soon as Lydia closed the door. 'I had such a great time with Lizzie. And she's coming here soon so that she and her mum can go and look at the school and see if she can start after Easter and I want her to stay here and we can have your room and you can have mine. She'd love to come to the picnic next Sunday, too. That'd be okay, wouldn't it, cos I already said it would be.' Sunny finally drew breath.

Lydia laughed and hugged Sunny. 'That'll be fine and great fun. But what about her mum? Where is she staying?'

'In Cahersiveen with the cousin who's going to put Lizzie up during the term.'

'I see. It looks like you have everything under control.'

'Yes, I do. So it's okay for Lizzie to stay here next weekend?'

'Of course. And we can swap rooms as soon as you want. I'll love looking at the ocean and hear the waves while I go to sleep.'

'Brilliant,' Sunny chortled. 'I knew you'd agree. I'm going to call Lizzie and tell her.' She stopped on her way upstairs. 'There's a note from Mrs O'Dwyer on the kitchen table. And I got some sausages for tea.'

'Great.' Lydia looked at Sunny, trying to pluck up the courage to tell her what she had been hiding ever since she had heard about Barry. 'Sunny, hold on a moment,' she said. 'I have something to tell you. Something important.' Her voice shook slightly, and she knew she had reached the point of no return.

'What?' Sunny asked, looking suddenly worried as she noticed the expression in Lydia's eyes.

'Sit down for a moment.' Lydia sat down at the kitchen table and Sunny pulled out the chair opposite and sat down.

'Fine,' Sunny said. 'I'm listening. Is it about you and Jason? That you're getting serious or something? In that case, I'm fine with it. I like him.'

'No, it's not about that. It's about your father. About those rumours you heard in Dublin.'

'What about them?' Sunny sat down, looking confused.

'All those things that were in the papers, the tax evasion and the money laundering…' Lydia started, taking Sunny's hand. 'They were all true. Your father did cheat on his taxes and there was some fiddling with money at his firm, which he knew about. I didn't tell you this at the time because I didn't want you to think any less of your dad.' Lydia drew breath.

'What?' Sunny looked at Lydia, her eyes wide with shock. 'You mean he did all that? Those things that were in the papers?'

Lydia nodded. 'Yes, I'm afraid so,' she whispered.

'And you knew that all along?'

'Yes.'

'Why didn't you tell me?' Sunny asked, her voice hoarse. 'Why did you pretend it was all lies?'

'I didn't want to make you even sadder,' Lydia said, squeezing Sunny's hand. 'I thought it was enough that you had lost your father. Finding out about what he was guilty of would have made everything a lot worse for you.'

'You should have told me,' Sunny said, glaring at Lydia. 'Maybe not straight away, but a little later. It was six months ago, Mum. Couldn't you have shared this with me?'

'Didn't you have enough to cope with?' Lydia asked. 'Moving from the house you grew up in, changing schools, coming here and having to get used to this house that was so cold and bare. I didn't want to pile anything else on top of all that.'

'Maybe, but...' Sunny stopped. 'It just seems so wrong not to tell me.'

'I know,' Lydia said, squeezing Sunny's hand. 'But I was trying to protect you.'

'Stop saying that.' Sunny pulled away, tears running down her face. 'You don't need to protect me, Mum.' She stopped and wiped her eyes with the back of her hand, staring at Lydia as what she had been told began to sink in. 'So… it was all true, then? He did all that and then ran away?'

'We don't know that he was running away. He might have just meant to meet with the business partners who had left to see if they could rescue the situation.'

'Yeah, but he still abandoned us and left us with nothing.'

'Not quite,' Lydia said. 'I got a letter the other day telling me that Barry took out a life insurance policy, the balance of which has now been paid into my account. Three hundred thousand euros. For your future. So he did think of us after all.'

'Oh.' Sunny blinked and stared at Lydia. 'That's good, I suppose. But still… I just can't believe it.' Sunny looked at Lydia with despair in her beautiful brown eyes. 'And I can't believe you didn't tell me.'

'How could I?' Lydia asked. 'It was bad enough to see you so sad. I couldn't bear to tell you the rest.'

'But now you could?'

'Well, I thought you should know the truth eventually.'

Sunny nodded. 'Yeah. I suppose you did the right thing. Both times.'

Lydia stood up and held out her arms. 'Come here, darling.'

Sunny let out a sob and rushed into her mother's arms, hugging her tight. 'I'm sorry for you, Mum. You had to carry all this on your own. And you had to look after me and do two jobs and organise this house and cope with all my moans about school and everything.'

'I did it for you. And you've been so brave,' Lydia said, stroking Sunny's hair. 'Such a huge support to me. I don't know how I would have managed without you, I really don't.'

'I didn't want to see you suffer either. That's why I tried my best to help you.' Sunny buried her face in Lydia's shoulder. 'I love you, Mum.'

'And I love you,' Lydia whispered in Sunny's ear. 'You have no idea how much.'

'I do.' Sunny pulled away and looked at Lydia, her eyes red. 'Oh, Mum, I don't know how I can forgive Dad.'

Lydia stroked Sunny's cheek. 'Maybe you will one day, darling. If there's anything I've learned in the last few months it's that even if time doesn't heal everything completely, it makes things easier to cope with. But a good cry really helps,' she added, remembering Jason's words.

'I know.' Sunny broke away from Lydia's arms. 'Oh, God. This was such a shock. I need to think about it. But…' She paused. 'I'm not going to tell Lizzie or anyone.'

'No. Maybe not,' Lydia agreed.

'I'm going to my room for a bit. And then maybe we can have the sausages for tea?'

'Of course,' Lydia agreed. 'I'll make mashed potatoes and peas to go with that. Okay with you?'

'Fine,' Sunny replied on her way out of the kitchen. 'Don't forget to read that note by the way,' she added over her shoulder.

Lydia found Helen's note and discovered it was an invitation to dinner on Tuesday night for her and Sunny and a request to call Helen when she had the time. *Better get that over with*, Lydia thought and picked up her phone. A good way to recover from the tumultuous moment with Sunny.

'Hello there,' Helen's cheery voice said. 'I didn't want to disturb you by texting or phoning on a Sunday. Hope you had a nice day in this glorious weather.'

'Lovely, thanks,' Lydia said, smiling at the memories of the day she had spent with Jason.

'Grand. Well, I have some good news. My golf group have donated a thousand euros to our cause. Great start, I have to say. And when the campaign kicks off tomorrow, I'm expecting a lot more. They have all promised to share it around. So we could split the money between Doctors Without Borders and The Simon Community. What do you think?'

'Good idea,' Lydia agreed. 'It's nice to do something for a local charity, too.'

'Perfect. So we can finalise everything tomorrow morning when you come to do the usual cleaning. Have you asked Saskia and Ella about contributing to our cause?'

'Yes. I saw them at the pub last night, and they have both agreed, but they will do it on their individual Facebook pages. We thought that was the best way.'

'Sounds good. Well, then, I think that was all. Except to ask if you're free for that dinner on Tuesday with your daughter.'

'Yes, we are. Thank you for inviting us,' Lydia replied.

'We're looking forward to having you.' Helen paused. 'I was going to save this for tomorrow, but I think I'll tell you right now to give you time to think about this.'

'Think about what?' Lydia asked, intrigued by the excitement in Helen's voice.

'My idea, which involves us working together. Not cleaning the house, even though you have become quite expert at it. I meant this fundraising thing. You said you had been doing it for a long time before you came here.'

'Yes?'

'Well, I thought that we might somehow do this together. I mean, start up a partnership in fundraising. This way we could use your experience and my network and raise money for all kinds of causes and have fun at the same time. Organise dinners and lunches and events all over Kerry together. And you have a lot of experience in marketing, too. What do you think?'

'Oh,' Lydia said, taken aback. She had never considered getting back into fundraising on a professional level. It wasn't something she could start up on her own. But with Helen's help and her huge network it could be very successful. Lydia weighed up the pros and cons while Helen waited at the other end. Could she work with Helen, who could be domineering and quite stubborn at times? But there was a warm side to her, too, Lydia had discovered, and they understood one another. She had worked with worse people and handled them quite well, so Helen's little foibles didn't seem too difficult to cope with. And in any case, Lydia suddenly realised, her heart beating faster, here was a job opportunity she hadn't considered in her eagerness to get back to Dublin. A job right here, in this lovely village that she had thought she wanted to leave but that now felt much more like home. And Sunny being so happy, and Jason, and…

'Hello?' Helen asked. 'You still there?'

'Yes.' Lydia laughed. 'Sorry I was just… It sounds like an interesting idea. But I need to think about it for a little while.'

'Of course,' Helen agreed. 'Take your time and tell me tomorrow. In the meantime I'll see if I can get a hold of my solicitor and he can draw up a contract. And then we might start a limited company for tax reasons. I'll get my accountant to look into that.'

'I haven't said I agree yet,' Lydia said with a laugh.

'I know. But you will.' Helen paused. 'I'm so happy you came here, you know. I feel we'll become very good friends.'

'I'm sure we will,' Lydia agreed. 'I'll write down a few points about the work of fundraisers and what they do. But let's do Pat's birthday campaign before we start anything else.'

'I agree,' Helen said. 'We'll discuss all that tomorrow. And, of course, once I've found a new cleaning lady, you can get on with the new job.'

'Oh,' Lydia said, not knowing whether to laugh or cry. 'I'll stay on in the present position until then.'

'Excellent,' Helen said, sounding happy. 'The kitchen needs a bit of a going over after the weekend.'

'I'll see to that,' Lydia promised. 'Bye for now, Helen.'

Lydia sat in the kitchen for a while, going over the conversation and the idea of working with Helen. It would be hard work, much of it done by Lydia, as Helen seemed to think it would be all about throwing parties and having fun while raising money for charities. It was a lot more than that. But something about it felt right. More than returning to Dublin had. She could earn some money while doing the kind of work she had always enjoyed. Life was short, Jason had said, and he was right.

Lydia pondered the situation with Jason for a moment, her aunt Nellie popping into her mind. Nellie had chosen independence instead of love, but in those days women had no other option. They couldn't have both a career and a family. Lydia suddenly realised how lucky she was. With Jason, she would have the freedom she needed with his support and love. It was only if she decided to leave that she would lose him. But here she was, in this beautiful little village where life was peaceful and people friendly. Big city life didn't seem at all enticing in comparison. The choice she had to make was suddenly no choice at all. Life in Sandy Cove won by far. Lydia's thoughts drifted back to Helen and the partnership she was about to embark on.

Helen was nearing seventy; she obviously wanted something to do before she was too old. She also needed a friend. With all her faults, Lydia had always felt a certain affinity with this woman, despite their age difference. So she was a bit bossy and snobbish. She was also quite fun when she let her guard down. But true friendships needed time for people to bond. It was, however, the beginning of a working partnership that would hopefully develop. It was all in the future that suddenly seemed bright and promising.

With a light heart, Lydia started to prepare the evening meal that Sunny now called 'tea'. Lydia smiled as she peeled the potatoes at the sink. Sunny had made this place her home in only a few months. After a difficult start, she had managed to fit into her new school, make friends and above all, she had accepted her new life, meeting any obstacle with courage and determination. She had done what Lydia hadn't quite managed. But now, with the money and the prospect of a new career, and above all, the love of a wonderful man, Lydia felt as if a huge burden of sorrow had lifted from her shoulders.

As she thought again about that money she had just received, she knew what she would do with it. It wouldn't be the move back to Dublin to pick up the threads of her former life, but something new and a lot more exciting. She would spend some of it on this house, the house her great-aunt Nellie had lived in, and make it a warm, comfortable home. She felt herself getting excited at the prospect of all that she could do. She would make a new kitchen and a bigger bathroom which could be done by extending the existing shower room into the boxroom and make it into a little spa room with a bathtub and underfloor heating. Then she would install proper central heating, buy new furniture and insulate the exterior walls. The little garden could be dug out and planted with shrubs and a flowerbed, as well. Lydia felt a surge of happiness as she thought of what she could do without leaving the house she had come to think of as home. She would never have to move again.

Lydia looked into the sink full of potato peelings, at her hands a little red and chapped from housework, and laughed. How shocked her former self would be to see her now. She would have thought it impossible to survive like this. But here she was, happier and more fulfilled than ever before, working hard, living in her little house, coping with the wild weather of the Atlantic coast in a small village where everybody knew your business. But it was those people, and the man she was falling in love with that had changed her into the woman she was now: someone who had learned to appreciate the little things in life. The view of the ocean, the sunsets, the wild winds, and most of all the starlit sky at night were things Lydia knew she couldn't live without.

Even if that insurance money hadn't arrived, she would still have this odd feeling of fulfilment and happiness. That other woman, the one she used to be, seemed to recede into the distance, along with all the anger and resentments that had been burning inside her. She was finally free.

Epilogue

Early summer was probably the most wonderful time of the year, Lydia thought, as she sat on her new deck having her breakfast, basking in the early morning sunshine. The shrubs and flowers she had planted last year were now in full bloom and the slopes down to Wild Rose Bay were covered in a mass of dark pink roses. More than a year had passed since she first came here, devastated after losing everything. She had arrived feeling lost and lonely, trying desperately to cope and look after her daughter. She had thought she would never be happy again. But now, here she was, in a newly restored house that she loved dearly, with Sunny heading into her final year in a school where she was now truly happy. And Lydia was a successful fundraiser, working with Helen – who had proved to be an excellent organiser of charity events all over Kerry.

After that first campaign, which had raised over four thousand euros, Lydia and Helen hadn't lost any time getting their fundraising firm started. They worked well together, Lydia doing most of the groundwork and Helen going to all the dinners, lunches, golf tournaments and coffee mornings like a star, always looking glamorous and cheerful. She often told Lydia how much she loved her new career and how it had given her life a meaning, not to mention the fun of dressing up and meeting people. Lydia was delighted to see Helen bloom, which had also resulted in her being great company. They had fun together, planning parties and choosing outfits for Helen. An unlikely friendship that had started awkwardly but was now something Lydia cherished.

And then, the house… Lydia glanced up at the newly painted façade, where the repaired windows gleamed in the sunshine. The interior of the house had been given a much needed facelift, the living room painted, big rugs on the floor, new furniture, the best of which was a big curved sofa Jason and George had designed where they often sat watching movies or reading in front of the fire. The new bathroom was now, as Lydia had wished, a beautiful home spa with a large bathtub, a shower, underfloor heating and shelves stacked with beauty products and fluffy towels. The bedrooms were also refurbished and now had comfortable beds, carpets and proper wardrobes. Lydia had stayed in the double bedroom at the back, while Sunny occupied the front bedroom with two single beds, as Lizzie often came to stay.

And Jason… Lydia smiled as she saw him coming up the path from the beach. How lucky she was to have him in her life. They were together, but still not in the same house. That could wait, they had both decided, as Sunny needed Lydia's support heading into her final year at school. She was hoping to get a place at Trinity College in Dublin, where both she and Lizzie planned to study environmental science, the career of the future, they said – wonderful plans that looked as if they would become reality if Sunny worked hard at her studies. This week she was staying with Lizzie in Cork and then they would both be in Sandy Cove, where Fintan was part of their happy little gang, with Lucky bringing up the rear on their excursions on the beach and up the mountains. Lydia enjoyed watching them having fun while she provided food and packed picnics, picking up wet towels and tidying up after them, like a mother hen.

'Lost in dreamland?' Jason said beside her, kissing her on the cheek.

Lydia laughed and caught his hand. 'You're cold. The water must still be freezing.'

'A little too warm for me, actually,' he said and sat down beside her, picking up the coffee pot. He poured himself a cup while he watched her. 'What were you thinking about?'

'Oh, this and that,' Lydia said, stretching her arms over her head. 'About the past year and how everything has settled down to a very nice rhythm. And how raw and hurt I was when I came here.'

'And how scared you were to commit to me,' he filled in.

'It was Aunt Nellie's story that affected me,' Lydia explained. 'I don't think I quite realised it. She couldn't bear giving up her independence to marry a man she loved. But in those days, women were forced to make so many sacrifices. These days, we don't. When I married Barry, I did give up my career and a lot of my independence to support him. I think that was a mistake, but it seemed the right thing to do then. In the end, it wrecked things between us. But with you…' Lydia paused and took Jason's hand. 'We're equals. You have never tried to influence me or force your opinion on me.'

'Except when you wanted us to have a long-distance relationship,' he countered. 'And I said I couldn't do that. Maybe it forced your decision to stay here?'

'No, it didn't. Not really. I was already on the verge of deciding that for myself, even though that job offer and the insurance money made me think I should go back to Dublin. But in the end, I couldn't do it. Mostly because of you, but also because Sunny was so happy here and because I had come to love this house, even in its earlier, dilapidated state.'

'And you and Helen started the fundraising thing together. Brilliant move by her, I have to say.'

Lydia smiled and nodded. 'Oh yes. Her idea was wonderful even though I was a bit doubtful at first. But now that I let her be the face of our business so to speak, we get on so well.'

'And so do we,' Jason said and kissed Lydia's hand. 'But I do hope that one day we will live in the same house.'

'We will once Sunny's left for college. You know that.'

'Yes, but I'm getting impatient. And where will we live? Your house or mine?'

'I think mine,' Lydia stated. 'It's the end of the terrace, so the garden is bigger and it's near the path to the beach. Then we can let yours and you'll have an income that way. What do you think?'

Jason smiled. 'I think it'll be grand. I'd live under a bridge just to be with you, you know. Or in a little mud hut on the beach, or even an igloo in Canada.'

'I wouldn't,' Lydia said. 'I need my creature comforts.'

'I know, my princess,' Jason said tenderly.

'And this house is my castle and I'll never leave it.'

'Neither will I,' Jason said.

Lydia laughed and leaned back in her deck chair, closing her eyes against the bright sunshine. And then she sat up and opened them again, looking at Jason enjoying his coffee, and thought again about the past year and the first time she had heard his voice over the hedge that night when she had been in such despair. She had made a wish that night. A wish that she would find a place called home and someone to love her. And now she knew it had come true.

A Letter from Susanne

I want to say a huge thank you for choosing to read *The Lost Girls of Ireland*. If you did enjoy it, and want to keep up to date with all my latest releases, just sign up at the following link. Your email address will never be shared and you can unsubscribe at any time.

www.bookouture.com/susanne-oleary

As I write this, the pandemic is still very much dictating all our lives. I do hope by the time you read this book, things will have improved for you and everyone else all around the world. This book was very special to me as it is set in this village I created, inspired by a part of Kerry I love so much. The village in the book is fictional, but very like any little village in Kerry, where people support each other and are always there with a helping hand if you need it. The craic is wonderful too and we love going to pubs and little restaurants that are so similar to the ones I describe in my books. But what is most striking is the beauty of the countryside, the views of the ocean, the wonderful beaches. I hope I have been able to bring you there in your imagination for a little while. There is so much more to explore in Kerry and I will continue to take you there in my stories yet to come.

I hope you loved *The Lost Girls of Ireland* and if you did I would be very grateful if you could write a review. I'd love to hear what you think, and it makes such a difference helping new readers to discover one of my books for the first time.

I love hearing from my readers – you can get in touch on my Facebook page, through Twitter, Goodreads or my website.

Thanks,
Susanne

authoroleary

@susl

837027.Susanne_O-Leary

www.susanne-oleary.co.uk

@susanne.olearyauthor

Acknowledgements

As always, I want to thank my wonderful editor, Jennifer Hunt, and also everyone at Bookouture, who work so hard on the production, marketing and publicity of my books. But most of all I want to thank all my readers, who buy my books and also take the time and trouble to let me know how much you enjoy them. In these troubled times, I hope I have managed to provide you with an escape from the harsh reality of life at this moment. Your enthusiasm and support are what inspire me to keep writing.